Mrs. Big

Also by Maryann Reid

Sex and the Single Sister

Use Me or Lose Me

Marry Your Baby Daddy

Mrs. Big

MARYANN REID

ST. MARTIN'S GRIFFIN
NEW YORK

This is a work of fiction. All of the characters, organizations, and events portrayed in this novel are either products of the author's imagination or are used fictitiously.

Published in the United States by St. Martin's Griffin, an imprint of St. Martin's Publishing Group

www.stmartins.com

The Library of Congress has cataloged the first St. Martin's Griffin edition as follows:

Reid, Maryann.
Mrs. Big / Maryann Reid.—1st ed.
p. cm.
ISBN-13: 978-0-312-34199-2
ISBN-10: 0-312-34199-7
1. African American women—Fiction. 2. African American basketball players—Fiction. 3. Wives—Fiction. I. Title.

PS3618.E54M77 2006
813'.6—dc22

2006046266

ISBN 978-1-250-85774-3 (trade paperback)

Second St. Martin's Griffin Edition: 2023

10 9 8 7 6 5 4 3 2 1

This story is dedicated to all the women who want a man workin'

with a little somethin' somethin'. . . .

Acknowledgments

As always, I like to thank the people who are on this journey with me. First and greatest is my mother, Veronica Reid, for her patience, thoughtfulness, and caring ways. You have helped me keep my focus and motivation. I love you.

For my sister Arlene, you are almost in your last year of college, girl. Go get it!

My grandmother, Pastor Phyllis Brown, a leader in the community, has always been an inspiration of strength to me.

To Lucy, Matilda, Marisol, and Anthony, you all hold special places in my heart with Mami and Papi. I will never forget the life we shared for many years.

To my best friend, Willie James Clark, may God continue to bless and prosper you and yours. Every woman needs a strong man like you to hold 'em down. You are keeping the seat warm for my man, and he's got big shoes to fill! For Latoya, Nicole, Carline, and all the women out there trying to make things happen!

A cute two-snap to the girls at the New York Helmsley Hotel who read my books and critique them, too! To Arlene Pimentela, you are a fast-reading lady and have a great eye for a story. Thanks for all your advice and love. Millie and Nancy, may God continue to bless you.

Now to the folks who keep a sister eatin' and writing. A big, fatty-armed mama hug to all the bookstores and students who supported me during my Northeast tour last year at Howard, Morgan State, and many more. Let's do it again soon! Valder Beebe of *The Valder Beebe Radio Show,* thank you for being the perfect host and for bringing your audience the profound message of family I am working hard to instill. Wendy Williams of *The Wendy Williams Experience,* I thank you with much love for bringing my books to a wider audience. I had much fun on the show! To Karen Hunter and the team at WWRL-AM, thank you for your interest in my work and message. Nancey Flowers, girl, you just got a good heart. Thanks for the love. Zane, thanks for being a wonderful vessel of advice in this business of publishing. You have my respect hands-down for the mark you've made.

And last but not least, thank you, God, for another blessing.

My life is very—*big!*

—Kimora Lee Simmons

Mrs. Big

One

"You got what?" asked Vernice, as she and Loletta sunbathed on the sunny, cerulean shores of the French Riviera.

"A Brazilian! I wanted to give myself a birthday treat." Loletta wiggled her behind further down the white leather beach chair, away from the direct sunlight piercing her eyes. She had left her Chanel sunglasses at the hotel.

"Girl, who in their right mind would put hot wax on their pussy?"

"It don't hurt any more than a toothache." Loletta smiled as she stared ahead at the foamy waters. She slipped her hand down her gold Chanel bikini bottom. "And it feels like silk. Ooh, I can't stop touching myself."

"Hmmph, you *are* crazy. Molesting your own body." Vernice smiled and shook her head. They laughed at Loletta blatantly fondling herself as they basked in the sun. "On second thought, we're in France. You fit right in."

Loletta and Vernice laughed it up some more, stopping only to sip cool, luscious piña coladas with a dash of champagne.

Loletta turned to her mother, who was lying beside her on a beach chair. Loletta and her mom were almost identical. Ms. Eve Landelton had a honey-toasted, smooth complexion, and at fifty-two she was still slim and petite as in her early modeling days. She still posed for catalogs and occasionally walked runways. But since she officially retired two years earlier, she had been hanging on to Loletta like her right hip.

"Mom," Loletta called out. She couldn't tell if she was sleeping or awake. "Mom?"

There was no answer, verifying that her mom was out for the count, most likely due to their serious partying. This was their fifth day at Cannes, and every night Vernice, Loletta, and her mom found a party. With some smooth talking and the connections they made at their deluxe hotel, they managed to get into all the hot parties, especially those for the black Hollywood glitterati.

Three French boys ran by so quickly that sand flew into Ms. Landelton's face.

"Oh, Jesus!" Ms. Landelton shouted as she wiped the sand off her white Gucci bathing suit.

Loletta and Vernice shouted some expletives as the French boys ran into the smashing blue waves. The sunny beach was so crowded that everyone was nearly shoulder-to-shoulder. All the women needed was a few hours to perfect their golden tans before they left in the morning for New York.

"Wow, why bother wearing Gucci when it ends up looking shitty?" Ms. Landelton said as she reached for her bottle of water. "Now I have to get in that cesspool to clean off."

"Or you can wash off at the showers over there," Vernice suggested as she pointed to the long walk at the entrance.

"I'm not standing around showering so these French perverts can get off," she said, standing up and straightening out her bathing suit. "I might as well look fabulous doing breast-strokes. I'll be back, ladies."

"Bye," Loletta said, watching her mother walk away. Her mother looked bad, she thought, as she closed her eyes. She prayed she'd have it going on like that twenty years from now.

"Loletta, wake up," Vernice said, shaking her arm. "Ain't that Carter Blake from the Eagles standing over there with the photographers?"

Loletta immediately pulled off her shades and zoned in. "Oh, yes, my dear. My black prince. I heard he is going to be at Le Chateau tonight."

"Girl, you didn't tell me. How do you know?" Vernice whined, her chest reddened from too much sun. Vernice was very light-skinned and burned easily; however, she insisted on getting as brown as possible.

"How do I know everything!" Loletta said, throwing back her head in laughter. "I played it off like I'm some reporter with *Vibe* who was assigned the story last minute when the real writer bailed out. I wrote a fake letter, and I'm in."

"Just you?"

"You and Mommy too. But ya can't be on my ass all night because I got to work. Not only do I get entry, but I get a one-on-one interview. And the last interview I read about Carter said he is very much available and the ink is still wet on his twenty-million-dollar contract."

"But what will you do when he finds out you ain't no writer?" Loletta gave Vernice a mischievous look and grinned. "I'll be whatever he wants me to be."

This was all routine for Loletta. When she was sixteen, she snuck backstage at an LL Cool J concert by saying she was one of the girls who won a free backstage pass from a local radio show. That night she lost her virginity to one of his managers. A few years later, she managed to sneak into the singing group Jodeci's trailer with Vernice, after paying the driver 150 dollars. That was nothing for Loletta because after two days on the road with Jodeci, she left with nearly three thousand in cash. All she had to do was be whatever they wanted. She split the money with Vernice. After she graduated college, Loletta stopped bothering with rappers and R & B singers. Their money came quick—and left quick. But then Loletta heard about Myra, her mother's longtime friend, who met and married the top black coach in the NFL within a year of meeting him at a party in Milan. It was then that Loletta, accompanied by her divorced mother, decided to take her lifelong quest for the "black and paid" to another level. With Vernice, they began taking expensive European trips in hope of snagging Loletta's version of black royalty—a professional athlete.

Le Chateau was just steps away from Loletta's hotel. Loletta had it all planned, including ditching her mom and Vernice early. *They would be fine at the party*, she thought. There were enough ballplayers to go around. In fact, she liked roaming around on her own, convening with her mom and Vernice later to trade notes. The one thing men hated was women who traveled in packs. Tonight she would be a lone wolf.

Champagne flowed like the conversations. Loletta noticed that she, her mom, and Vernice were almost the only sisters in the place. The bar, the steps, and the dance floor were dominated by white or multiracial-looking women trying to outdo each other by dress, dance, or the handsome brother they snagged. The few white men in the place seemed to be satisfied with the leftovers, but Loletta was not going out like that.

"Do you see how desperate these women look?" Vernice asked, wrapping her red chiffon shawl over her neck. She pulled down the bustier to her dress to show more cleavage.

"Yeah, just like us," Loletta snapped as they stood by the door. She scanned the room to make sure no one else was rocking her cheetah-print bodysuit and black boots getup. She thought it was a little bold, maybe a little 1980s, but nothing made her feel sexier than animal print. And no one else wore anything close.

"I'm a sophisticated woman with class," Ms. Landelton said, her chin up. "I'm only here for the food, honey."

"Very classy thing to say, Mommy." Loletta rolled her eyes as they walked down the steps to the party. But she had to admit, her mother did look classy in a short black cocktail dress with the back cut so low it showed the dainty curve of her behind. "But we know why we are all here."

"That's right," Vernice chimed in, long bangs nearly hiding her thick-lidded eyes that looked half asleep. "We are here to give these men direction, purpose in life, help them invest that ten or twenty mill. We're sort of like financial planners."

"I'm an investor, baby," Loletta said, "and I see a nice piece of property right over there." She nodded in Carter Blake's direction.

"And he's alone," Ms. Landelton said, turning around. "I wonder if he has a father around here somewhere."

"He's always alone, even when I see those party photos of him in a magazine. He rides for self," Vernice said, picking a baked clam from an hors d'oeuvres tray.

"I like a little challenge. All I need to do is strike up a conversation about golf. I hear he is obsessed with it. I did my research."

"That's a lonely man's game. It figures," Vernice said, with cynicism. "I got my eye on Calvin Winnerby. Give me some time, give me some time." A throng of white women were surrounding him, each dancing to her own beat.

"What you got in common with him? Did you do your research?" Loletta asked as she took a glass of champagne from a waiter and passed it to her mother.

"I read he can eat chicken wings all day, everyday. Now you know I can finger-lick my way to high heaven with a bucket of KFC all to myself. We don't have to talk chicken; we can *eat* chicken." Vernice shrugged.

Loletta had enough with the talk; she was ready to let the games begin. Brushing her long weaved hair off her shoulders, she said, "I have some business to take care of, ladies. You both do, too?"

"Ooh, baby!" Ms. Landelton blurted out as she flung her newest wig, the blond one, to the side. "This is my groove." Ms. Landelton rolled her hips from side to side, as did several older-looking folks who seemed to get into it with her.

"Mommy, we leave tomorrow. You better handle yours," Loletta said, directing her mom's attention to an older, distinguished Hispanic gentleman blowing kisses at her.

"Ha, honey, who do you think taught you what you know? I had that the moment I stepped down those stairs," Ms. Landelton said, dancing into the crowd around her.

"Vernice, let's hook up here by two a.m., but if you don't see me, I'll check you both later," Loletta said, taking out her vanity mirror and applying more gold lipstick. "I ain't leaving this town without putting twenty percent down on my investment."

"Ha, ha! Girl, make that two of us. This sexy ass is pulling up on Calvin any minute. Bye, bitch." Vernice laughed as she sauntered away to the other side of the room, where Calvin and his boys were.

Loletta had to admit that Vernice was smooth with hers. She was thick in all the right places; depending on how she did her makeup, she could look Hispanic one day, and light-skin ghetto the next. She was a game talker and could talk a hustler out of his own money, whereas Loletta relied more on her exotic dark-skinned looks and brains to get her way.

As Loletta made her way to Carter, she didn't know what she wanted to start off with. She couldn't be too pushy or too calculated. She wanted to fuck him, consume every inch and ounce of his essence. Who was she kidding? she thought. She could care less about conversation and golf to get his attention. She was going hard. She had plans, and by next year she wanted to be staring down at a six-carat engagement ring, not another MasterCard bill.

She kept her eyes glued on him as she walked across the crowded room. Carter's eyes grew bigger, as if he were watching a speeding train come directly at him, and his feet were frozen. Loletta was just as nervous as Carter looked. She had also read he was intensely shy. What if he turned her down? She was in no mood to work hard tonight.

Then he turned around and disappeared behind a closed door.

Loletta didn't stop her approach, but now she wondered if she'd have to get through some locked door or bodyguards. Two petite, short-haired women in matching body-hugging outfits stood at the door.

Fuck it, Loletta said to herself. If she had to pound one of those bitches to a pulp, she would.

"Excuse me," Loletta said, bumping one of the women out of the way. Loletta pushed on the door, and to her delight it swung open.

"Looking for me?" Carter said. He was sprawled out on a

white leather sofa, looking delicious in dark jeans and a white linen shirt with dangling platinum chains. He smiled.

Loletta smiled back and closed the door behind her. "I'm Loletta. I don't usually have to chase a man."

"I don't usually get caught so easily," he said, standing up and walking toward her. "When I saw you charging at me with that look, I knew we needed some time alone. Like now." He dropped his hand down to her round, fat ass.

Loletta backed him down to the couch and straddled him. She cupped his face in her hands. "I read that you were shy. I was hoping to be the one to break you out of that."

"Please do," he said, gripping her thighs. He pressed her body down onto his hardened dick.

"You need this?" he said, handing her a pill.

"Not at all. I create my own ecstasy. I don't need any fake one," she said, sliding down the straps of her bodysuit.

"Man, Loletta, your eyes are so fucking sexy. I know a lot of niggas say that, but it's true," he said, seemingly mesmerized by her. Loletta smiled to herself; her almond, bedroom eyes were the bomb.

"You know, Carter. I have been watching you since your college days. I just want a chance to get to know you," Loletta purred, squeezing her breasts together. "I know I can love you."

"Come on, baby, you know we hear that all the time," he said in between licks of her nipples.

"Ooh," Loletta said, bending forward so her breasts smothered his face. But she was real about loving Carter or anyone who could love her back. "Tell me anything, please."

"I love you," he said with a slight grin. "You have beautiful titis. And I can't wait to see that ass."

So much for the shy-guy role, Loletta thought. She stood up and peeled off her bodysuit. He tore off his jeans and underwear. Carter touched her fleshy hips and nearly sent her head spinning. He pulled her naked body down on his. She crawled down to his dick, and let the smooth, warm texture invite her to taste him. Overcome by everything Carter—the MVP, the multimillion-dollar endorsements, the power, the respect—she came sucking his dick.

This drove Carter wild. He climbed down on the floor with her, and licked the juices from her thighs like a little animal.

"I love you, Carter," Loletta moaned, as he kissed her mouth with her own saltiness. "But I ain't done yet." She wiggled down to between his legs and feasted on his dick, a tree that bared all the fruits that would make one woman set for life.

"Hold on, baby. Damn! I'm about to come. But I want that pussy first," he panted, whipping out a condom.

Loletta helped him slip it on, ready to make him say her name out loud. Then two minutes later, it was over.

"Call me," he said, slipping on his jeans. He scribbled his number on a pack of matches. "Wherever I am, you'll be."

"Okay," Loletta nodded, half naked as she stood up and gathered her things. He helped her clean herself up in the bathroom. He rubbed her inner thigh clean with a cloth, slipped on her panties, and assisted her as she got it together. "Thank you," she said as she left the room.

"Call me when you get home. And let me tell you, what you did just now was gangsta. Most bitches try to act like they know me, telling me about golf and shit, trying to tell me about my plays on the court. But you handled yours. Straight nasty, straight up about what she want. Even if it's just sex," he said, sounding a bit disappointed. "I ain't like these other ballplayers. I'm real different, Loletta. I take my women as serious as I take my game."

There was something different about Carter, and Loletta

didn't think it was that. She closed the door and left. *Whatever*, she thought. He was one among many for her. He was gullible, twenty-two, and easy to control because he was still unsure of himself behind that big talk. At least she could count on her bills being paid for the next two, three months.

Two

"Loletta, would you mind giving out these petty-cash envelopes when you're done inputting these food bills in the system?" Jared Mckinney asked. He was her boss of two years. Loletta thought that her job as a receptionist at the luxury Jaguar dealer would be all about looking cute and answering phones, but it kept her buried in paperwork instead. But she liked it. It put her right in the faces of men with disposable income.

"Sure, not a problem," Loletta said, as she took the two stacks of envelopes from Jared. As she entered the bills into the system, she wondered how much longer she would be there. Her goal of working there in the first place was to get a man within her first six months. But she was going on year three and nada. A car dealership was one of the few places men frequented, outside of Home Depot and ball games. "Do you need me to print out a list of today's appointments?"

"Yes, great idea, Loletta. Always one step ahead," Jared said, as he patted her desk and walked away to the showroom floor.

Great, great, great, Loletta thought. If she was so great, why hadn't she had a raise in a year?

"Good morning, Ms. Loletta." Jordan Jones was one of the highest paid salesmen on the floor. He would collect nearly ten thousand dollars in commissions a month. He also hooked up Loletta with one of his clients, who couldn't stop sending her flowers. He was an investment banker on Wall Street, Italian, married, and bipolar. But Loletta looked at the relationship as a few free fancy meals at exclusive restaurants all for the price of stroking his bruised ego and giving him respite from his domineering wife. The dates also helped Jordan close the deal, and he gave Loletta a smooth ten percent, which was twenty-five hundred dollars.

"Hey, Jordan. So who you got for me today?" Loletta asked, as she kept her eyes on the screen.

Jordan smiled his bright white teeth and stroked his thick goatee. He was dapper, dressed in a gray flannel suit, black shirt, and wingtips. And very gay. "I got two players from the Knicks and one A & R guy from J Records. Total sum of their money about 16.2 million; the A & R guy is at the bottom, around one to two mill. He's VP, so he gets paid. I also got this chick from J Records who got her advance. Dumb ass wants to spend 100,000 of her 250,000 deal on a car. Black folk. You gotta love us, right?"

Loletta laughed. "Well, dumb asses keep you paid. It's beyond me how you get these people to spend 500,000 when they came for only 70,000," she said, tapping away at the keys.

"Is the appointment sheet ready?" he asked, leaning over her desk. "Mmm, nice legs."

"Jordan!" Loletta snapped with a smile. She had on a short, fitted yellow Italian suit with yellow heeled sandals to match. It looked gorgeous on her licorice skin.

"Here it is," she said, taking the sheet off the printer. She scanned the names on the list for anyone she might be interested in. "Here . . . rookies."

"Don't you love those?" he teased, rubbing his hands together as if that made his day.

"I like my players a little more seasoned. More settled. Those rookies still ain't used to all that pussy. They go crazy. I don't need my heart broken anymore," she said, resting her chin on her hand. "I did meet one in Saint-Tropez this weekend. Got his number and everything."

"Name?"

"Carter Blake."

"Hot damn! Carter 'Da Bluebird' Blake?"

"Bluebird?"

"Yeah, because he does that whistling sound every time he slam dunks."

"Oh," Loletta said, amused. "Well, I'm supposed to be hooking up with him soon. I have to call him today."

Jared Jones. Jared Jones. Come to the floor, the announcement said.

"Time to get my slam dunk," he said, blowing down on his freshly manicured nails.

Loletta smiled as Jared went to handle his business. She wanted to call Carter right there, but decided to wait till she was in the privacy of her home. The things she wanted to tell him were not for everyday ears.

Dressed in a white tee and black-boy shorts, Loletta sat down in the middle of her studio apartment on West 134th Street in Harlem. She shared the apartment with her mother, who sometimes seemed like a younger sibling. Loletta did the cooking, cleaning, bill paying, and organizing. All the while, Ms. Landelton shopped, lunched with friends, and took temporary stints as a secretary. Loletta avoided complaining because her mother's heart condition always loomed over her. Though she had never seen her mother take a pill, she'd never forgive herself if her mom got sick because she upset her. She loved her mother more than she loved herself. Since divorcing her father, her mother had handed over the responsibilities of the house to her daughter. Loletta hated playing mother hen to her own mother. But this was all new. When they lived together as a family, her mother was the perfect mother. She had attended to all of Loletta's needs, cooked for the family, nurtured and cared for everyone. Loletta understood that the divorce broke her father down to pieces. But she didn't expect her mother to stay down. Almost living life as if she didn't have a care. Loletta was already grown, but she often wondered why she had to pay the price for being an adult. She wondered if her mother would ever stand on her own again because right now Loletta was about to break down herself.

Bills and a paper shredder surrounded her as she sorted them on the gray, stained carpeted floor in their ground-floor apartment. She owed $75,000 in credit card bills, mostly for clothes and exotic trips. Every cent of her French Riviera trip had been charged. Her mother demanded that they take these types of trips together. She called it "mom and daughter bonding," but Loletta felt it was more like bondage. Her mother would convince Loletta that these kinds of things would lead her to find that man who would take care of her, like her own father took care of them. So Loletta would book the tickets and hotel.

She shook her head. How did this happen? St. Bart, Bora-Bora, and Tortola. She did have great memories, but her bills were over a hundred K until she met Andre Jackson, a retired

NFL linebacker in Bora-Bora, who hit her off with twenty-five K during their three-month affair. She had to break her mom off with ten K for minor "nose surgery." Andre was kind enough to keep giving Loletta money for her own personal maintenance, until he caught on that her mother was also living off it. This was not the life she had planned for herself, living with her mom at twenty-eight in a studio in Harlem. They took Cristal taste on an Asti Spumante budget to a whole new level.

She dialed Carter's number. Her heart beat so hard she felt like she was choking. She had never been nervous doing this before.

When a man picked up, she said, "This is Loletta. Carter?"

"Yes, baby girl. How is you?" There was lots of laughter and music in the background. It was eight p.m. on a Tuesday night, and he was already partying, while she was coming off a long workday.

"I'm okay. Where you at?"

"Vegas, baby," he laughed. She heard him call out a bet and then squeal in delight.

"Sounds like you doing good?"

"Listen, be at the airport in the morning. I'm gonna have a ticket there for you," he said.

"Um." Loletta hesitated, feeling bad about leaving her mother. "To Vegas?"

"Yeah, baby. We can live it up all week. All expenses paid."

"But I work, Carter. I can't be just disappearing for a week. I just came back from a two-week vacation."

"If you play your cards right, you may not have to work a day in your life anymore."

Loletta rolled her eyes and lay back on the floor. "Unless you plan to pay me for my time, I can't accommodate you. I may not have a job when I get back."

"Come on, boo. I'll take care of all that when you here. I know what you into. Get your ass over here."

Oh, hell no, Loletta thought. She was the one calling the shots. "Okay, well, why don't you and I go away together when you get back? I really don't feel like doing the Vegas thing with you and your boys."

Carter grunted, and his tone drastically changed. "Damn!"

"What?"

"I just lost fifty Gs."

"Did you hear what I said?"

"Yeah, but there is something you should know. And if you cool with that. We cool."

"I'm married."

"Okay."

"Well, good. Now, I will call you when I get back. What's your checking account number?"

Loletta sat frozen in shock because she thought he had divorced. She stared at the bills around her and at the phone. "Six-seven-seven-eight-seven-seven-eight-nine," she said, as she fiddled with her checkbook. She wanted to be the wife, not the "pay girlfriend." This was a definite sign that she had to change her game. She didn't want to be a thirty-five-year-old chick still hanging out, with no commitment. *Oh, hell no.* She didn't want to be like her mother.

In the morning, she called her bank and found she had ten thousand dollars in her account, which would hold her for the next few months. She knew it wasn't for her lovely smile, but for keeping the secret and for agreeing to be Carter's jump-off. She immediately put the money in her savings and took it as a good-bye gift instead. She was never going to talk to Carter again, and she was sure he'd understand why.

At work later that afternoon, Loletta called Vernice. She was about to declare the end to all of this bullshit going on.

"Are you gonna give him back his money?"

"I'm fed up, not crazy," Loletta said, as she talked low into the phone. "I just am getting too old to be some tasty side dish. I am filet mignon, baby."

"Well, you could be eating filet mignon if you just stick by his ass. He may leave that chick someday, and you want to be right there."

"Okay, how many NBA, NFL divorces have you heard of? We hear about Hollywood divorces every week. Juanita, Cookie, Shaunie, and the rest of them heffas are standing by their trifling men until they die. So now, come on. Juanita tried to leave Michael, and he nearly went fool. Them negroes do not divorce, and those women are getting nicely compensated for the stress. I wouldn't be going anywhere either."

"I never thought about it that way," Vernice said.

"What's up with Calvin?"

"Girl, he's in New York this week. Last night, I went to his hotel suite. He had Popeyes laid out everywhere like it was caviar. We must have ate about ten whole birds."

"Did ya fuck?"

"We was too full. We ended up falling asleep on his Persian rug."

"What?" Loletta laughed, but it wasn't real. She could see that Calvin and Vernice might actually work out into something. She was into this long enough to know. Not too long ago *she* had the stories, while Vernice was on the listening end. "What happened when y'all woke up?"

"We played video games," Vernice laughed.

"Oh." Loletta tried to downplay it. "Well, he sounds like a little boy to me."

"Girl, please. That's the difference between you and me. I'm just in it for the fun, while you in it for the ring. More power to you," she said sarcastically.

"I've been fucking up lately." Loletta pretended to be typing when she saw Jared flash by her desk. "Just satisfied with the money. Those rich motherfuckas are gonna marry somebody, and why can't it be me? There's no way I'm gonna stop living like I do, but I'm gonna make it work for me, instead of me working for it."

"Well, I'm gonna be working for it until I get laid off. Once you drink Cristal, you can never settle for Korbel." Vernice giggled on the other end.

"And they both turn flat and taste the same." Loletta said. "Eventually."

Three

Right before Christmas, Loletta and her mother went to a spa. It was a ritual they followed every couple of months. Another expense Loletta took care of. December was a time of year when people were more concerned with shopping and reveling than with getting microdermabrasions or salt scrubs. Neither Loletta nor her mother shopped for anyone but each other. That was one thing her mother was good for, she thought. It had been just the two of them since her mom moved back to the states from Switzerland when Loletta was nine. Loletta's father, Mr. Walter Hightower, was alive and well and living with his Italian wife, Mirella, in Milan. He was a successful businessman earning millions in real estate. Every summer she'd go visit them, and her mother often went too. They all got along, and Loletta attributed that to her father's charismatic, humorous personality. He didn't have one mean bone in his body. And it was Loletta's mother who broke his heart, when she left him after he lost his pro contract because of a disability.

"So, baby where will our next trip be? I was thinking we

should do Brazil or maybe even New Zealand," Ms. Landelton said, as she lay facedown, her back smooth with sugar and papaya.

Loletta was getting the same treatment. Last thing she wanted to do was think about more bills. "Are you paying this time?" she said sarcastically, while she looked at her mother's thin fifty-six-year-old body. It saddened her that her mother was getting older. As much as she disliked her mooching ways, she couldn't live without them either.

"Sweetie, you know my cards are so maxed out that I have to borrow from your daddy. I don't like doing that," Ms. Landelton hissed. "It's so embarrassing, and I know Mirella knows, even though I told him to keep it hush."

"Why are you still bothering Daddy to take care of you? And like a fool he does," Loletta said, slurring her words. "I pay for everything anyway."

"Because he still loves me," she sang, like a little girl on a seesaw. "And he's always trying to pay me back."

"Mommy, Daddy is just being a good man. I really don't like to see you use him like that."

"Look at you telling me about using people, Ms. Thang. I've never seen you refuse to take anything them rich ballplayers give you."

"They give it to me. I never ask," Loletta snapped. "With everything I pay for, I need someone to take care of *me* for a change."

"Well," Ms. Landelton huffed, "if I have to pay for the next trip, I will."

Loletta must have heard her mother say that a hundred times before. She closed her eyes to calm herself from going off in the massage room. A minute later she flashed them open. "Look, I'll take care of it. But I pick the place. It ain't gonna be Brazil either. Nothing but men go there."

"That's what I mean, sweetie! Men, men, everywhere!"

"Yes, but they are looking for native Brazilian women who don't speak a lick of English and don't mind getting their asses slapped for an American dollar. All there is for us there are poor Brazilian men. 'Cause their women are long gone."

"New Zealand it is then. Or Australia!"

"Mommy, I will let you know. I am not rolling in dough like I was when I was dating Andre. I'm rolling for self right now."

"What about Carter?"

"He's married."

"Oh."

"I need a break. I don't want to start the new year off like this anymore! Last New Year's it was me, you, and Vernice."

"Andre jetted us to his LA home for his midnight party."

"Yeah, and he didn't show up till about four a.m. We toasted the new year together—you, me, and Vernice. Though I love y'all, I ain't about to spend the new year all up in your faces. I want me a man of my own, on my terms, who loves me—"

"Is rich."

"Who listens to my ideas, takes his time in the bedroom, understands who I really am—"

"Is rich."

"And"—Loletta tried to say this with a straight face—"Richer Than Sin White Chocolate Cheesecake!"

"Mmm, don't forget to break Mama off some."

"I always do," Loletta said, as she closed her eyes and let her mind sail away.

After their treatments they sat in the lounge drinking champagne and eating a spa lunch of salad and a neatly prepared chicken quesadilla. Loletta felt refreshed and relaxed, as if she'd had a spiritual makeover. Maybe it was all the stress she was feeling lately that just had her down and cynical. Her mother always managed to make her laugh at these times.

"Honey, I was thinking while I was back there in that room with you. And someone popped in my mind," Ms. Landelton said, swirling her glass of champagne.

Loletta looked in her direction, licking her fingers. Somehow, she was always famished after a spa treatment, as if all the food she had eaten for the last few weeks was rubbed away.

"Kavon. What ever happened to him?"

Kavon. He was the all-star basketball player at Drexel University in Philly, where Loletta went for a year before transferring to Hunter College. She was a freshman; he was a senior. He had a definite crush on her, but she thought he wasn't cool enough because she was still hung on chasing R & B bands and following rappers. Last she heard, he was drafted by a top team and married. Even the sound of his name made her feel foolish.

"Loletta?"

"Um, Mommy, Kavon is off married somewhere. Besides, I think he's benching now. I have not heard about him since he got into the league five years ago."

"Well, I have. And I heard he just got a divorce. Real hush-hush. Delores, grandmother to Derrick Nickey's child and my industry insider, said they annulled about a year ago. No kids."

"So where is he?"

"He's a free agent and supposed to be in talks with the Knicks. Honey, you are really slipping."

"I just feel like I lost my chance with Kavon. If I hadn't been so foolish, all caught up with the shine, I wouldn't have to go through all this. I could be married and pregnant right now."

"You still can be."

Loletta looked at her mother through the corner of her eye.

"Find him."

"Mommy, I—"

"Girl, with that computer access on your job, all you need is his social security number and you can get his background info."

"I don't have his SS number."

"I do," her mom snickered. "And don't ask how."

Loletta thought about it. She did have that credit-check system that could basically pull up anyone's latest info.

"Or you can just use those online services. I would do the search for you or ask Delores, but I don't want to force you."

Loletta picked at her salad. The possibility of having a second chance with Kavon "Big" Jackson. *Kavon "Big" Jackson.*

At home, Loletta prepared dinner for her mother and herself. Two green plates of lemon chicken, Asian noodles, and green beans sat on opposite ends of a small round table near the kitchen.

"Oh, honey, these beans are delectable. Just the right crisp texture. But I would have laid off the salt a bit," she said, forking up several green stems.

Loletta nodded, while she dabbed the corners of her mouth with a napkin. Her mother was an exceptional cook. In fact, that was who she learned from. But it was like Loletta could never get a dish perfect. Her mother always had an armchair critique, even though she was home and could have made the meal herself.

"I like how the green beans taste," Loletta said, sipping from her glass of water. "Can't do everything like you do."

Her mother shot her an icy glare. "Excuse me?"

Immediately, Loletta felt like she was sixteen again. "I mean, I like how you make them, too. I just don't see why you always got something to say."

"Because I am a better cook than you," she retorted, putting down her fork. "And if I didn't have to live with these daily chest pains, I could do more around here." Her voice became feeble, and she quickly reached for her glass of water.

"Are you okay?" Loletta said, as she took her mother's trembling hand. It felt terribly cold and clammy.

Ms. Landelton touched her forehead. "I feel fine. Maybe it's a hot flash," she said, fanning herself. She adjusted her white silk blouse and tightly tucked it in her fitted jeans.

Loletta sat back down and watched her mother gingerly eat the food. They both sat in silence, each looking up when the other looked down.

Halfway through dinner, Ms. Landelton asked, "When are you planning to reach out to Kavon?"

Loletta knew that she couldn't ignore their earlier conversation. She needed more time to think about it. But so far, she couldn't think of a reason not to reach out. "I'll do some research tonight. I don't want it to seem like I am tracking him down." Loletta zipped up her black cashmere hoodie. It was particularly cold in their apartment, mostly because Loletta had not been able to meet the last heating bill. She reminded herself to call the company on Monday and tell them payment was in the mail. This usually gave her a few more days to get the money together.

"Well, Christmas is coming. Who knows what can happen or what he can give you? It's three weeks away. Plenty of time to make an impression on someone," Ms. Landelton said, pouring herself more water from the crystal pitcher. Her long, red manicured nails firmly wrapped around the handle. "Plus he liked you so much in college."

"He could have another girlfriend by now. Mommy, I just don't want to keep living like this. I just want to meet a nice, normal man."

"Kavon is nice and normal. He just happens to be rich. Don't penalize the man for that."

"I'm not. It's just going to be so obvious when he sees me or hears from me that I'm pining over him. I missed my chance with him, and I should leave it at that." Loletta picked up their empty plates from the table and walked to the kitchen.

Her mother followed closely behind. "Then don't make it so obvious," she said, with her hands on her hips. "Make it a coincidence."

Loletta met her mother's eyes. *That could be pretty easy,* she thought, as she began to rinse out the dishes.

"You're the one who said you don't want to spend another New Year's Eve with me and Vernice. If that is so, then do something about it," she challenged. Ms. Landelton smiled and gently drew Loletta's chin toward her. "Because, honey, I don't want to be with you two heifers either."

Loletta laughed. Her mom had a point. But she wouldn't go that far to admit it. There was no reason why she should be down on herself. A new year was starting, and if she wanted it to be a harvest year, she had to start planting the seeds.

After midnight, when her mother was sound asleep on the pull-out couch, Loletta went online. She Googled "Kavon," and several articles popped up about his negotiations with the Knicks, his sizable contract of twenty million, and little or nothing about his divorce. He lived in Fort Lee, New Jersey, and was thirty-two. Loletta felt overcome by a surge of energy and emotion. She decided to go a bit further and access the background-check system she used at her job. She plugged in Kavon's social security number, year of birth, and a few other small details she was able to muster up online, and nailed it. In minutes, a report was compiled that contained his address and home number.

Now what? Loletta thought, as she sauntered to her bed. If she called, it would be obvious she was digging, and if she didn't call, she'd torture herself with what-ifs. Not to mention her mother would absolutely disown her, at least figuratively.

In the midst of deep thought and fantasy, Loletta heard her cell phone ring.

"Hello?" she answered, looking over at her sleeping mother. She didn't want to wake her.

"Hey, bitch, get up! Calvin wants to take us to Mister Chow's tonight."

"Vernice?"

"Loletta, he is sending a car to you in twenty minutes. We'll be waiting," she said, and hung up.

Loletta touched the wrap around her head. She would need to work some magic on it to make it presentable for human eyes. She carefully tiptoed around the apartment, ran a hot comb trough her short tresses, and threw on some jeans, furry boots, and a short black mink jacket.

"Mom, I'll be back," Loletta whispered as she opened the door.

Her mother grunted, then mumbled. "Don't forget to bring home a doggy bag or something."

Loletta slowly closed the door, promising herself that no matter what, next year she needed to be on her own. She didn't care at what cost. Her mother was entirely too much up in her business, she thought. But tonight Loletta was relieved Vernice called. She needed to get her mind off things and maybe get a little something out of this evening too, something besides overly priced dim sum.

Mister Chow's was known as one of the premier gathering spots for black celebs and their ghetto-fabulous counterparts. Loletta remembered how she and Vernice would save up money from their paychecks to eat like queens whenever they found out someone hot was going to be there.

Calvin sat hugged up tightly next to Vernice. Loletta didn't mind flying solo this time because there were plenty of wandering eyes in her direction. Unfortunately though, more than half of the men had women with them. Vernice watched Loletta feed Calvin a succulent piece of duck that he sexily pulled off the fork with his lips.

"Calvin, you are just too crazy." Vernice giggled, as he helped himself to some more from her plate.

"We like to eat in case you didn't notice," Calvin said, chewing his food and smiling.

Loletta found Calvin about a six in the looks department. He was a short and stout NFL safety for the Patriots, with a junior beer belly, but beautiful hazel eyes that looked strangely alluring in contrast to his dark skin. She thought he looked like a buff, pretty-eyed version of Teddy Riley. She noticed he did pay lots of attention to Vernice, even ignoring a few calls on his cell. Vernice, on the other hand, just seemed to be more concerned with several dipping sauces and which one went with the right meat. It was times like these that Loletta worried more about Vernice than herself. They were both getting older, and they still didn't have any concrete plans for the future. Loletta didn't want to be a receptionist all her life. Loletta thought that Vernice wasn't as interested in companionship as she was, but more in the fringe benefits. And just by looking at Vernice and Calvin, Loletta believed that Vernice was going to leave Calvin's pockets as dry as his ashy elbows.

"So, Ms. Loletta, you think I can get your girl to settle down with a simple brother like me?"

Loletta looked at his half-full glass of wine. He couldn't be drunk. *Why wouldn't any woman want to settle down on the stack of cake he was worth?* she thought. But she knew her friend.

She looked at Vernice, who looked up at the ceiling and shook her head.

"I guess you can, but she's a lot to handle. You gotta make sure she's number one," Loletta said.

"Come on, girl. I'm not that complicated. Calvin, just make sure you got my ones. That's all." Vernice laughed.

Calvin laughed too.

Loletta thought they were probably made for each other.

"You ain't got a man with ya fine self?" Calvin asked Loletta.

"I'm working on it. Got any friends?"

"Yeah, I may be able to give one of my boys a holler. He may not be a player though."

"I don't deal with regular men," Loletta said, giving him an icy look. "They're a waste of time."

"He's our team doctor. Young cat. But I gotta warn you: he got mad bitches. But he may be able to hit you off with something here and there for your company." Calvin fed Vernice another piece of duck.

"Interesting," Loletta said, unimpressed. "I need my own man, all to myself. I ain't cut out to live my life like this forever."

"She's more like the serious type," Vernice said to Calvin. "Always talking about that marriage crap."

"I don't want crumbs anymore; I want the cake. Mama need

a contract, signed, and would even sign a prenup if my well-being would be taken care of indefinitely."

"See, I'm the type of bitch that would disappear on a nigga for two days. Loletta will stay for two days!" Vernice said.

Loletta covered her face with her hands. Vernice was the drunk one. *What an ass,* she thought.

Calvin looked over at Vernice with a screwed-up face. He was not feeling what came out of her mouth. "Now a nigga know what time it is."

"I'm only playing, Calvin," she said, stroking his cheek. "You know you got me."

"You two are just insane. Pussy must be the fucking bomb, Calvin," Loletta said.

Calvin nodded and kissed Vernice right on her mouth. Their tongues stayed tangled for at least twenty seconds. Loletta was about to excuse herself to the bathroom when it dawned on her.

She faked a cough to signal an interruption.

They both looked at her like she had mud on her face.

"Do you know a player named Kavon Jackson?"

Calvin adjusted himself in the seat and leaned in. "Why?"

"I want to know."

"You got his baby." He grinned.

"My mom asked about him. We went to school together."

Vernice nibbled on his ear while he spoke.

"Big? Kavon 'Big' Jackson. He's my boy. We in this real estate group together."

"I heard he divorced. You know why?"

"Man, we don't be putting all our biz out there like that with each other. But what I heard was the chick couldn't take the life. You know, he tried to make her happy, but you women be impossible sometimes."

Loletta tried to play it off, but that was some good news

right there. What woman would be impossible with what a man like Kavon could offer?

"Do you know who she was?"

"Some chick he met out one night. Got married real quick. Big is that type of nigga, when he see something, he bags it, tags it, and brings it home."

Loletta's panties started to feel moist. She had to have Kavon. He was her final shot at that life.

"I haven't seen him since college. Is he the same person?"

"Yo, out of all the dudes I know, Kavon is most laid-back, real to himself; he gives to charity, and even does volunteer work. I just get on his ass when he let these bitches play him."

"Play him?"

"Yeah, he got a real big heart. He'd buy a bitch the world without even smelling the pussy. I at least got to get a lil' bit of pussy juice on my fingers," he said, staring at Vernice.

"Calvin!" she whined.

"Can I ask you to do me a favor?" Loletta asked Calvin, knowing that everything she wanted was right in her reach.

Four

A week later at the dealership, Loletta waited at her desk with a fresh brewed cup of coffee and her eye on the door. Like every morning, Jordan walked up to her for his daily appointment sheet.

"So, how much would you like to split this one for?" he asked, with the smile of a Cheshire cat.

"I don't have to settle for the milk this time. I'm getting the whole cow," Loletta said, winking at Jordan and blowing down on her smoking yellow mug.

"Good. More for me." Jordan's smile stayed like it was plastered on his face.

"Jordan, maybe you should just go to your desk? I don't want him to see us chatting. He may recognize me off the bat, and I want it to be natural."

"Well, you worry about that while I seal the deal. Trust me, I need to make a quota this month, and I will do it if I have to buy the damn car myself!" He laughed. "But I know your boy will come through."

"Don't forget to walk him through here," Loletta reminded him.

Jordan walked away when his name was called to the showroom. Loletta stuck her neck out to see. Would she recognize Kavon? If not, she would definitely spot Calvin. If everything worked out right, Kavon will walk out the dealership with more than a car.

A few hours had passed when Loletta heard Jordan's voice getting closer to the reception desk. His voice boomed as he chatted with a few people who were laughing. Loletta's insides jumped around as she strained to hear the conversation. She recognized everyone's voice except one that was particularly low. But when Loletta laid eyes on the man with the low voice, she knew exactly who he was. Gone was the tall, lanky, goofy college senior with a pimple-ridden forehead. Kavon was still tall, standing at six-five, but he was built like an ox, with broad shoulders, rich tea-black skin, a bald shiny head, white piercing eyes, and full, thirst-quenching lips. His sharp curves were a perfect solid formation of a man. He was dressed in a gray and black suit and black wingtips. He looked like the millionaire he was. Suddenly, Loletta felt shy, but this was Kavon, she told herself. *Tall, goofy Kavon.*

"Look, gentlemen, it was great doing business with you. If you don't mind, please give your information to our lovely receptionist, Loletta. We want to make sure you're on our VIP list for events . . . ," Jordan said, as he ran his mouth about Kavon's new Mercedes Maybach.

Loletta didn't hear anything. She fixed her attention on Kavon, who glanced at her only a few times. She had worn the perfect outfit. Not too revealing like her usual. Today she was dressed in a chocolate brown Calvin Klein suit that cost her three paychecks. It gathered around her curves, with a tiny jacket that squeezed in her waist making her hips jut out. Her short black shiny hair was tapered neatly on the sides, with feathered edges. Light cherry blush kissed her dark chocolate skin, and white eyeliner showcased her almond-shaped eyes. In her mind, she had him.

"This is Loletta Hightower; she'll be happy to assist you with any further questions," Jordan said, shaking Calvin's and Kavon's hands.

Loletta tried to play off that she didn't know Calvin, but he kept grinning at her.

"Loletta," Kavon said, squinting his eyes as she tried to jog his memory. He touched his bearded chin with his forefinger. "You didn't go to Drexel, did you?" By the sound of his voice, he already knew the answer.

Loletta squinted too. "You know, I thought it was you!" She laughed. "Yeah, I did go to Drexel. Oh, my God," she said. She pointed at him with her pencil. "What a small world," she said and batted her eyelashes. Her mother would be so proud, she thought.

"Damn, girl." He laughed nervously, then whispered. He rested his large body against her marble desk. "Times is hard? You working at a dealership?"

Loletta couldn't have been more embarrassed. What was wrong with her job? she asked herself. She flashed him a smile.

"I guess fucking with them R & B niggas got pretty old after a while," he said, baring down at her with a sweeping smile that brightened up the room, most of upper Manhattan, and all of Loletta.

Damn, damn, damn. Of course, she thought, *he would remember*. She really felt played. "Well," Loletta said, sitting up straight. She looked up at him. "You know, I was a little girl then, doing little-girl things. But I'm a woman now, and I gotta work to take care of myself. And it may not be all that, but I like what I do."

"I like it too," he said, his eyes warming up to her. It sent chills down her legs. "If it wasn't for your job, we wouldn't be here in each other face right now. Right?"

"Right." Loletta nodded. "I get to meet a lot of people, and I make good business contacts. Some of us have grown up," she said. Then she mumbled, "But I see you are still as arrogant as ever."

Kavon backed up and so did Loletta. She didn't expect it to happen like this. He was already supposed to be asking her out. They were supposed to be reminiscing. But she was hip to his game. He was trying to pay her back for dissing him many years ago.

"Anyway," Loletta huffed, "you can fill these out, and someone will call you in a few days." She shoved a stack of papers in front of him. By now, Calvin had wandered off to chat on his cell phone. Loletta could tell by his animated conversation that it was no other than Vernice.

"I don't do paperwork," Kavon said, pushing the papers gently back in her direction. "You can fill it out for me."

"Why?" Loletta said, as she cut her eyes at him. She wanted to be angry at his smart remarks, but she forced herself to remain focused.

"Because you gonna be mine eventually." Kavon picked up her hand and kissed it. His lips grazed her skin like silk.

Loletta breathed in deeply, like she was inhaling his very essence. "I can't forge a signature," she said, pretending not to be moved by him. But she couldn't hide her smile.

He smiled too, took the papers, and signed them. "Well, it was good seeing you again, Loletta. Take care," Kavon said, handing the forms back to her.

"Um, okay," she said, wondering what would happen next. She didn't want him to just walk out of there. But she didn't want to push too hard.

Kavon nodded in Calvin's direction, as they both walked to the exit.

No, no, Loletta thought. She couldn't move from the desk; at least she wasn't supposed to. He was feeling her, and she knew it. She couldn't let him go again.

"Kavon?" she called out behind him. "You forgot your pen!"

Kavon stopped in his tracks and smirked. He turned to Calvin, who shrugged. Then he looked in Loletta's direction.

"Do you want it?" Loletta asked, begging inside for him to get his behind right back to her. If she had to, she'd leave her desk.

Then Kavon slowly walked over. "I didn't have a pen," he said in a collected, smooth tone. "But I do want it."

"Want what?" Loletta asked, as she left her curvy, glossy lips slightly parted.

"It ain't the pen," Kavon teased.

Loletta rolled her eyes. "Then what is it?"

Kavon leaned in and spoke softly into her ear. "I want you. I always have."

Those words resonated in Loletta's spirit. She knew he meant it. She could have him. She laid her eyes on him and twirled the pen in her hand. "What now?"

"I'll call you," he said, gingerly caressing her chin.

"But you don't know my number," Loletta said, getting ready to scribble it down.

He put his hand on hers. "I know everything. Just chill."

Loletta sat there with her mouth open as she watched him stroll his way out of the dealership. His new Maybach was being imported and shipped to his door. And Loletta pictured herself in it, enjoying the ride.

After work Loletta met her mother for drinks at Olive's. A swank bar in the Lower East Side. Her mother was already there when she arrived, throwing back glasses of port wine. It was in a hotel bar that her mother had met her father. A hotel bar in Milan frequented by many top basketball players. Her mother had had no idea that a drink would lead to a child, a marriage, and a five-million-dollar settlement that she basically squandered on plastic surgery, clothes, cars she banged up, and bad investments.

"Hey, Mommy," Loletta said, planting a kiss on her mother's powdered cheek. She took the empty bar stool next to her and signaled the bartender.

"Awfully chipper this evening," her mother sang. "And what do we owe this good mood to?" she asked, scanning Loletta's corporate outfit up and down.

"I'll get into that in a minute," Loletta said, patting her mother's shoulder. She also looked especially nice in a sleek black pants outfit, with a black fitted blouse with gold dangling chains decorating the front. Loletta asked the bartender what her mother was having. They'd both enjoyed the smooth, intoxicating flavor of port ever since their trip to Portugal a few years earlier. Out of that trip came a brief affair between Loletta and a popular Spanish soccer player. She got pregnant and had an abortion. Till this day, she still heard her screams as she lay on the cold hospital bed in her dreams. Not even her mother knew. Sometimes she felt they were like two familiar strangers.

The attractive waitress, a Hispanic woman with lush, thick black hair and blazing blood-red lips, laid a delicate small glass before Loletta. She took a long sip and sighed. "Mmm, I haven't had a good glass of port since our trip."

"Okay, okay," Ms. Landelton said impatiently. "Enough small talk. What happened today?"

Loletta put her glass down. "I saw Kavon today."

Ms. Landelton swirled her chair around to face Loletta head-on. "You didn't! Already?"

"Yes," Loletta said, grabbing her mother's hand. "I had Calvin, Vernice's friend, bring him in. They're both ballplayers. It's a long story. But it wasn't obvious that it was planned. He bought a Maybach."

Ms. Landelton had to put her own drink down. "Now tell me everything that happened. Moment by moment."

Loletta looked up at the bar ceiling. She wasn't in the mood for her mother's analysis. But she would just be badgered all night for info if she didn't give up the details. "At first it seemed like he didn't remember me. So I play it off like I didn't remember him. But we both knew," Loletta said, as she picked up a black olive from her mother's plate.

Her mother listened intently, despite the loud voices of an aggressive, after-work crowd.

"Then he tried to talk down to me a bit, like why was I working at the dealership. I know he is still holding on to some hard feelings. So I let him know that he was being an ass."

"What?" Ms. Landelton said, disappointed. "Now why would you say such a stupid thing—"

Loletta raised her hand to cut her mother off. "Wait, it gets better. Then he tells me that I should fill out his paperwork, and he walks away."

"Did you stop him?"

"I didn't at first because he was being an arrogant ass. But I did. He came back like he had wanted to the whole time. He told me he wants me. And that he always has." Loletta beamed. "I can have him, Mommy."

"Well, did you get his number? Did you arrange another time to meet?" Ms. Landelton seemed confused, like she couldn't figure out why Loletta sounded happy when it all sounded pretty bad.

"No, he said he'd call me."

Ms. Landelton exhaled loudly. "Did you give him your number?"

"He said he had it. That he knows everything and I should wait."

Ms. Landelton spun back around to face the bar and nursed her drink.

From the look on her mother's face, Loletta could tell she was not impressed.

Then she finally said, "I would have written my number down and gave it to him. Those men are too busy to try to get some girl's number."

"Well, obviously, I'm not some girl to him,' Loletta said, offended by her mother's snippy remark.

"Loletta," her mother said, as she spoke with her hands, "how do you know he will call you? I mean, it was really asinine to just let the man go like that. And call him names? Haven't I taught you better? Those men have options. For your sake, I hope he does call you."

"Just because I don't stake out hotel lobbies like you did and have a script to go by doesn't make me any less savvier in catching a man like Kavon. I've thrown myself at men before, and it gets me nowhere. Kavon didn't have to chase me; I bought his black behind to me. The least I can do is let him do a little of the work. And I know he'll call. And if he doesn't," Loletta said, snapping her fingers, "it's his loss."

"And another woman's gain," Ms. Landelton said.

They both sat immersed in their drinks and private thoughts.

Loletta thought her mother would be just as happy as she was. At least she'd made a connection with Kavon again. She despised the way her mother placed so much pressure on her. She wanted to show Ms. Landelton that she could have that life they once lived, a life they both deserved. But Loletta began to feel like she was doing it more for her mother than herself. It just wasn't fun anymore. It was business.

Five

When Loletta returned from her Brazilian-wax appointment on Sunday afternoon, she was pleasantly surprised to have the apartment all to herself. Her mother had left a note that she was on Madison Avenue and would be gone for the next few hours. Loletta thought it would be the perfect time to call her father. They usually spoke at least once a month. But if her mother was around, Loletta could forget having a private talk with her father. Ms. Landelton always competed with her for attention from Hightower. Loletta recalled times when her mother wouldn't give her the message that her father called, and if he called to speak to her only, it would be an issue.

"Daddy?" Loletta said when she heard him pick up the phone. She always felt like she might be interrupting a special family moment. She twisted the telephone cord around her fingers. "It's Loletta."

"My baby, Loli. What's going on?" he asked, excited to hear her voice. "Man, it took you long enough to call your daddy back."

Loletta sighed hard. "When did you call?"

"Like two weeks ago. Your mama didn't tell you? I wanted to see how your trip to the French Riviera was," he said, faking a French accent.

"Oh." Loletta tightened the cord around her finger, so tight it became numb. "She must have forgotten or something."

Her father grunted. "Well, how my girls doing back in the States?

Loletta wanted to jump right through the phone onto her father's lap. She always felt safe with him. He was one of the few people she trusted. "It's okay," she said, her eyes somewhat watery. She didn't know why she felt like crying.

"Okay? That's it. What's new?" he asked, his voice lower with an urgent tone. "You know you can talk to your daddy."

"I'm okay, really. We both are. I just wanted to call to say hello. I miss you. How's Mirella?"

He chuckled. "We doing fine. She got me gaining weight out here. You know how those Italians love to feed their men. Everyday it's a feast," he said, laughing.

She laughed too. She could picture her father rubbing his belly and his light skin turning beet red. "Just keep it healthy, Daddy. I know Mirella will take care of you."

"Are you girls okay with money and all? You know, your mama called me and asked me for about ten Gs the other day. And that was after I gave her five Gs the month before—"

"Daddy, you can't keep taking care of Mommy like that. She will have you do that till you die. Don't let her use you," Loletta said, wondering why her mother needed so much cash, when she was already milking Loletta for everything she had. Loletta had just let her mother use her Bloomingdale's card, and she charged almost two Gs worth of clothes.

"You know your mama always trying to put on the guilt trip.

How I left her high and dry for some Italian woman. And you know I didn't. Your mama counted me out when I got on disability—"

"I know, I know," Loletta said, having heard the story a thousand times. "Mommy sometimes worries me. She borrows money from me. If one of my boyfriends gives me something, I have to hit her off. It's like I can't have anything for myself. Not even my own privacy." Loletta curled up on the couch and grabbed a piece of Kleenex.

"What kind of boyfriends be giving you money?" Hightower asked with a tone of concern. "You still messing around with those NBA-type cats?"

Loletta didn't answer. She knew her father disapproved heavily of her choice of men.

"Come on, Loli. I was there. Those men will string you along with money forever. That's how they end up controlling you. I hope you at least doing something with that money, like investing or saving?"

"Yeah," Loletta muttered. Though she had done neither and hadn't the slightest clue how to begin.

"Shit, I did that to your mama, and you see where that got us. She still can't be independent and have her own things. Man, Loletta. I don't want to see you end up like that."

Loletta had never heard her father say that about her mother. She sat up on the couch and smiled. "Damn, I thought I was the only one who thought something was wrong with Mommy. But how do I fix this? I feel bad if I move out and leave her alone. I feel awful when she asks for money and I don't want to give it to her—"

"Loli, at some point you have to be your own woman, and so does your mama. Now I have no problem giving you something if you need it. I hate to know that you need to ask one of those clowns for money, because they can cut that off whenever. Come to me if you need something. Promise?"

Loletta agreed, but she didn't know how to go about that. She liked the money she was able to get from her conquests and had become dependent on it. Living off her own money would drastically lower her standard of living. And borrowing money from her father, she thought, would make her more like her mother.

"Daddy, I gotta go. But I promise to come visit you." Loletta felt that a "daddy speech" was about to come on.

"You know, I would like to see you with a nice, regular man. Like a doctor, lawyer, banker, maybe even a jet-setting politician. But to see you become one of those gold diggers—"

"Daddy!" Loletta said, embarrassed. She considered herself higher than that. "I don't be asking these men for nothing. They just want to help."

"Loli, it's a dangerous game. I'm an old cat. These new guys out here play by different rules nowadays. You give up a lot to get so little in the end," he said in a warm, caring tone. "I love you, baby."

"I love you too, Daddy," Loletta said, snapping the phone shut. She buried herself in the futon and flicked on the television, when she heard the front door slam. It was her mother.

Ms. Landelton glided her way into the apartment, dumping her Louis Vuitton and Henri Bendel handbags on the ground. "Did you hear from him?" she asked, as she slipped off her black mink gloves.

"Not yet," Loletta said, switching channels. She was actually surprised too and somewhat worried that she'd missed her chance. "I just got off the phone with Daddy. Why didn't you tell me he called?"

"Baby, please," Ms. Landelton said, sitting beside her and

opening one of the bags. "I thought I did. Besides, talking to your Daddy, you should be finding out where the hell Kavon is."

Loletta stuffed her hands into her hooded black Juicy Couture sweatsuit and curled back up on the couch. "Whatever," she hissed.

"Sweetie, look at what I bought you. You can wear this on your first date with him," Ms. Landelton said, her mouth practically watering as she held up a black and gold, mini cocktail dress. Very vintage Chanel, circa 1929."

Loletta ran her hands down the dress. It was absolutely not her style, she thought. "Mommy, it looks a little too old-fashioned."

"It's knee-length!" Ms. Landelton said, tugging at the edge. "It has an open back and V-shaped front. What do you plan to wear? A thong?"

"The man hasn't even called me yet," Loletta said, exasperated. She hopped off the couch and marched to the kitchen. "Just back off for a bit. I doubt for a first date he's gonna take me anywhere I can wear that dress to."

"Baby, your standards are just too low for me," her mother huffed, as she stuffed the dress back in the bag. "I can take it back." She carefully opened the other bags and removed the tags from the clothes. From the corner of her eye, Loletta could see at least five thousand dollars' worth of clothes, bags, and shoes. "Oh, and here's your card," Ms. Landelton said, putting the Bloomingdale's card on the yellow kitchen counter. "Thank you."

"Sure," Loletta said, stirring some honey into the tea she was fixing. "I'm gonna take a nap."

"Oh, I thought we could go out to dinner tonight," Ms. Landelton said. "Maybe go to Serendipity and have some of that frozen hot chocolate everyone is talking about? Or maybe we can go to the Gotham Grill?"

Loletta remembered that she and Vernice had plans. "I'm going out with Vernice to Javon Hudson's birthday party at 40/40." Loletta squeezed a bit of lemon into her tea.

"Only you two?"

"Yeah, Vernice tried to get another ticket, but she hustled for these. You said you ain't never liked that place anyway." Loletta didn't want to tell her that this was the one in Atlantic City because then her mother would really feel like she was missing out.

"I hate that club, too small to dance," Ms. Landelton said, with half a smile. "You two go ahead. I'll just stay here tonight and"—She looked around the tiny studio apartment—"watch a few movies on the DCR."

"You mean DVD?"

"Of course. Just make sure you tell me all about it," she winked.

"Don't I always?" Loletta smiled, and dumped the dried-out lemon in the garbage.

Later on that night, Loletta and Vernice were perched up in the VIP lounge sipping luscious saketinis and nibbling on spicy chicken wings. Loletta realized that she had to look supertight tonight, so she sported a winter white Gucci bodysuit with a zippered front, furry beige Gucci boots, and a matching suede belt. She loved catsuits and would wear them every day if she could. She had a killer shape: flat stomach, tiny waist, and curves like the number eight. Her high ass elongated her slim, shapely legs, and its thick roundness made it picture-perfect. Besides, she thought the catsuits were classy, simple, and most important, comfortable. She needed to be able to slip in and out of her clothes really fast.

Vernice, dressed in a Baby Phat cheetah-print fur-trimmed

skirt and red halter top, was more hip-hop video girl. Loletta felt that Vernice complemented her, and they usually didn't attract the same type of men, which was good.

"Damn, can there be more white bitches up in this piece?" Loletta asked. She surveyed the room and counted Vernice and herself among the few black girls at the party.

"Well, thank the white bitch who gave us these tickets. Nobody got these. At least nobody black I know," Vernice said, as she savored her purple-colored saketini.

"All these negroes in here gotta know some black bitches. This is crazy," Loletta laughed. "You think I would be used to this by now."

"Hey, just to think about it," Vernice smiled. "We look exotic now. Anybody who step to us—you know, he like the chocolate."

"True. I ain't complaining." Loletta and Vernice bopped their heads to the latest hip-hop hit as their entire row started singing the words to the song. Loletta and Vernice stood up and danced their way to the middle of the room, careful not to spill their drinks. It didn't take long before they attracted a couple of fine brothers, one who slid up on Loletta's bumper like a traffic cop.

"Mmm," he moaned, as he stroked Loletta's thighs from behind. She couldn't see his face, but felt the power of his muscular arms around her. Slowly turning around, she met his eyes drinking her in.

"Who are you?" Loletta asked, as her hips gyrated to the music.

"Twan," he said, following Loletta's rhythm.

Loletta held in her laugh, but she thought he was somewhat cute. Standing at five-eleven, maybe no more than 170 pounds, with a top hat tilted to the side and big, muscular tattooed arms. "Interesting name," she said, looking around for Vernice, who was already hugged up with an unidentified dude in the corner.

"Your name, precious?" Twan asked, rubbing her shoulders.

"Loletta," she said loudly, over the music. She tried to place his face. She was well educated in all the players top and bottom in the industry all the way back to 1996. "Why do you look so familiar?"

He managed a playful grin. "Well, you may have seen me run across your screen a few times," he said, gently bumping his hips against hers.

"Okay," Loletta nodded. "Basketball, right?"

"Yeah," he said, with a goofy laugh.

"I'm sorry but I don't know who you are. Who do you play for?" Loletta asked, with a smile. It was possible she may have overlooked this one for whatever reason.

"I'm a towel boy at the Garden. It's one of the best workouts I've ever had," he said, putting his large hands around her slim waist.

She carefully removed them and said, "Oh, excuse me." She quickly walked to the ladies room and locked herself in a stall. *Oh, hell no*, she thought. She could not be seen talking to those types. It just made her look bad, and no brother of any money stature would waste any time on her. She slid on a coat of her rum-raisin lip gloss, dabbed some red blush on her cheeks, and exited. She walked down the steps to the main floor where she spotted Javon with his wife and family. *Damn*, she thought, as she watched him gloat over his wife, who looked like any average black girl with extra weight. She had read about his whole story. He and his wife met in high school, and she stood by his side the entire way until they got married last year. Before they walked down the aisle, she had five of his babies. As Loletta watched from the top of the steps, she thought about where she would be now if she had given Kavon a chance.

"Do you mind?" she said, tapping on the back of a guy who

had been standing in her way for a few seconds. She tried to wait patiently.

He turned around and gave Loletta the nastiest look, like something smelled bad.

Loletta gasped and covered her mouth. *Out of all the parties in town, he had to come into mine.*

"Yes, I do mind. That you take my motherfuckin' money and can't even call a brother to say hi," he said, with a wide grin.

Loletta saw that several women were staring her down. She thought about giving them something to look at, but she didn't forget why she didn't call Carter back in the first place.

"Where's the wife?"

"Home, where she belongs," he said, pulling her toward him. He kissed her gently on the forehead. "Damn, even your forehead taste good."

Loletta ran her hands down his peach-colored silk shirt and remembered what happened the last time she looked into his eyes.

"You look so fuckin' bad in this bodysuit. Turn around," he said, spinning her around one time. "You a bad bitch."

Loletta smelled the alcohol on his breath. She threw back her saketini until it was gone. She thought she might as well enjoy the evening. It was no fun if she was gonna party with Carter to be the only sober one. He grabbed her hand and walked her back up to the VIP room, where he sat down at his own table.

He ordered a few more drinks for them, but they didn't talk much. He smoked a blunt; she watched. He kept his arms around her the whole time, and she admitted she liked feeling like his bitch for the night. And slowly, his hands and lips began to wander around her neck and mouth.

Then a slow reggae tune came on, sending an air of sick, sultry sexiness through the club. Carter passed the blunt to her and played with her zipper, lowering it inch by inch. Loletta nursed her third saketini as she puffed out circles of smoke, each covering up the lies she was telling herself. It wasn't okay, but fuck it, she thought. She lay back on the couch, as she fed Carter the blunt and the drink interchangeably. Then their lips met in a long deep kiss.

"Girl!" Vernice said, standing over her. "I was looking for your black ass. I'm leaving."

"Why?" Loletta said, her mouth still glued to Carter, who didn't even look at Vernice.

"Come on, baby, let's get a room," he whispered in her ear.

"It's cool, girl. I'm leaving with Calvin. His crazy behind is here. He told me he was going out of town," she shouted, as she flung her long black weave off her shoulders. "I'll call you tomorrow?"

Loletta nodded to both Vernice and Carter. And within minutes she and Carter were in a car heading to the Taj Mahal.

Loletta and Carter stumbled into the penthouse suite of the Taj Mahal, both barely able to stand. Loletta tripped every other step, and Carter did the same until they made it to the bedroom. But once they landed on the bed, all their body parts were fully operational.

Loletta watched Carter undress as she lay across the bed. She wondered where Kavon was. Why hadn't he called? Maybe this was it? This was her life. Who was she to think that maybe she and Kavon were meant to be? Never.

She looked on as Carter did a naked dance like he was a Chippendales dancer, pumping his blessed, sepia-skinned body like a pro. Loletta's mouth salivated as she looked at his dick harden and lengthen. She crawled up to the edge of the bed and gripped his thigh, squeezing his hard ass in her hands.

"Let me help you with that." When Carter pulled her zipper

down, her C-cup breasts flew out like birds from a cage. He slipped her bodysuit off like a glove and climbed on top of her silky brown nakedness.

"Here," he said, popping a tiny white pill in his mouth and giving her one.

She swallowed and closed her eyes, ready for the journey.

Loletta felt like her body was suspended in thin air as Carter sucked on her bald pussy like an icy pop.

"Aah, aah!" Loletta yelled, her legs shaking. Carter's tongue felt like ten tongues delicately licking her pussy. She raised her hips feeding Carter who grunted and moaned in pleasure.

He slowly crawled his way back up to her and threw her legs over his shoulders, pumping her until she begged him.

"You want me to stop?" he asked, his eyes rolling to the back of his head. Beads of sweat trickled down on the side of his face, down to his lips to her chin.

"Never, never," she panted. "Kill me with this dick, you big nasty black—"

"Aah!" Carter yelled, finding a spot in her that drove both of them insane. But he slowly pulled out his dick and invited her to taste it.

Loletta knelt down before him on the bed and gave him a spit shine that he'd never forget. She didn't know what came over her, but Carter's dick in her mouth felt good enough to eat.

"Shit, I don't wanna come yet," he said, his bald head covered in sweat. He bent Loletta over and tossed her salad, careful not to miss any nook or cranny. She pumped her ass into his face and bent over further until she felt his dick push in between her thighs.

"Ooh, ooh." Loletta trembled, as he had her doggy style on the edge of the bed. He slapped her ass hard several times. He slapped her so hard that she fell over. But that didn't stop Carter, as he pumped his dick back inside her, while she lay face-down on the carpet. Finally, he came, all over Loletta's back. And there they lay asleep until the morning.

A few days later, Loletta had an eight-thousand-dollar check delivered to her via FedEx and a note from Carter that read, "Love don't cost a thing." Loletta deposited the check in her account. She couldn't agree more.

Six

On Wednesday after work, Loletta returned home from Christmas shopping with Vernice. But she neglected one thing: her light bill.

"I told them I would send them my payment on Friday!" Loletta said, as she hopelessly flicked on every light switch in the apartment.

"Where's your mother?" Vernice asked, finding her way to the futon near the window. She opened the blinds to let in some street light.

"Probably out profiling with one of her associates like she's living large, with no clue that she'll be lighting a candle tonight." Loletta plopped herself on the couch. This was the third time in six months that her lights had been cut off.

Loletta rested her chin on her hand. Vernice moved closer to understanding what it was really about. She had the same problems too, but was better at hiding them. "Didn't you get some money from Carter?"

"Girl, don't even go there. You know what happens to that money."

"True," Vernice said, folding her hands between her legs. "But you know, maybe if you plan better—"

"Please," Loletta said, shaking her head adamantly. "Bills are the last things that get paid with that money we get. We gotta go shopping, keep up our look, dine at the right places, and travel so that we can keep getting that money. If I have a little left over, then my bills come in. You think I really want to live in this dump?"

"Look, you need to get you somebody steady, like Calvin."

"He taking care of you like that?"

"Girl, yes! That negro has not been able to get rid of me. I control everything in that relationship."

"Everything?" Loletta asked. Their lifestyles never allowed them to control nothing.

"Well, he is married, with four kids. I can't control that. But I've already made up my mind that I am not going to be anyone's wife in this game. It's too much stress for too little appreciation. I can get fully appreciated by being his side bitch without all his bullshit," Vernice said.

"What about security, Vernice? Don't you want to have a family?"

"I got you, our mothers, my sisters. I got a family."

"I mean your own kids, a husband, a backyard, holidays together."

Vernice looked up at the ceiling like she was bored. "That is what I'm saying. You are so caught up in a fantasy world. That shit is not happening. It's never like that anyway. Calvin is spending Christmas with me, not his family."

"And how you know?"

"He told me, but I know he got other bitches to see that day. As long as he sees me last, I'm good. Save the best for last!"

"Girl, I think we both are getting dumber with age." Loletta laughed nervously. "But you're right about one thing. I do need a steady."

"Carter?"

"That man will get me knocked up and pregnant. I ain't about to be his third baby mama."

"Kavon." Vernice smiled like she hit the jackpot.

"Yeah," Loletta said, picking at the fibers on the couch. "But he hasn't called me. It's been almost two weeks."

Vernice shrugged. "He's probably all caught up in business. They are preparing for their season. But I really did think he would be at the party."

Loletta walked to the kitchen, opened the refrigerator door, and slammed it shut. "Great, now everything is spoiled and stanking," she said, emptying out the milk, cheese, wilted lettuce, and a half-eaten plate of chicken teriyaki from Mister Chow's. Vernice helped her as they wiped the inside with Fantastik and bleach.

"Ladies!" Ms. Landelton called as she entered the apartment. "What the funk is up?" she laughed, slipping off her black mink coat.

"It's the food. They turned the lights off on us again, Mommy," Loletta said, holding a roll of paper towels. "Feel free to jump in and help." Loletta threw the roll in her mother's direction, but she missed.

"Baby, now you know I don't do housework. Never did. I think Vernice can continue to help you out because I have a long day tomorrow," she said, looking at Vernice.

Loletta didn't even bother responding. She was used to it. Her mother was the definition of a prima donna.

"Oh, and about the light," Ms. Landelton said, peeking out from the bathroom. "I have a very nice set of candles we can burn. It'll be fun." She blew them a fake kiss and closed the door.

Loletta and Vernice had to laugh. Her mother usually knew how to make a party out of nothing. And within an hour, Ms. Landelton had the whole place lit up like the tree at Rockefeller Center. Loletta and Vernice maneuvered carefully around the candles on the living room floor to the table, where they began to eat their Chinese food. They watched Ms. Landelton run around the small apartment, gathering her bathroom items and shoes, and folding her clothes.

"So, you're gonna stay at a hotel or something? The lights will be on by tomorrow," Loletta said, looking at her mom as she ate.

"I've actually booked a trip for myself. I'm leaving Friday. Have to get out of this cold mess." Ms. Landelton flipped open her suitcase and gingerly began packing her things.

Loletta stopped chewing as she and Vernice stared at each other blankly. "Where you going? I didn't know you were planning a trip."

Ms. Landelton gave them both a sympathetic look. "The NFL Coaches Conference is this weekend, and Delores invited me to accompany her. I was going to tell you, Loletta, but I knew you probably wouldn't be able to take time off from work."

Vernice frowned. "Ms. Landelton is about to get her freak on. Don't try to act like it's all about keeping a friend company. You could have told us!"

Loletta stayed quiet. She was in fact thrilled that her mother would be away. She could finally have some privacy. "It would have been nice to go with you. I'm sure I could have taken time off," Loletta said, trying to sound regretful. "When are you coming back?"

"The twenty-seventh."

Vernice flash Loletta a surprised look. "That's after Christmas."

Then it occurred to Loletta that she would be alone for Christmas again. Vernice and her mother would be gone. And there was no time to plan a trip to visit her father in Milan.

Ms. Landelton looked at Loletta sadly. "Sorry, but I'm sure you'll find something to get into." She playfully nudged her.

Loletta forced a tight-lipped smile, but she had expected this year to be different. Her mother usually traveled around the time of Christmas. Last year she was shopping in Aspen. Loletta was looking forward to sharing the day with somebody she truly loved and who loved her.

"Good," Ms. Landelton said, as she held up a gold, string bikini. "Because I definitely plan to be working that day, too!"

Vernice gave Ms. Landelton a high five. But all Loletta could think of was being alone. It seemed like everyone had somebody or something that interested them. It was gonna be a new year, and the only thing new in her life was a pair of overpriced Christian Louboutin stilettos.

Loletta took the day off from work Friday. On top of her light bills, there were several other things she had to take care of before the holidays. She took the day to run errands and busy herself as much as possible. Her mother had left that morning, leaving the apartment in a disarray of hair strands in the bathroom sink and puddles on the floor. As soon as Loletta picked up the mop, the doorbell rang.

She opened the door and was overwhelmed by a mountain of white orchids.

"Loletta Hightower?"

"Yes," she said, inhaling the sweet fragrance. She didn't think Carter would try this hard. But, she thought, how would he know white orchids were her favorite?

"I have a delivery for you. Can we come in?"

Loletta moved out of the way and let several men pass her as they descended on her apartment. They placed over twenty luxurious arrangements anywhere they could find. Her apartment now looked as white as the snow outside her window. After Loletta signed for the flowers, she pulled the card out of the largest bouquet.

It read, "When I first saw, you had one of these in your hair. Since that day you've never left my mind. Love, Kavon."

Loletta unconsciously touched the right side of her hair. In college, she loved wearing flowers in her hair when she'd pulled it back in a ponytail. And that very day she met Kavon in the cafeteria, she wore jeans and a white tank, and had a white orchid stuck behind her ear. She couldn't quite remember when she stopped wearing flowers. As she read the note for the third time, the phone rang, and the answering machine soon picked up.

"Loletta? This is Kavon—" he was saying.

"Kavon!" Loletta said, as she snatched up the phone. "Thank you. These are the most beautiful—"

"You're welcome. And there's more where they come from. I want to get to know you, Loletta," he said in a somber, serious tone.

She wanted to ask him what took him so long to call, but now was not the time for that. "Where are you?"

"I'm in New York. I had some meetings this week, and I have a press conference on Monday. I'm gonna be a Knick," he said, with no emotion.

"Really? Congratulations. Now are we gonna celebrate?" she

asked, already doing a mental check of her closet and what to wear.

"Tomorrow night. How about we go out someplace? I got so much I want to tell you," he said.

"Like where?" Loletta laughed as her fingers played in the soft petals of the orchids.

"I'll have a car pick you up tomorrow at nine p.m. See you soon."

"Bye, Kavon." Loletta held the receiver and exhaled.

Seven

Le Bernardin was a top-rated restaurant on the Upper West Side where socialities and celebrities alike dined. Kavon had arranged a private room, just for the two of them, with their own waiter and sommelier. Loletta had never dined at Le Bernadin, but her mother had. Her mother would without question fly back just to watch and critique Loletta's night with Kavon. But as Loletta stared across the table at Kavon, looking handsome in a coffee bean–colored suit with matching ostrich-skin shoes, her mama's shadow was getting smaller. Loletta thought she wasn't looking too bad herself. Her short, black, shiny hair was tapered to the sides, showing off her high cheekbones and bedroom eyes. Her lips were a glossy cherry red, and her fake eyelashes made her face look as faultless as a doll's.

"Where did you get that little dress you got on? You look good enough to put on my plate," Kavon said, before he took a bite of his steamed halibut fillet.

"I bought it at Bloomingdales a while ago. Almost forgot I had it," she said, looking around at the grand wood-paneled room. She was terribly nervous. Loletta almost forgot that she was wearing the black-gold Chanel cocktail dress her mother had bought her. She came across it when she was looking for a Louis Vuitton bag in her mother's closet. Ms. Landelton innately knew that her daughter would need the dress at some point and was smart enough not to take it back. Loletta silently thanked her mother, because most of Loletta's clothes were too revealing or too corporate for her special night with Kavon. Kavon was someone who knew about her past of chasing men with money, which hadn't changed much since. She couldn't understand why he was willing to even see her again when she had ignored his advances for selfish reasons.

"You ever thought about me?" Loletta neatly forked up some of her Vietnamese beef salad. She wanted to get a moment to clean things up. Kavon was different than the other ballers she pursued. She actually felt she could have a future with him. She didn't know him well at all, but for the first time she was willing to.

"I did. Sometimes." The sommelier arrived with a sampling of a new South African wine to complement their fluke ceviche. He briefly explained its merits. They both sipped and enjoyed it together. Loletta didn't know exactly what a sommelier was, but she liked the way Kavon confidently handled it. He seemed to have more class than anyone she'd been with recently. One thing she did remember was that Kavon came from a well-to-do family. He would have been rich with or without basketball.

"Like when?"

"When I signed my first NBA contract. I wanted to share it with someone, even though I didn't have enough to give you at the time."

Loletta dabbed at her mouth, as she saw an opportunity to straighten things out. "I was young, silly. I was just going after what was hot, what was popular. The girls I was hanging with were all caught up with sleeping with the next R & B star, chilling with them on the bus until they got kicked out—"

"And you weren't a part of that?" He smirked.

Loletta wondered if she was talking too much. She didn't want to sound like a liar either. "I mean, I was. I was doing that and loving it. I wasn't really into college like that, so I didn't know anything about you or how the scouts was checking for you. Aren't you glad I didn't?"

"I am, because a lot of females was doing that. But you straight-up dissed me for the next man, like I was a straight-up bum. And you may not have known, but I was checking for you every day. I wanted you so bad," he said, in that familiar somber tone. Then he laughed. "Maybe I was even in love."

Loletta stroked his sharp, freshly shaven chin. Love, she thought, had been the furthest thing from her mind at that time in her life. She wanted to sympathize with Kavon, but she couldn't feel where he was coming from. But she was going to follow his lead, even though her feelings were not that deep. She hoped they eventually would be, for her own sake. "Let's look at it this way," she said. "We have a new chance to get to know each other. Thank God you signed with the Knicks in New York. Maybe we're getting a little nudge from heaven." She wanted to sound convincing. She didn't know Kavon well, and she had to be careful about appearing too eager. She knew she had feelings that could grow, but she had to have fertile ground to plant her seed.

Kavon smiled warmly at her. "I guess you heard about my divorce."

Loletta nodded. She thought it was too early to go there, but what the hell, she figured. "Who was she?"

"A girl I met when I moved to Denver. I signed with the

Denver Nuggets at first. But that didn't work after a few years. So she bounced."

"She left, just like that?"

"Yeah, I guess she didn't have faith in a brother." He leaned over and took a polenta fry from her plate.

"That's it?"

"Let's just say she couldn't handle the life I lead. Look at you; you know what this is about. You know how the life is—constant traveling from state to state, not to mention whenever I get traded and I have to uproot my entire life; the media; the tabloids; the groupies. That ain't for the average female. She was average. I need a woman who is down for whatever," he said.

Loletta scratched her forehead. "*Whatever* means what exactly?"

He let out a quiet chuckle as the waiter removed their empty plates. "I need someone to stand by me when I have a knee injury, get suspended, or need a career change. You know, bullshit like that. I didn't get the name 'Big' for nothing."

Loletta sipped her red wine as she gazed between his legs. "Is it a name the ladies gave you?" She smiled.

Kavon chuckled. "That's part one. But part two is for my big mouth and my extravagant taste. I do everything big. I'm sure you remember years ago when I refused to stand up for the flag and nearly caused a riot in redneck Denver. I also called the NBA racist and was suspended, but I'm not that hotheaded anymore."

"That was you?" Loletta said. "Of course, I remember that time with the flag. Man, I must have really been out of it then." She remembered at that time she was dating TK, the lead member of Silk Five, then one of the top R & B bands. With him, she was caught in an alcohol- and marijuana-infused haze for at least two years.

The waiter placed down their desserts of banana crème brûlée with peanut caramel and slow-baked apple confit with raisins. As Loletta savored her crème brûlée, she tried to figure out if she had unconsciously blocked Kavon from her memory; after all, he had been all over the media when he was drafted. Perhaps she had, because all the time she was out chasing a dream, she had found hers years ago and he was right under her nose.

Kavon rested his hand lightly on hers. Loletta wiped away a smudge of chocolate from his lips. "I know you arranged for me to come to the dealership," he said, his eyes lingering on her cleavage.

Loletta ran her fingers slowly across it. "I ain't gonna lie; I wanted to see you. I do feel like we missed our chance. Maybe if you had communicated more, or maybe if I had been more mature, things would have been different. But really, no time is better than now."

He squeezed her hand gently, then kissed it. "Let me ask you one thing."

"Yes?"

"This industry is small, and everyone talks. So tell me, who you fucked with already?"

Loletta's eyes widened. There were many. Some retired, some overseas, some married, and some the star of their team. "Just a few. It's really part of my past now that we're together."

"I know, and it's okay," Kavon said, as he sniffed the aroma from the inside of his wineglass. He lifted his head and looked at Loletta. "Trust me, I know you follow these cats, and it ain't for the free courtside tickets. But anybody I should know about?"

Loletta's eyebrows rose slightly. Kavon's face reflected some kind of sinister pleasure from their conversation. "Kavon, a lady doesn't talk about the men in her past. Don't make me."

"I won't," he said, leaning in closer to her. "But I'm still a man, and some things matter to us. However, there's nothing to be ashamed of. We go way back. I knew when I first saw you that you're a good woman, with a good heart. All I ask for is that heart be mine," he said. She opened her mouth for him. He kissed her longingly, like he wanted to suck away her breath.

He made her feel safe enough to reveal everything, but she wouldn't. The last place she wanted to be was Le Bernardin. After they finished their desserts, Loletta asked, "Do you want me to come back with you?"

Kavon wiped his hands with the table napkin. "No, I don't. I just want this night to stay like it is. I don't want to be like those other guys. I want this to be special."

"Oh, it is very special. When exactly are you gonna make your Knicks announcement?"

"Tomorrow, right before Christmas. I want you to be there."

"Okay, I'll be wearing my cute little Knick cheerleader outfit," Loletta said, as he laughed and motioned for her to sit next to him. He put his arm around her so that her head was lying on his chest.

"Speaking of Christmas. What do you have planned?"

Loletta's smile faded. She didn't want to seem like a charity case. "I may be alone, but I got some things to do."

"How about you come over Christmas Eve and stay as long as you like?"

"I can't think of anything more special than that," Loletta said, as her lips touched his. "Thank you, Jesus," she said silently, as she lost herself in the warmth of Kavon's mouth.

The next morning, Loletta met Kavon at a press conference at Mickey Mantle's in Manhattan. She invited Vernice, who was going to be there anyway because of Calvin. All three sat together among the reporters, the media, and a small gathering of fans. Loletta was glad to have Vernice by her side because she was really the only other person she knew there. She looked around for anyone who might look like a member of his family, but saw no one. Kavon was on the podium standing next to Knicks general Manager Jeffrey Abramson and Madison Square Garden President Kenneth Klein. Several people took to the podium and began to talk about Kavon.

Loletta listened intently until she saw Kavon signal for her to join him on the stage. She looked around to see if he was talking to anyone else.

"Girl, he is asking for you to go up there. Give it your best sexy walk." Vernice laughed, as she nudged her friend out of her chair. Loletta had no problem showing off her goods because she had dressed elegantly, in a winter white knit dress and grey suede boots, just in case this happened. A girl like her always had to be prepared, she thought. She was flattered that Kavon would want her by his side. Kavon whispered into the ear of a young blond-haired guy, who escorted Loletta onto the stage. A few cameras flashed in her direction, but she played the back and stood to the side, behind Kavon. How did she get here? she asked herself. She wasn't really quite ready to make her television debut, she thought. She had to stop herself from laughing at the goofy looks Vernice was giving her. She knew it was to make her laugh and lighten up a bit.

"I'm so happy you came. These types of things you're gonna get used to," Kavon said over his shoulder.

"We are honored to have Kavon 'Big' Jackson as the newest member of the Knicks. We haven't seen his likes in at least twenty years. Here's to you, kid," said Abramson as he adorned Kavon with a Knicks jersey and hat.

Kavon took the spotlight without hesitation. A small crowd outside the restaurant shouted, "Big! Big! Big!"

"Okay, okay, calm down, everybody. I just want to thank most of all the New Yorkers who have supported my move. I want to thank Mr. Abramson for bringing me to New York and making me a part of this legendary team. And I'm ready to bring that ring home, baby!" he said, as the small crowd cheered and clapped. Vernice and Calvin cheered the loudest. And Vernice kept winking at Loletta.

Loletta clapped too. Kavon just seemed confident, like he could get through anything. She saw a genuine happiness in his eyes that she hadn't seen in anyone in a while.

"I also want to thank my beautiful girlfriend, Loletta Hightower," he announced, taking Loletta's hand as she reluctantly walked to the front beside him.

Girlfriend, when did that happen? Loletta thought, as she looked at a frozen Vernice.

"Will you marry me?" he asked, getting down on one knee. He opened a small blue box with a bright, shiny solitaire diamond that nearly blinded Loletta. She smiled and looked at Vernice, who sat there with her mouth open wide enough to fit a fist. Loletta shook her head at her like she didn't know this was coming.

"Loletta," Kavon said through his teeth, to draw her attention back. He held both of her shivering hands.

Loletta didn't want Vernice to think she was holding out on her. But if it looked like it, so be it. She could explain to her later, but now was her moment. She planted a fat juicy kiss on Kavon's cheek and screamed, "Yes!" He breathed a sigh of relief.

Television cameras zoomed in on her finger, and cameras flashed erratically as the couple were flooded with questions about his career and their relationship.

She let Kavon handle most of that, while she smiled and cheesed for the flashing lights. Kavon also entertained more questions about his new team. She thought she might as well get into it, because now the world knew and nothing was ever going to be the same.

Eight

Kavon lived on a two-acre estate in northern New Jersey. The trees and lush green bushes outside his mansion were covered with thin slithers of snow and ice. Loletta thought the landscape of white, silver, and green was fitting enough to be on a Hallmark card.

As she peered out the window of the master bedroom, she was afraid to close her eyes in case she was in a dream. This was the life she was meant to live. This was what she had been accustomed to. Just last week she was counting on being all alone for Christmas. Now she had a lifetime of everything she had been looking for. Kavon hadn't mentioned a prenup yet, and she wanted to keep it that way.

Today was Christmas Eve. Kavon had arranged for a driver to pick her up in his Bentley and bring her to his home so they could spend the holiday together. Kavon was on his way back from Manhattan after signing some last-minute papers with his agent. He had left a brief note on the bed telling Loletta to make herself at home.

An elegant Hervé Léger dress wrapped in a Bergdorf Goodman box sat on the wooden sleigh bed, and Manolo Blahnik shoes were in a box on a nearby matching bench. A cook was downstairs stirring up Indian dishes, which coincidentally were Loletta's favorite food. Inhaling the fragrance of cardamom, cinnamon, and other roasted spices, Loletta heard her stomach begin to growl. She took her time and dressed in front of the mirror, slipping into a turquoise silk gown. Every few minutes she'd hold her diamond up against her to see how it looked in the mirror. The light patter of snow on the window excited her. She had always liked making love on a snowy night. Tonight would be their first.

She took her Hanae Mori fragrance from her weekend bag and sprayed some around her neck, elbows, and knees. Sitting on the bench beside the window, she felt Kavon's presence in the room even though he wasn't there. His sandalwood scented cologne clung to the air, covering the linens that draped the windows and his bed. The floor-to-ceiling windows were adorned with only a thin piece of mint green, chiffon-like material hanging over a decorative brass wrought-iron rod. A large brown and white, fluffy fur rug tickled the bottoms of her bare feet. Tall bamboo plants in rectangular glass vases sat on separate mantels throughout the bedroom, giving it an Asian touch. Stacks of books and magazines rested on a vintage red leather trunk across the room near the entrance. A few framed photos of Kavon's game-playing style embellished the wall behind his bed. She joked to herself that he probably got off watching himself make a slam dunk. She reclined on a nearby armchair and flicked the channels on the spanking new fifty-four-inch flat-screen television. It seemed to beg her for some attention, and she was happy to oblige.

Loletta answered her ringing phone when she saw Kavon's

number flash on the screen. "I'm here," she sang, standing up and walking toward the snow-covered window. She saw the headlights of a black Escalade in the distance.

"I'm here too," he said, with a smile in his voice.

"Thank you for the dress and the shoes. How did you know my size?" she asked, as she watched his car go around several bends up to his house.

"I got a good eye; let's just say that." He finally exited the Escalade and handed one of his assistants the key. "Whenever you're ready, Loletta, come downstairs."

Loletta hung up and prepped herself in the mirror. The halter-top dress was perfect for her shape, defining her shapely breasts and shoulders and ending right above her knees to show off the results of intense leg lifts at the gym. She slid on her blue and green jewel-embellished Manolo Blahniks and did a model-like catwalk up and down the bedroom. She had several Manolos, but these took the cake. She felt giddy and wound-up about Kavon, even though she knew he probably had one of his "people" buy her these things. That's how it was done—with his approval, of course.

"Hey, baby." Loletta glided down the spiral steps and stood by the seven-foot Christmas tree adorned in white lights and gold and red ornaments. Kavon was walking out of the kitchen, where he had been doing a little taste-testing.

"Damn, damn, damn. You gonna really ruin our evening looking this good. I don't think I can wait till later," he said, playfully smacking her behind.

She put her arms around him as their mouths met briefly. She thought he would be in a suit and tie, but he was dressed in a black designer sweatsuit that fell nicely over his tall thick build. It made her feel overdressed.

He looked into her face with those alluring, dark brown eyes and assured her it was fine. "I know I'm not in a million-dollar suit, because tonight I want you to be the star. *My* star," he said, and kissed her again, gently tugging on her full bottom lip.

She followed him down the hall to the left, to a small room with a table set for two with fine linen and sterling silverware.

A fresh-faced waiter at their beck and call came and pulled out their chairs as they sat shoulder-to-shoulder facing the crackling fireplace. Loletta couldn't wait to get her hands all over Kavon and on the food as well. But she composed herself. There was time.

"Do you do this every time you eat?" Loletta asked, as she picked a strawberry from the bowl of fresh fruit.

Kavon fiddled with the thick, gold pendant on his chain. "Not at all. Sometimes I eat in the den upstairs, but I hardly ever eat on that big-ass marble table. I mean it's for twenty people; I'm only a man of one. Now two and, hopefully, three and four, five—," he said, kissing her bare shoulders each time.

Loletta unzipped his sweatsuit jacket to reveal a chiseled chest with a thin coat of fine hair down the middle. She loved a man with hair on his chest. She ran her fingers up and down the center. He felt as strong as an ox.

"Mmm." He moaned, as she fed him a strawberry. Then she lay across him as he fed her juicy green grapes. His hardness poked her back, and by its length she could tell she was going to be getting a different kind of dessert.

The waiter reappeared with platters of chickpea-and-vegetable fritters; fried, flat paratha sprinkled with coconut and raisins; small, tender beef-and-lamb kebabs; sweet scented chicken biryani rice; and an assortment of internationally inspired desserts, like mango ice cream.

After their meal was set on their plates, Loletta and Kavon wasted no time indulging in their grand feast.

"Open your mouth," Kavon said, as he fed Loletta a succulent, sweet beef-sausage kebab.

"Ooh, this is better than Outback's ribs," she laughed.

"Just a *little* better," he said, and he laughed too.

Loletta watched Kavon as he licked his fingers and belched every now and then. She didn't mind one bit. She had always loved the little nuisances of a man.

"You know when you proposed to me yesterday, that came out of the blue." She wanted to get more into his head. Did he really love her?

"Hell, yeah. That's how it's supposed to be, baby," he said, as he bit into a crusty pakora. "A surprise."

"You know people are gonna say we jumped into this." She passed him a napkin as he passed her the bowl of fragrant rice.

"Well," he said, wiping some food from his mouth. "That's the kind of man I am. I do what I please. I've known you since college. People make things too complicated. I don't want a prenup because we're either in this together or we're not."

Loletta wanted to do a "hallelujah" church dance right there. She was dreading the prenup talk because usually wives fared better, in case of an emergency, without one. She didn't want to acknowledge Kavon's statement directly because it was good enough. "We know we're in this together, but I want to make sure we stay together," she said.

"Come on, Loletta. You want to be married, and I want to be married again. I made a mistake that I won't ever make again. I've always loved you. I got all this shit here. I want to make a family, start a legacy."

They both held their glasses up as the waiter poured a rich, dark red wine. Then the waiter disappeared again.

Loletta didn't know if she was in love with Kavon, but everyday it felt more like it. "I can't wait to see the look on my mother's face about this. But fuck it, you have people been married for twenty years and still surprising the hell out of each other with bullshit," she said.

Loletta gave him a funny, look. "You don't have any bullshit, do you?"

"Nobody's perfect. But you got my heart, Loletta. Word," he said, beating his chest. He tore the flattened bread in half and spread some mango chutney on it. She did the same and gazed at him. He probably was the one she should have married years ago, she thought. There was a small flame in her heart for him that grew bigger and stronger. They were like lost souls reunited, she thought.

Kavon caressed Loletta's chin and turned it toward him. "I love you, Loletta. And I want you in my life. I will do anything I have to do to be the best husband. Will you be the best wife you can be?"

"I will," Loletta said, as she rolled her head to the side. "I'm sure you'll make it all worthwhile." The flames from the fire flickered in his eyes, making them look fiery red. Then he closed them, as she kissed both of his eyelids.

After dinner, they ended up in the master bedroom sprawled on the black and gold silk sheets. Loletta still had her dress on.

"Can you take it off for me?" Kavon asked, as he pulled off his sweatsuit.

Loletta's eyes danced all over his deep mahogany skin, which seemed to never end. His legs were defined and muscular and looked like they had the strength of a tree trunk. Lying back on the bed, with one foot up, he looked like he was posing for a *GQ* spread.

Loletta slowly peeled out of her dress and her thin black

thong, letting them fall to her feet. As she went to slip off her heels, he said, "Keep those on." She then crawled into bed beside him, the warmth of his body sucking her in.

She climbed on top of him ready to stake her claim. Holding him down by his shoulders, she ran her tongue and lips around his neck, nipples, and belly button. She pretended she was licking a cone of rich, chocolate-batter ice cream. His hardness jabbed her chin a few times as she teased around it. But she couldn't resist. She wanted to taste the fiber of who he was. He lay back with his legs slightly bent at the knees, as she sniffed around his dick like a little animal. The tip of her tongue patted the head, which released dots of sugary juice. She glided her mouth over the entire length of him, able to leave out only about an inch.

He grabbed the back of her head, pressing her down further as he moaned in complete surrender to her will. Careful with the power she held in her mouth, she managed to fit in the last inch, which she deep-throated to his satisfaction. Her cheeks sunk into her mouth as she got a rhythm going. She could tell by his high-pitch moans and tighter grip on her hair that he was about to bust soon. But she wasn't ready for it to be over that quick.

His dick felt like it belonged in her mouth. She sucked it like she was talking to it, telling it all about her insecurities and anxieties. It was giving her back the perfect answers.

"Damn, baby, damn!" he said out loud, as he fought to hold back. "Get on your back."

Loletta slid his dick out of her mouth and did as he requested. By the time her back hit the mattress, Kavon was returning the favor. He engulfed her pussy in his mouth like a clam sucked out of its shell. She pressed her hips down on the bed and squeezed her pelvic muscles to make her orgasm more intense. Kavon lightly ran his tongue across the bare skin of her pussy, sucking gently on its lips. Loletta spread her legs wider, feeling her body elevate to a state of pure bliss.

She dug her fingers into his shoulder blades and wrapped her legs firmly around his neck as he licked her to a puddle of wetness underneath. She thought she could get used to this.

"I can't get enough of this pussy," he said, with her juices glistening on his mouth. He muttered a few other words. He was talking to himself, she thought. *My pussy is so damn good, I got the negro talking to it!*

When he'd finally had enough, Kavon slipped his dick into her like a special delivery. He kept his eyes on her for any reaction to his blessed package. She held her feet up by her hands as he buried all of himself inside her. She rubbed her hands all across his back like it was made of silk. Their sweat-slicked bodies rolled around the bed several times until Loletta was on her knees. Kavon bit her shoulders as he pumped into her with power and grace.

She got up on her knees—her preferred position and, obviously, his too. He slapped her ass several times as he fucked her from behind.

"Slap it again," she begged, and he smacked it even harder.

"I love you," he said into her ear. When she turned around to look at him, his eyes were bearing down on her. That turned her on like hell. A few more adjustments and she was on top. She wanted to fuck Kavon so hard he'd want to suck his thumb to sleep.

She held down his shoulders and abused his dick for her pleasure as she rode it back and forth, up and down. Kavon's eyes closed, and he gripped her sweaty thighs. "Take it, baby. Take this dick."

Loletta's eyes rested on a photo of Kavon doing a slam dunk

at last year's NBA All-Star Game—he was hanging on to the rim, with his legs dangling over everyone below. That was her man, she said to herself. That was gonna be her husband. *He's a bad motherfucka.* Her head bent back, she cried, "I love you." Then she collapsed on top of him.

Nine

The next morning Loletta awoke to the quiet stillness of a snowy Christmas Day. Kavon was beside her, gently snoring. Her inquisitive mind had questions. She needed her mother to help her sort out these things. She was about to get everything, but why did she still feel something was missing?

Kavon's arms pulled her into him. She kissed his hand and turned over. "Merry Christmas," she said. She wondered what he could possibly have gotten her, because she thought nothing could top that rock on her finger.

"Merry Christmas," he said, stretching out his body. He pulled out a tiny black box from under his pillow.

"How did you get that under there?"

"You can sleep through the LA riots. That's how," he laughed.

Loletta untied the red ribbon and lost her breath. "These are—oh, my God—these are . . ." She was at a loss. She held one of the diamond-stud earrings in her hand. It was almost as big as the entire nail bed of her thumb. She covered her mouth with her hands as Kavon put them on her.

"You needed something to go with that ring," he said, touching her earlobe.

She grabbed the mirror from the nightstand. "Thank you," she said, turning her head from side to side. "These are at least eight carats, right?"

He just nodded.

Loletta was good at this stuff. She estimated that the earrings cost at least twenty-four thousand dollars. The cut and clarity of the diamonds were first-rate.

"And whatever you're thinking, it cost twice as much," he said, rubbing the sleep out of his eyes.

She felt guilty. She didn't have any kind of gift to give him. Shit, she thought, she hadn't even expected to ever hear from him again. In less than a week she was engaged and laid up in his mansion. There was absolutely no time. "I'm sorry, but I left your gift at my apartment. I promise—"

"You can't buy me anything anyway," he shrugged. "I got everything I need, including you."

Kavon walked into the bathroom, leaving Loletta to admire herself in the mirror some more. She raised her diamond-crusted left hand to her left ear. She had never owned diamonds this big. She promised herself she would buy something for Kavon; she didn't care what he said.

"Oh, one more thing," he said, as he walked out of the bathroom naked and took something else from under his pillow. He handed her an envelope and a box.

She opened the envelope and found a key, and in the box, an American Express platinum card.

"That key is for the Maybach; if you gonna be my wife, you got to ride in style. The card is for whatever you need; you gotta start shopping like her too," he said, as he hugged her from behind.

She turned around and squeezed him as hard as she could. "This is crazy. I mean, thank you. I don't deserve all this," she said, locked in an embrace.

"Okay," he said, and took the card and key from her.

"On second thought, I can get used to this," she said, carefully sliding the items out of his hand. She couldn't wait to hit Fifth Avenue.

While Kavon showered, Loletta called Vernice.

"Hey, Merry Fucking Christmas," Loletta said when she heard Vernice's voice. It was eight a.m. but she sounded wide awake.

"What's up?" Vernice said dryly.

"What's wrong?" Loletta didn't like the tone of her voice.

"Nothing. I'm just here waiting for Calvin. He was supposed to have been here since last night. I hate waking up alone."

"So call him."

"I did; I got the voicemail."

Loletta shook her head. She didn't want to see her friend down like this. It was the kind of life they led. Anything could end at any moment.

"You with Kavon?" she asked.

"Of course," Loletta said, wanting to brag about her earrings, the Maybach, the card, but she figured Vernice would see them for herself. "You want to come over?"

"Can I?"

Loletta wasn't sure. But she would feel awful if she was laid up in this big house with her man, and her girl was alone on Christmas morning. Vernice was wild, but she had a good heart and was always there when Loletta couldn't talk to her mother. "Sure, girl. I'm sure Kavon didn't make any plans for us today. Just get over here soon."

A few minutes later Kavon walked out of the bathroom

wrapped in a navy blue, Egyptian-cotton bathrobe tagged with his alias, "Big."

"You ready to have breakfast specially prepared by the one and only?"

"You cook breakfast?"

"Hell, yeah, I may have grown up with some uppity black folks, but one thing my mama showed me was how to make good pancakes and omelets," he said, sitting on the edge of the bed.

"Um, well, I'm hoping you can make a big breakfast because I invited Vernice over for a little while. She's all alone—"

"You mean Calvin's chick?"

"Yeah," Loletta said, massaging his bare shoulders. "Is that all right?"

Kavon chuckled and sighed. "I invited Calvin and his wife over today."

"Oh," Loletta tapped herself in the head. "Why didn't I ask you first?"

"I don't know. You should have," he said, lotioning his feet and putting on some socks. "But it ain't a big deal."

Loletta picked up her cell phone. "I gotta tell her she can't come."

"Forget it. Let it ride. She can come. Calvin is gonna come. The only person who won't know anything is his wife. Your girl is cool with that, right?"

Loletta wrapped the cool silky sheet around her. She felt cold suddenly.

Kavon rubbed her leg. "Right?"

"She knows he's married. I'll let her know when she gets here because I'm sure she's already on her way."

Loletta, Vernice, and Kavon assembled with Calvin and his wife, Darva, to enjoy a delectable Christmas dinner in the elegant dining room. Vernice was well aware of what was going on and had adapted herself well to the situation. Vernice was not ready to give up Calvin, Loletta thought, but it pained her to see her friend fake the funk.

"Kavon, you have to tell me the name of your interior designer because Calvin and I need a serious home makeover," Darva said. Her blond bangs were combed neatly to the side of her shoulder-length hair.

"She want to make our house look like something outta a Martha Stewart handbook. I like my ceramic tiles, my rare paintings of Tupac and Biggie. Woman, I want to keep my shit," he laughed. Loletta and Vernice joined him.

"I love those Tupac and Biggie paintings," Vernice blurted out as she cut into her duck breast. "Those are hot."

No one said anything. Everyone looked at Calvin.

"Yeah, see what I'm saying? It's a hood thing," Calvin joked.

Darva squeezed Calvin's cheek. "You can keep the paintings if I can give the kitchen a country-style makeover complete with his-and-her oven mitts." Then she kissed him and wiped some food from her mouth.

Loletta felt the anger radiate off Vernice, but she played it cool.

"Wow, I'm full," Vernice said, pushing away her dinner. "I haven't had duck like this in a while."

"That was my idea, sweetie. I recommended the perfect caterer to Kavon. He did my mother's fiftieth wedding anniversary—"

Loletta just listened as Darva went on and on. But she and Vernice knew the truth. Darva had been married to Calvin for only three years. She was one of the highest paid, most popular publicists in black entertainment. She repped some of the best known actors, rappers, and singers. But she was known to sell out her clients and rev up the media frenzy by dishing their dirty laundry on Page Six. Rumor had it that she had become pregnant by several of her high-profile clients, including Calvin. By the second time, he caved in and married her. Darva Braxton had a reputation as both a whore and a genius.

"It all comes down to everyone's personal taste. That is why Calvin and I are opening our own catering business."

Loletta and Vernice just stared at her as she continued her annoying banter.

"No, you are," Calvin said, smirking at Darva.

"And I am so glad to have Kavon as our first client for his birthday party in March."

"Well, I'm not having a party because Loletta and I plan to get married on my birthday."

"We do?"

"Yeah, it's only three months away."

"Oh, my God, that's fantastic. I'll do the catering—"

"Wait, wait—" Loletta said, putting her hand up. This was her show, and she was running things. Plus her mother would have a well of ideas of her own. She wasn't going to let Darva run her life, like she'd been running Calvin's. "Yeah, we have our own way of doing things around here," Loletta said, as she glanced at Kavon, who looked at her with loving bedroom eyes.

"I just was trying to help," Darva said.

"Thank you, but we can figure this out," Loletta snapped. "Anybody want more sweet potato soufflé?"

Vernice snickered as she stuck her finger down her throat to symbolize how sick she was of Darva. But Darva was too busy filling up her plate to take notice.

"I'm going to pass on anything else," Vernice announced, as she gave Calvin the eye. "I need to keep this body beautiful, and a third plate would just defeat the purpose of me holding on to my size four jeans." Vernice was a proud size six, smaller than Loletta's eight and sometimes ten.

Loletta said. "I am through. Another plate and I will be nodding off at this table."

"Suit yourself," Darva said, grinning. Her plate was stacked with sweet potato, duck, greens, and macaroni and cheese. "I've got an excuse. I'm eating for two."

"Ooh," Kavon said, with a mouthful of macaroni and cheese. "Congrats, man," he said to Calvin, as he gave him a pound. "Darva, I did notice you picked up some weight."

"All for the right reasons."

Vernice stood up and quietly pushed in her chair. "That's very nice. Excuse me," she said, disappearing down the stairs.

"Yes," Loletta said, smiling at Calvin, who looked embarrassed for some reason. "Um, congrats to the both of you. Excuse me," she said, as she followed Vernice down the steps.

Loletta found Vernice checking out Kavon's mantel in his Championship Room. It had every award he ever coveted since he was in high school.

"Vernice," Loletta hissed, as she closed the door behind her, "that bitch is pregnant."

Vernice turned her head slightly to acknowledge what Loletta said, but she kept studying the mantel.

"Vernice, did he tell you?"

Vernice stood up straight and put her hand on her hip. "No, he didn't. His ass probably just found out today. That woman is scandalous. She would say anything to upstage anyone."

Loletta touched Vernice's shoulder. "Calvin looked like he knew. So how do you feel about it?"

Vernice walked away to another mantel. She stroked a gold-plated medal, one Kavon had received for MVP for the U.S. Olympic team. A sly grin fell across her lips.

"What?" Loletta asked, as she stepped toward her. She folded her arms. Vernice was up to something, she thought.

"If she's pregnant, better for me because we all know she ain't gonna be fucking him for a long time. He's gonna want this pussy even more," she said, snapping her fingers like a magician. "And who knows, the bitch may miscarry or keep it. Either way, I know she's lying."

Loletta thought Vernice was gambling a bit too much. "You can keep having sex with him, but when she does eventually have a baby, it may change him. He will get attached to that child and may not have the time with you like he do now."

"That's why I'm gonna enjoy it while it lasts. I ain't like you. I don't have to know everything right away. And not everybody can get married like you," Vernice said, as she examined a gold-plated award from the Boys Club of America.

Loletta fixed her lips as if to say something about Vernice's smart comment, but she didn't. She took the award from her and placed it on the mantel.

"Excuse me, ladies. Can I have a word with Vernice?" Calvin stood in the doorway, looking like a lost puppy with his stout build and pensive eyes.

"Sure," Loletta said, giving Vernice a last look. "I'll be upstairs if you need me," Loletta told her, as she walked out.

But Loletta didn't go anywhere. She stood by the door and listened carefully. About fifteen seconds later, she heard Vernice's gentle moans and heavy breathing.

Loletta wanted to bust in there. *They better not be messing up Kavon's fine furnishings with their nasty selves,* she thought. Now she had to go upstairs and play dumb.

She walked back up the stairs and found Darva chewing off Kavon's ear with more catering talk. He just sat there like a lump on a log. "Anybody need anything?" Loletta said, as she walked back over to the couch. "I'm feeling a little tired. I may lie down for a bit."

Kavon looked concerned and signaled for Loletta to sit on his lap. He rubbed her thighs and asked, "I should be asking you if you need anything. I know I kind of kept you up all night."

Darva let out a loud, obnoxious sigh. "Where's Calvin? I think we should get going."

"Um," Loletta said, looking at Kavon. "I think he went downstairs for something."

"I'll get him." Kavon eased out of the chair and walked down the steps to the basement level.

Now Loletta and Darva were alone. Something she didn't want.

Darva slipped on her winter gloves and put her Prada bag over her shoulder. "Tell your bitch friend that I got her card. And I'm the wrong one to fuck with."

Ten

Sunday, two days after Christmas, Loletta was at her apartment sorting out the life she had neglected. She was supposed to meet Kavon at his game against the Miami Heat at the Garden. She was running late because plans were to meet him there in the next hour or two.

Loletta had a pile of mail on the kitchen table. *Bills, bills, bills.* These had to go, she thought, and they would. She wasn't sweating it at all. She called her bank just to check on her funds. When she heard the automated voice, she nearly passed out.

Your current checking balance is $500,700. For more information on your account, please press one.

Loletta pressed it. *A credit of $450,000 was deposited into your account on December twenty-fourth. A credit of $10,000 was deposited into your account on December twentieth—*

Loletta hung up the phone, having heard all she needed. Kavon's Christmas gifts just didn't stop. She pulled out her checkbook and happily paid all her bills, totaling around fifty K. As she wrote her last check, her cell phone rang.

"Thank you!" she shouted into the phone when she saw it was Kavon. "I got both of your deposits, and I am writing my checks out now. We are *both* debt-free now, baby," she said, licking the envelope.

"Both?"

"Yeah, weren't there two?" Loletta sealed the envelope shut as she went back to the recording in her head.

"I just made one," he said coldly. "For 450,000 dollars. That's supposed to jump-start your monthly allowance."

"Oh," Loletta said. *The ten K must be from Carter.* "My bad; I think I may have mixed it up with my job's direct deposit. I forgot I got a holiday bonus."

Kavon was dead silent. She was afraid to say anything. She didn't know what else Carter was expecting, but the money in her account meant things were still on for him.

"Listen, if another nigga is putting shit in your account, dead that. Give that nigga back his money."

"Kavon—"

"Who is it?"

"I don't know!" Loletta said, frustrated; she wasn't about to be a fool and tell him.

"Give that nigga back his money. And I want you to close your account."

Loletta's shoulders fell. She hated being told what to do. But this was the price. Nothing was ever free. "Fine, but I can't control people from doing what they want."

"That's why you do the thinking for them. Close the account today. We'll have a joint account where you can take out whatever you need. I wouldn't be a man if I let you keep that account. See you later."

Loletta hung up the phone. There was no way she was going to close her account. She realized that there were some things she would have to give up, but money was something she would never part with.

Loletta's attention was drawn to the door when she heard someone fiddling with the lock. Then the door busted open.

"I'm baaack, my lovely!" Ms. Landelton said, as she waltzed into the room with her Louis Vuitton duffel bags and with her sun-kissed skin looking radiant and bright. She dumped her bags and charged at Loletta.

Loletta felt limp in her mother's embrace and relieved to see her at the same time. "You're back early?" Loletta asked. "Something happen?"

"Well, hell yes! I had to come back early and take care of things," Ms. Landelton said, grabbing Loletta's left hand. "Honey, I read all about it in the papers!" Ms. Landelton squeezed Loletta even more tightly. She felt suffocated by her mom, even though she was only 5'4," barely 100 pounds wet.

Loletta and Ms. Landelton sat down on the kitchen chairs. "Well, baby, we got a wedding to plan."

"I know." Loletta finally smiled, eyeing her ring. "Everything happened practically overnight. I feel like it's all a dream."

"Then why do you look like someone stole your only pair of Prada boots?"

"Because a lot of things happened. And—"

"And?" Ms. Landelton asked, holding on tightly to Loletta's hands. "Those earrings are spectacular."

"I just got off the phone with Kavon. I found out that he put some money in my account. But I had another deposit, and I thought it was from him too. So he caught on and basically told me to close my account."

"Who put the other money in? How much was it?"

"Carter put in ten K. I don't know what his ass wants."

"Close the account. Then call Carter and tell him you are an engaged woman. Don't go making Kavon have second thoughts about this."

Loletta rolled her eyes at the ceiling. "I'm going to give Carter the money back."

"You sure as hell won't. Open a new account. And tell Carter you've moved on," Ms. Landelton said.

"I don't even know how Kavon got my account number," Loletta said.

"Who cares? Those men have their sources. Has he offered you the joint account?"

"Yes, but I need my own account, too."

Ms. Landelton waved her hand at Loletta like she was hopeless. "I want to get down to the real business. Is he making you sign a prenup?"

"Nope." Loletta grinned. She saw the twinkle in her mother's eye.

"Fantastical! So when is the wedding?"

"He mentioned March. That's only three months from now."

"Plenty of time. How much money you think we can blow on this thing?" Ms. Landelton asked, taking a notepad out of her bag. She jotted down a few things.

Loletta opened the refrigerator door and poured two glasses of week-old wine. "As long as it took me to get here, it's a cause for celebration." They clinked their glasses, and she added, "I'm thinking the sky's the limit."

Loletta and her mother staked out the courtside seats as they cheered Kavon and the rest of the Knicks. Her mother took snapshots of Kavon every time he made a leap for the basket. He scored over twenty points just in the first half.

"Don't you think you got enough pictures?" Loletta asked Ms. Landelton. She tried to grab the digital camera from her, but Ms. Landelton was too swift.

"Honey, relax," Ms. Landelton whined. "I want to be able to show these off to Delores. My daughter is going to be the wife of an NBA star."

"Mommy, it's too embarrassing," Loletta said, taking the camera. "And it's distracting to the players." Loletta was tucking the camera away in her Chanel bag when she saw Kavon run down the court and deliver a flawless slam dunk over the Miami Heat center's head. It broke the tie in the game, and there were only a few minutes left.

"Yeah, that's my baby!" Loletta said, flying out of her seat and pumping her fists. "Don't hurt 'em!"

The crowd shouted their approval as they broke out in their "Big" cheers.

"He's so handsome," Ms. Landelton squealed, as she fixed her eyes on Kavon.

Loletta stayed on her feet with the rest of the Garden crowd as the final seconds were counted down. The Knicks needed three points to win the game. The next thing she saw was the ball being passed several times, finally making it to Kavon. He posted up on the three-point line and made a shot that was all net.

"Yes!" Loletta, Ms. Landelton, and the crowd roared as the buzzer went off. Everyone surrounded Kavon. This was his first game as a Knick, and he had started the season off just right.

After the game, Kavon took Loletta and Ms. Landelton out to dinner at B. Smiths. Loletta was charmed by the restaurant's yellow walls and soaring ceilings. Years ago she used to meet Vernice there for drinks after work. She had always admired its welcoming presence and felt it was just the right environment for her mother's first official meeting with Kavon. But she feared that even though a nice mood was set, her mother would find something to criticize.

"How was your vacation in Aspen?" Kavon asked Ms. Landelton. She was relishing her potato leek pancakes topped with smoked salmon and caviar.

"It was the usual Aspen. Same folks, same stores. I missed my baby as soon I left," she said, delicately moving a strand of Loletta's hair off her face. *Right*, Loletta thought. *She missed me like she missed that fake-ass tan and that suitcase full of new designer threads.*

"And then I heard the news!" Ms. Landelton waved her fork at both Kavon and Loletta. "I just know you two are right for each other."

Loletta shot her a look, as she held her barbecue ribs to her mouth. Then she looked at Kavon, who was happily munching on fried catfish. "Baby, you really did your thing tonight. Man, getting you was the best thing the Knicks have done since they signed Latrell Sprewell."

"Well, you don't want to compare Kavon to that lunatic."

Loletta stabbed her fork into caramelized sweet potatoes. "I wasn't comparing them. I'm saying that—"

"Babe, it's okay. I feel honored. Latrell did his thing when he was with the Knicks. I'm trying to go for legendary status. It's only the beginning. And hey, if I can have people still talk about my skills years after I leave the game, then I can sleep at night," he said, rubbing her knee with his free hand. She felt energized whenever he touched her. It was like turning on a light in a dark room.

Loletta didn't know what Ms. Landelton was trying to start, but she didn't like the vibes she was getting. She could tell her mother liked Kavon, but she wasn't sure what was bugging her.

"So, what kind of wedding are we talking about here?" Ms. Landelton asked, as she poked around in a salad of fresh field greens.

"Actually," Kavon said, putting his arm across Loletta's bare shoulders. She wore a pink silk shawl over her green sweater and couture jeans. "I was hoping we could do it in Las Vegas. The season is on, but I've always wanted to get married on my birthday, in March."

"Well, let's wait till the season is over," Loletta said, looking at him.

Ms. Landelton interrupted Loletta's thoughts. "Oh, please. We can do it in Las Vegas. Michael and Juanita Jordan got married in Las Vegas."

Loletta winced at her mother, but thought a Las Vegas wedding might actually be fun. She prayed that this interaction between she and her mom wouldn't chase Kavon away. "I'm okay with it. I just want to marry this man," she said. Loletta turned her face to look Kavon square in the eye.

"I'm thinking for the dress we should go for that same designer who did Shaq's wife Shaunie's platinum dress," said Ms. Landelton.

"Michelle Roth?" Loletta said. "I had someone else—"

"Follow me," Ms. Landelton said, as her hands moved wildly before her. "Platinum silk, beaded chiffon, sprinkled with Swarovski crystals. But we have to give it a different look, something short and sassy," her mother laughed. "It's Las Vegas, after all!"

Loletta was liking some of what she heard. She looked to Kavon for a reaction, but he was just nodding and chewing. He finally said, "I just want to marry Loletta any way I can. I waited this long," he said, stroking Loletta's shoulders.

"Aah," Ms. Landelton moaned. "That is adorable." She lodged a kiss on Kavon's stubbly cheek.

Loletta's head felt like it was being squeezed by a wrench with the wedding talk. Her mother could be very aggressive in getting her way when she wanted to. After dinner, Kavon had arranged for a car to pick up Ms. Landelton and another to take Loletta and Kavon back to his house.

"So, honey . . . you're not coming home tonight? It's my first night back," Ms. Landelton asked Loletta in the ladies' room.

Loletta felt awful. Here she was going to this sprawling mansion in New Jersey, and her mother was going back to their studio in Harlem. That would eventually have to change too, she thought. But not tonight. "We just got engaged. I don't think I can be away from him more than a few days at a time," Loletta said, slicking down the sides of her hair with a comb. It had grown fast in the last few months and was now chin-length.

Ms. Landelton cut her eyes at Loletta. "Already sending your mother off to the dogs, I see. You know I have trouble sleeping alone," she said, faking a pitiful tone.

Loletta didn't answer but opened the door to the bathroom as they both exited.

At night, as Kavon explored her body, she asked him, "Can my mother come live with us, at least until we can arrange for her own place?"

"My thoughts exactly. But I'm busy right now," he said, as the tip of his tongue traced circles around her hard raisin-colored nipples.

New Year's Eve. Loletta was lounging on a beach chair at Nikki Beach on the chic island of Saint Bart. She was waiting for Kavon to return from the bar. Ms. Landelton and Vernice, sans Calvin, were nearby. Kavon had paid for both of their trips so they could join Loletta and him at an exclusive party given by one of hip-hop's pioneers. Everyone from real estate moguls to fashion designers congregated at the luxurious club, which was known only to the rich and richer. Kavon was putting every effort into being with her, Loletta thought. He showed her mother respect, and he seemed to like Vernice too, aside from her indiscretions. He put Vernice and Ms. Landelton in their own separate master suites in a nearby hotel and gave them expense accounts so they could shop for their needs during their stay. At times like this, Loletta didn't feel bad about the gold-paved road to life she chose for herself. Even though it was someone else's gold. It was a shortcut to marry a man who was paid, and no matter what, anything less would never do.

"So why don't you ever talk about your family? What are they doing tonight?" Loletta asked, as she took her glass out of Kavon's hand.

"I don't speak to my parents. Since I left college to get into the NBA, things never been the same. I do my own thing, but they don't have any problems accepting my money or season tickets for their friends." Kavon lay back on a lounge chair beside Loletta and held her hand.

Loletta found that strange, seeing how close she and her parents were. Her father lived across the Atlantic, but she had him in her heart. She wondered what Kavon's mother and father would be like.

"But," he said, sensing Loletta's pensive state, "you can meet them soon. But probably not before the wedding."

Loletta swung her hand with his, as both of their hands acted like a bridge between them. She picked up on a pain or distant sadness in his voice. "I know everyone got their family issues. Whenever you're ready, baby," she said, captivated by the beauty of Christmas lights, fresh pine, and make-believe decorative snow along the sandy beach.

Kavon glanced at his diamond-crusted Rolex just a few minutes shy of midnight. "It's that time," he said, as Loletta took his hand. They all gathered on the extravagant yacht where the party was being held. Loletta looked around to see her mother and Vernice waiting for her on the deck.

"Girl, there's only three minutes left!" Vernice said. She and Loletta waved wildly, holding individual glasses of champagne.

Loletta and Kavon joined them on deck as they counted down in unison with the other guests. *Five . . . four . . . three . . . two . . . one . . .*

Happy New Year, Loletta thought, as the boat erupted in cheer. Kavon grabbed her close to him and enveloped her in a sumptuous kiss that nearly knocked her over. Ms. Landelton had to break them apart, and soon all four of them were spreading the New Year's love.

This was a year Loletta was looking forward to like no other. This was her moment of arrival. She finally got her cake and could eat it too.

Eleven

The last three months had been a flurry of activity. Loletta had become Mrs. Kavon "Big" Jackson on a weekend trip to Las Vegas in March. But this wasn't any drive-through wedding. This was the real deal. Loletta and Kavon married in a famous chapel used by celebrities on beautifully landscaped grounds with a gazebo and elegant waterfall, and held a reception at the MGM Grand, where they stayed in a lavish suite. Ms. Landelton and Vernice had one of their own.

After the wedding, it was back to Loletta's new normal as the wife of an NBA star while her husband traveled. Most of her time was spent at Kavon's New Jersey mansion. He had other homes. There was one on Star Island in Miami, where she would meet him for his games at the AmericanAirlines Arena, and another in LA. He also had a colonial-style mansion on the Caribbean island of Tortola, complete with butler and maids. All his properties he rented out to celebrities during his season on the road. Loletta wished she could be at all the homes at the same time. But she knew she and her mother could visit each home any time they wanted. Now that was living, she thought. But she also knew that Kavon was spread out, and the more homes he had, the more he needed to fill them.

They didn't have a real honeymoon because of Kavon's busy season schedule. When the wedding was over, they headed straight to Utah for his next game. This didn't bother Loletta one bit. She knew as an NBA wife there would be certain adjustments she'd have to make. She didn't want to delay her wedding just to take an exotic honeymoon.

There was another major change in the Jackson household. Ms. Landelton moved into Kavon's mansion right after the New Year. Loletta thought it was exemplary of Kavon to invite her mother to move in. He even gave her access to one of his cars and her own "apartment" in his home. Loletta liked the idea that her mother was nearby. She didn't want to leave her alone in their tiny Harlem apartment while she lived the high life in Jersey. She also worried about her mother's chest pains and wanted to keep an eye on her.

One thing that hadn't changed was Loletta's job at the car dealership. After convincing Kavon that she needed to work because she actually liked to and didn't need to, she was back on the job. But her mother and Vernice ridiculed her for keeping her job, and Ms. Landelton even called her selfish. To Loletta, however, it was more than just a job; it was something she was good at, and she liked the people she worked with. They liked her, too. It was something she could look forward to, a place where she could meet different people and feel helpful. She took the PATH train to work like everyone else. However, on days when Kavon had kept her up the night before, she'd take a private car with a driver. Everyone at the job knew about her new status, and they sometimes harassed her about clients. They thought she could bring in all the Iversons, Marburys, and

O'Neals. And there were those who couldn't care less and would purposely still call her by her maiden name. Loletta liked the attention. She dressed the part too, wearing the latest couture suits and summer dresses made of the finest linens and fabrics. She was no longer the receptionist but "Kavon Big's wife." Needless to say, Jordan no longer needed to cut her a slice of his commission for her assistance in his deals.

"Well, there, if it isn't the working girl helping her poor slumming husband," Ms. Landelton teased, as Loletta walked through the door after work. She was filing her nails on the couch, dressed in a white yoga suit and with her hair gathered in a swinging ponytail. A glass of green energy drink was set on a coaster on a yoga mat beside her feet. Ms. Landelton had taken up healthier eating habits as advised by her doctor.

"If it ain't mother goddess, queen of the yoga mat that has never seen any yoga," Loletta said, as she gave the maid her coat and bags. She dropped her body next to her mother on the sofa. "Are you gonna keep getting on me about that forever?"

Ms. Landelton switched the nail file to her other hand. The small specks of white dust were caught on a towel on her lap. "Sorry, honey, it just pains me to see you struggle when you have everything."

"I'm not struggling. It just gives me something to do. I don't need the money. But what am I gonna do? Sit here all day with you?" Loletta said, a bit too abruptly.

"If that's what it's about, then forgive me for breathing. It was your husband's idea to move me in," she snapped as she bore down hard on a nail. "And I'm not going anywhere until he says so."

Loletta shook her head. "I didn't mean it like that. And it was my idea too to have you here. I couldn't sleep at night if I left you in that horrible apartment by yourself. It just wouldn't be right. It wouldn't be me," Loletta said, searching her mother's face.

"I know, baby," Ms. Landelton said, as she shaped her nails to perfection. Her mother didn't need a manicure, but Loletta remembered her mother filing her nails in deep moments of contemplation, which wasn't often. "I just think it's so wrong for you to stay in a job when there is a more deserving, probably financially needy girl out there just waiting for something like it. It's selfish."

Loletta sulked in her chair. Was she really being selfish? she thought. She was tired of hearing her mother say it. "But Mommy, I haven't met any of the NBA wives. I don't have any friends besides Vernice, and she has been acting really shady since I got married. All I have is you."

A quick closemouthed smile appeared on Ms. Landelton's face, then disappeared. "Yes, honey, I know that. But you gotta get out there. This is the life we wanted. I mean, *you* wanted. Live it."

"I'm scared," Loletta said out of the blue.

"Scared? Oh, God, please don't start with that Dr. Phil psychobabble." Ms. Landelton took a sip from her green drink and commenced to file, file, file.

Loletta took the nail file out of her mother's hands. "Maybe I've seen too much with my own eyes. But ninety percent of the athletes I slept with have wives that do nothing. They shop until they're exhausted, sleep all day, and blow their cells up keeping tabs on their husbands. The ones with kids are even worse, because they practically consume the children and have nothing of their own. They sit back and wait for their cut in a divorce, if that ever happens. I want to be different."

"Ha." Ms. Landelton made a curt laugh. "This game has been played for years, baby. You cannot change it. And I can assure you if you keep that job, Kavon is going to start questioning why you need him. He's going to seek validation in someone else's panties. Mama knows. I've been there," she said, reminiscing on her trysts with athletes in her heyday.

"But you got a divorce. So I don't know if you're the one to talk about how to keep a man happy," Loletta said, her eyebrows raised.

"You're right. I was greedy, and I dissed your dad when he became disabled and could no longer play. However, you are not like me. You have an extra something that can sustain a marriage. And hopefully that won't make you a divorcee at my age. Hopefully it will have you celebrating another anniversary together."

Loletta gave her mother back the nail file. She was touched that her mother thought she had something. She had never thought of herself as having anything extra. Her mother was who she looked up to. She was always in the mix, always full of life, and always looking good. "Thank you, Mommy," Loletta said, kissing her mother on the cheek.

"So be a good wife," Ms. Landelton said, as she put the nail file against her fingers. "Let's get out there and find some things to do. Make Kavon happy. And I know you think because you seen the other side that it happening to you is inevitable. It will happen to you. The good thing is when he cheats you know at the end of the day he's not leaving you to be with his wife—"

Loletta, Vernice, and Ms. Landelton were in their appointed courtside seats at another game. It was a home game at the Garden, Loletta's favorite, because it meant Kavon would be in town for a few days. Tonight Kavon would be scoring high, performing his signature dunks and three-point shots, and bringing his team to another win, she hoped. But tonight was difficult, as the Detroit Pistons stayed on the Knicks, matching them for every shot. Kavon was overworked. He'd shake his head every time he looked her way. It wasn't going to be an easy one. As Vernice and Ms. Landelton stayed absorbed in the plays, spotting celebs in the audience and buying expensive drinks, something caught Loletta's eye. There was a young woman a few seats away who cheered louder than anyone whenever Kavon scored. Loletta was often flattered when the fans rooted for her husband, and she was his number one. But he taught her to be subdued at his games for fear of distracting him. That was cool by her, she thought. But this young woman would stand up every time. She was attractive too—dark skin, long thick black hair, impeccably dressed in a tailored suit with shiny platinum bracelets and jewelry. Every strand of her hair was in place. Her suit couldn't hide her curves, which were many.

During halftime, Loletta wondered if what she was thinking was crazy. "Vernice, you see that chick a couple of seats down in that butter-colored pantsuit? Who the hell is she?" Loletta asked, as she directed Vernice's attention to her. Ms. Landelton zoomed in as well.

"Hmm, she look like some businesslady," Vernice said, looking at Ms. Landelton, who remained quiet.

"I'm gonna keep my eye on her because she is acting a little too excited. Every time Kavon makes a play, she is out of her seat," Loletta said, as she smiled at Kavon coming toward her. He kissed her cheek.

"Sorry, baby, tonight is crazy. If we don't win this, you may need to peel me off the floor," he said, wiping his face with a towel. Then the coach blew his whistle to gather the players, and Kavon was off again.

"That man is so attentive to you, girl. I don't know why you trippin'," Vernice said, handling her bag of popcorn.

"Look, look." Loletta poked Vernice's shoulder so she could pay attention to Kavon talking to the mystery woman. All three women watched as Kavon and the girl smiled, and she hugged him a few times and held his hand.

"See that look on Kavon's face. Whoever she is made him damn near blush," Loletta said, giving the girl the evil eye. Kavon whispered something in her ear, and the woman waved to Loletta. But Loletta didn't wave back.

Ms. Landelton tapped her knee. "Don't be so rude. She's probably some business associate. He wouldn't point you out to her if he's seeing her. They're about to start," Ms. Landelton said, giving Loletta a stern look. But she looked at Vernice, and they both knew that was a rule for normal folks, not for them.

At home, Loletta waited for Kavon. It was midnight, and her mother had retired a few hours earlier. They were home about nine p.m. They had left as soon as the game ended because Ms. Landelton was feeling unusually tired. Now Loletta tossed in the bed and checked the clock continually. Finally she heard Kavon's car pull up in the driveway.

They hadn't had an argument yet, and that was about to change, Loletta thought, as she ransacked her brain for the right words. She wanted to bring up what she had seen earlier. She planned to have an adult conversation about it and then forget it.

Kavon turned the light on low when he entered the room. "You asleep?" he whispered in the dark.

Loletta mumbled. She wanted to act like she was sleeping.

"After we did the press conference, some of us hung around and talked to Coach Randall. I thought you'd be up waiting," he said, running his hand up her naked thighs. "You feel warm." He gently squeezed them.

Loletta sat up, moving the covers slightly off her. It was a misty, humid summer night, but the air conditioner made it feel comfortable. She massaged the corner of her eyes. "Sorry about the loss tonight," she said, rubbing his broad back, which was still clothed in his tailored, black Gucci suit and matching wingtips. She loved how most of the players dressed up after their games.

Kavon got up and began removing his clothes. "You were looking real good, tonight." His underwear fell to his feet. "Those tight-ass jeans had some of my teammates talkin'." He smiled smugly.

"Oh," Loletta said, remembering which jeans he was referring to. She had so many now. She diverted her eyes from his swaying dick. It swung heavily as he moved around the room to get ready for bed. It was really distracting her, and she wanted to stay focused.

He slipped under the covers with her and turned off the lights. He climbed on top and lost his head all over her body.

"Kavon," she said, as she felt herself getting wet for him. "Can I ask you something?"

He stopped instantly. "What?" he said, rolling off her and turning on his side to face her. He rested his head on his hand.

She had his full undivided attention. She knew if she let this go it would get harder and harder to discuss.

"That girl at the game tonight," Loletta began, as she traced her fingers around the tattoo of an angel on his forearm. "Who was that?"

Kavon nibbled on her earlobes; then he asked, "Which girl?"

"The one who waved at me?"

"Kia?"

"I already don't like her by the sound of her name." Loletta pushed her body up against Kavon, feeling what was hard, not soft.

"She works for the management office. She coordinates all our events and stuff like that. She ain't nobody special. Just a chick with a good job," he smiled, as he took a handful of Loletta's ass in his hand.

She liked that. She sucked on his lips. She loved his lips, with the bottom one slightly curled underneath. Then she paused. "Have you had relations with her?"

He laughed. "Hell, no. She's talking to Brian Jones on the team. Don't tell me you don't trust me already."

"I trust you. I do."

"Then why go there?"

"Because I used to be the girl on the outside. I know what kind of games these chicks be playing. I can see it a mile away."

"So you saying she trying to get with me?"

"Maybe."

"And I can't handle it?"

"Maybe."

Then he flicked the light on bright. "What you think? I'm some new jack-gonna-get-all-open because some bitch smiled at me? I don't appreciate you undermining my experience with this."

"I trust you, but no matter how long you been playing, it is hard to resist pussy when it be around like your next breath."

Kavon rolled over on his side away from Loletta. "I don't need to be stressed tonight. You know we lost the fucking game, and you come at me with some bullshit."

She prodded him to turn over, but he didn't. She felt shut out when the plan was to get closer, to handle this like adults. "Forget I mentioned it. I guess I'm just paranoid because of what I know."

"Whose problem is that exactly?" he asked coldly.

"I guess it's mine," Loletta said, cringing at the sound of his voice.

"Then deal with it, because I'm getting me some sleep." He turned the lights off and pulled the covers up to his neck.

If she was going to find out anything, she had to get more creative, Loletta thought, as she stayed up all night wondering just what to do next. There were lots of unanswered questions, and she wasn't going to sit around waiting for the answers to fall out of the sky.

Twelve

On Monday afternoon at work, Loletta decided what she had to do. Clearly labeling what needed to be filed, sent for departmental approval, and followed up on, she organized her desk. She updated her Rolodex, throwing out old entries and transferring new ones onto small index cards. Temporary Excellence was sending over a temp to cover her. She made sure all her bases were covered. Her company had taken care of her, and she wanted to take care of them.

"Jared, can I talk to you for a second?" she asked, as she peeked in his office after lunch.

"Hey, you finally got my basketball signed!" he said, rolling his chair back as he got up to examine it. "Thanks, Loletta. You're an absolute angel."

"No problem. I did promise." She watched him roll the ball around his hand and bounce it around a few times. Kavon had signed it for her this morning before his trip to Houston.

"You know, if Big was the only player on that team, they'd have more of a chance for a championship. The poor guy is playing with scrubs." He bounced the ball a few more times. "I can't wait to add this ball to my collection," he said, sitting on the edge of his oakwood desk.

Loletta wanted to talk. She waited for him to come on down from his high.

"What's up?" He stopped bouncing the ball. "Want overtime?" he laughed.

"Not exactly," Loletta said, handing him a folder. "This is my letter of resignation. Everything is taken care of; a temp is coming in the morning. I told them to send Betty."

Jared sat on his swivel chair and set the ball on his lap. He scanned the letter. "I knew this was coming," he smiled. "Did he make you leave?"

"No." Loletta crossed her legs, which were covered at the knee by a white Ralph Lauren pleated skirt. She wore a gold chain belt around her waist. "I want to focus my full attention on my marriage. This is what I wanted, and I want to be fully present in it."

"Hey," Jared said, putting his hands up in the air. "If it were me, I would have told this place to shove it. You're living a life most women would die for. You must still be on cloud nine."

Loletta uncrossed her legs. If she was on cloud nine, she was coming down fast with a life jacket, she thought. "I've only been married for a couple of months, so I guess I still am. But Kavon and I want to have kids. So I want to prepare for that."

"Man, oh man. So Big is about to have some little Biggies running around," he said, walking his fingers across his desk. "You got my best wishes, kid." Jared stood up and shook Loletta's hand.

"Thank you," she said, feeling a little down.

"I remember you as this little miss diva coming in here while you were in college. You told me all the things you couldn't do.

But I hired you anyway because you had the guts to walk in here and tell me why you wanted this job. You wanted to meet a millionaire. And if there's one thing a woman will commit to, it is finding that man of her dreams, especially if she knows where he goes car shopping," he laughed.

Loletta laughed too. That was a while ago, she thought. She hoped she had changed some since then.

As she turned to leave, Jared asked, "So are you gonna mail my season tix, or are you gonna drop by?"

"I'll mail them. Thanks, Jared," she said, and her former self closed the door tightly behind her.

After getting a hundred-dollar manicure at an exclusive salon, Loletta quickly took to Madison Avenue. She had called her mother to join her, but she had a doctor's appointment. Loletta went in and out of every designer store like she was on autopilot. While she was paying for her purchase at the Prada boutique, she turned to her right and saw Darva. She was sipping champagne while one of the salespeople showed her some of the latest additions. Loletta watched Darva shake her head no each time the harried, petite guy came out with a new item. Just when Loletta slipped on her shades and tried to leave before she caught Darva's attention, she heard that annoying voice.

"Loletta! Congrats on your wedding," Darva said, taking quick strides toward her.

"Hi, Darva," Loletta said, glancing at her own watch. She didn't want to chat. Besides, she thought, this woman was married to Vernice's boyfriend. She didn't want to get in between them because she'd always be on Vernice's side.

"Welcome to the club." Darva threw Loletta a smile and

kissed both of her cheeks. "I actually didn't think you would be getting married so soon."

"Or getting married at all?" Loletta said, struggling to hold up her bags. "Listen, I have to go."

"No, wait," Darva said, following her. "Here's my number. We should talk. I mean, you never know when we'll need each other."

Loletta freed up one of her hands and checked out the card. "Yeah, okay," she said, dropping it in one of the bags. "Nice seeing you." Then she walked out the door. As she slid inside the black sedan that awaited her, she thought about Darva. There *was* something she needed. It was something she couldn't ask just anyone about. And she knew Darva had to have one; most famous and rich people did. She was determined to try anything to understand Kavon better and to protect their future. This was not a time for pride, she thought.

In the car she dialed Darva's cell. "I think there *is* something you can do for me," Loletta said, and Darva listened.

Around eight p.m., Loletta was in a dark room that smelled of frankincense. A chime went off outside every time a summer breeze hit the window of the East Eighty-second Street brownstone. Loletta sat on a purple velvet couch and waited. The room was a serene blue with red-colored crown molding. Darva had arranged a last-minute appointment for Loletta. Lady Anise was kind enough to accommodate her, despite the demand on her time. Loletta felt her face flushed with heat as she heard a woman's footsteps approach. A young, olive-skinned Indian woman dressed in an ankle-length khaki skirt and white tunic blouse walked in.

"Welcome, Ms. Jackson. Glad you could make it," she said, embracing both of Loletta's hands.

"Thank you. I only have a few questions. I heard you were very good." Loletta's chest heaved up and down as she had a flashing thought to head out the door. But she stayed put.

"Come with me," Lady Anise said, walking to another part of the room, which was covered with a curtain.

Loletta followed her. It was a plain white room, with two wooden chairs. Loletta took note of the woman's white-painted, manicured nails. She must be living really good, because she had repeat customers, thought Loletta. Everyone from Jennifer Lopez to Starr Jones had used Lady Anise. Darva swore on her life that this woman had helped her win legal battles that had impeded her business. Loletta reasoned that if she was a phony, she would have been ousted long ago. Her hair was neat, rolled into an artful twist, and silver earrings with orange beads framed her small oval face.

"Sit," Lady Anise said, pulling a chair close to Loletta's. "Now I'm going to ask you some things. You answer them. Then we talk. I don't use any balls or cards. I read your energy, and I am open to the third-dimensional plane. Which simply means your guides can communicate with me. I can use cards if you want."

"No . . . whatever." Loletta wanted to get this done.

Lady Anise was poised, and her conservative demeanor didn't seem to be shaken by Loletta's nervousness. And in turn, Loletta felt more relaxed.

"Close your eyes, and take five deep breaths," Lady Anise instructed.

Loletta did just that and tried to make herself concentrate as Lady Anise squeezed her hands.

"Open them now." Lady Anise placed a clear bowl of water

on the table and lit the two candles next to it. She opened a plastic bag, which was labeled "Gooferdust." She sprinkled the light-colored dust in her hands, and rubbed them together. Then she took Loletta's hands and rubbed the dust on them too. Loletta examined Lady Anise's hands, thin with fat veins that looked like vines wrapped around a tree.

The lines around Lady Anise's eyes deepened, as she quietly recited a prayer to herself.

"Your mother, is she sick?" whispered Anise in an affectionate low voice.

Nina shook her head. "This is about my husband. My mother is doing just fine."

"I can only tell you what I see, even if you want to know something else. Please be patient. It will come."

Nina took a deep breath. She had enough things on her mind. She didn't want to hear her mother was sick.

"Your mother is sick, my dear. She has a heart condition that is more than chest pains. Tell her to go to the doctor and ask him to check it again."

"She went today," Loletta said.

"I know," Lady Anise smiled warmly. "But tell her to go to another doctor, or she will end up in the hospital."

"Wait a minute. Is my mother seriously sick?" Loletta clenched Lady Anise's hands tightly.

"Not very sick. But it seems to me that she is the type to fake sickness for so long that now it is real."

"Okay." Loletta took another deep breath. "We'll get another doctor."

Lady Anise was in a trancelike state. Then she said, "Your husband is very talented."

"I know," Loletta said, a little impatiently.

"But he's not at peace. He's a *jutha* and a *kachcha vaidya*."

"What's that?"

"A liar, charlatan. These people are very toxic. They aren't true to anyone and attach themselves to hide. This is very serious."

"It sounds like it."

"You are, too. You're like him."

Loletta didn't say a word.

"You are both looking for acceptance. You are accepting a lot from him. He had another woman."

"Yes, yes," Loletta said, sitting on the edge of her chair. "What happened with that?"

"Shhhh . . . ," Lady Anise said, as she contemplated for a minute or so. "This was a very unstable marriage. Your husband physically abused this woman. He threatened her. She was very young. She's now remarried."

Loletta lost her breath. *Beating women?* Not Kavon. But before Loletta could correct Lady Anise, she continued.

"There is another woman standing near you. She is a little younger, very dark, and her name is Lia or Mia. Something like that."

"It's Kia," Loletta said, her body tightening.

"This is the woman who will destroy your marriage. But understand that your husband is not the composer of this relationship. She keeps it going."

"Can you be more specific?"

Lady Anise's eyes fluttered to the back of her head, then closed fully. "She is a *veshya.*"

"What is that?" Loletta asked, tears beginning to cascade down her face.

"Not all, but some women like this are dangerous and can cause serious harm. I can't be any more specific than to say she is holding on to your husband. She is holding on with forceful will and powerful focus. This is more potent than any spell."

"Okay, that's enough," Loletta said, shaking her head and letting go of Lady Anise, who was breathing heavily. She handed Loletta a napkin, and they both wiped their wet foreheads. Loletta had sweat profusely, which puzzled her because she was in such a cool ventilated room.

Loletta quickly paid Lady Anise and dashed for the door.

"Wait," Lady Anise said, still sitting. "Take this." She handed the money back to Loletta. "I'm giving it to you because I've stopped taking payments. I live good and am quite well off. I love doing this and helping people. And I want to help you. Don't be afraid, Ms. Jackson."

Loletta fell onto a nearby chair and broke down in more tears. "I am out of my mind right now," Loletta said, blowing her nose in a tissue. "I don't even believe in these things."

"It is up to you to use the information or not. However, I don't think it would hurt to pay more attention to clues around you. Nothing is more powerful than our intuition. Did I say something new?"

"No."

"Well," Lady Anise said, lighting a cigarette in the dark room. She opened a window. "I think you should go home and act yourself. Do not confront him."

"Oh, he's gonna catch hell tonight," Loletta said, laughing nervously.

"Don't. Sleep on this. It is my take. But yours is more important. Come back in a few weeks, and let's talk more about you. Maybe I can suggest a way to make this easier."

Loletta left.

When Loletta got home, she walked into a sea of white orchids. The same type of flower Kavon had sent to her when they first began dating. She inhaled the scent, and wished she could go back to that moment when things were new. Now she had to think about her next move. Lady Anise had dropped a load on her, and it wasn't something she could sweep under the chinchilla rug.

"So how did everyone take it today?" Ms. Landelton asked, referring to Loletta's leaving her job. "I see you're doing mighty fine. When I got in, all your Prada and Bergdorf bags were all over the place."

"I know," Loletta said, her face long and withdrawn. "The job wished me luck because I'm gonna need it." She walked to the bar and fixed herself a drink of Coke and rum. She made a drink for her mother too. She needed to talk—to anyone.

They both sat on the stools and took quiet sips.

"How was the doctor?" Loletta asked, her eyes looking up from her drink. She thought about whether Lady Anise could be right.

"It went great. He said not to worry about my chest pains. It's just stress. He said to sleep more." Ms. Landelton poured an extra dash of rum in her Coke.

Loletta guzzled hers down at once. She needed the strength to stand by what she was about to say to her mother. "I want you to see another doctor."

"Why?" Ms. Landelton asked, as they walked to the kitchen and sat down at the table in the nook. "I feel fine."

"Yeah, but we can afford a better doctor now. I want you to get a thorough checkup."

Ms. Landelton picked at a bowl of black grapes. "I hate doctors, and I like the one I have," she insisted.

"I have to tell you something, Mommy." Loletta reached for Ms. Landelton's gold-crusted wrist.

Ms. Landelton stirred her drink with her fingers, looking bored.

"I went to this lady who told me you could have a serious heart condition. She's a lady that is well known, and a lot of people trust her."

Ms. Landelton looked at Loletta from the side of her eye. "And what else did she say?"

Loletta saw that her mother looked interested. Maybe her mom could help her sort through what Lady Anise had told her, and maybe they could come up with a way to get through it, she thought. "Darva, a friend of Kavon's, gave me the name of a spiritual adviser. I went to see her to talk about Kavon and some other questions I had."

A grin came across Ms. Landelton's face as her posture changed. "I love those people! Oh, my God, what did she say about Kavon?" Ms. Landelton pulled her chair closer to Loletta like she was being let in on the world's best-kept secret.

"Too much." Loletta felt knots in her stomach as she began. "She said some things I never would have guessed, like—"

"Did you ask her about his next contract? How much?"

"That's not for a few more years," Loletta said, taken aback by her mom's focus. "I didn't ask her."

"What about the championship? You know if the Knicks win, everybody gets a bonus. It's prestigious, and he will get more endorsements than ever. *Chi-ching,*" she said, pretending to pull open a cash register drawer.

Loletta covered her face with her hands, and the tears fell.

"Okay, sweetie. Wait, is he gonna be cut? Injured?" Ms. Landelton asked, putting her arm around Loletta.

"No," Loletta shot back. She pushed her mother's hand away. "She told me he is cheating. That he beat the hell out of his ex-wife. That he is with a woman now who is dangerous, who wants him, who may even be using covert tactics to get him. And I think we both saw her that night."

Ms. Landelton sat limp in her chair, staring into space. "How did she know about me being sick?"

"Because she can see things and predict. Now it's all sinking in, huh?" Loletta said, grabbing a napkin and dabbing her eyes. "And she said you fake your sicknesses."

"It can't be," Ms. Landelton said, not denying that last bit of information. Her hands shook slightly as she held her drink. "I'm fine and so is Kavon. You would have to go play Sherlock Holmes and start a mess." She brought the drink to her forehead.

"Are you hot?" Loletta asked. Ms. Landelton's face was damp with moisture.

"I'm fine," she said, hitting Loletta's hand off her. Then she began breathing in short breaths.

"Shit," Loletta said, darting to the sink for a glass of water. She held it to her mother's mouth and forced her to drink.

Ms. Landelton took long, thirsty sips until she finally exhaled loudly. She fanned herself and said, "I think I need rest."

"I'm sorry," Loletta said, feeling like this was all her fault. Maybe she was looking for problems, but she could see it with her own eyes. Her mother was not well. She lent her mother her shoulder for support, as they both walked carefully up the steps to her bedroom.

Loletta pulled the covers back as her mother undressed from her jeans and blouse. She helped her get in the bed; then she knelt beside her. "Look, just get some rest. But I know what this lady told me is one hundred percent true. I'll deal with Kavon. But I need to get you to a new doctor tomorrow."

Ms. Landelton nodded and then pulled the covers to her

chin. "I wanted so much for you to be happy Loletta," she said, her eyes slowly closing. There was a glimmer of some understanding behind them, a sympathy for Loletta. But then they flashed open. "Kavon is a good man. Don't ruin this for us."

Loletta knelt beside her mom until she dozed off.

Thirteen

"So how long has she been feeling this way?" Vernice asked Loletta, who was waiting impatiently in a green dress and golden jewelry. They both sat in the waiting room while Loletta's mother was being attended to by a cardiologist.

"She hasn't been looking well lately and was complaining about chest pains. But the doctor she was seeing said she was fine. That it was stress. I told Kavon this morning, and he had his team doctor contact some other big doctor." Loletta recalled that it was one of the hardest and shortest conversations she'd ever had with him. "Supposedly this doctor is the best heart surgeon in the Northeast."

Vernice bit her nails as they both pondered what was going on inside. "Why didn't you go in?" Vernice asked.

"She didn't want me to."

"I just think it's a blessing to have a man like Kavon who can pay for this kind of treatment. That is why I love me a rich man. Life is just better when you have somebody who wants to take care of you." Vernice didn't look at Loletta when she said it. Loletta picked up a tone of resentment.

"I'm his wife. He's supposed to help me when I need help."

"I'm just saying, dating an average guy ain't making one of the busiest doctors in New York change his schedule to see your mother."

Loletta ran her tongue across her teeth. She didn't want to bring it up here, but she couldn't keep acting like nothing was wrong. "Kavon is not so perfect."

Vernice made an irritated sound and asked, "Does he leave the toilet seat up?"

Loletta turned to Vernice, who was looking especially nice in cranberry-red matching Capris, tank top, and heels. "I went to see this lady who told me Kavon is cheating with some woman. The one we saw at that game. She warned me that she is not a regular woman, but someone with serious intentions. Kavon lied to me, lied about everything since I met him."

Vernice gasped. "Did you ask him?"

"Not yet. He's gonna deny everything. I want to catch him when he's home. I just can't live like that. But I ain't letting no bitch take my husband," Loletta said.

Vernice fell silent. Loletta was sure she'd have more to say. "What should I do, Vernice? We just got married. If I walk away now, I get nothing. And it looks like Mommy is gonna need some treatment. I won't be able to afford that on my own."

Vernice nibbled on a nail as she pondered Loletta's situation. Then she said, "Deal with it."

"Deal with what?"

"Kavon and this woman. It's our karma. We were once there. She'll eventually fade to black."

"Yeah, but I never seriously pursued a married man. That's your shit," Loletta said.

"Fine, but don't try to act like you wouldn't have. Carter was married. Lest we forget."

"But he came after me. Kavon is not doing that. And I didn't know until after we fucked that Carter was married."

"Listen, Loletta. That chick at the game looked close to Kavon. But I wouldn't question him as much as I would check that bitch out."

Loletta surveyed the hospital room and the harried nurses as she thought about getting a private investigator.

"Besides, how do you know that Kavon is not the one pursuing this woman?"

"Because that lady told me Kia, which is her name, is hell-bent on getting Kavon. Which means fucking up everything we have planned together."

"How did you hear about this lady? Who is she?"

"Darva introduced me to this spiritual adviser. Everybody uses her."

"Darva?" Vernice laughed. "Please, if she was using her, she'd know about me and Calvin."

Loletta wanted to tell her that she did, but passed. That would be a whole other can of worms, she thought. "Trust me, Vernice. Her name is Lady Anise, and she is good."

"You don't need a Lady Anise to tell you that you must do all you can to keep your marriage. You've gotta talk to Kavon *now*. At least to see his reaction. It looks like you brought it up if you know the girl's name."

"I did, but it was brief and he got pissed off."

Vernice tilted her head to the side. "You need to regulate on his ass. We know the game, Loletta. Don't get played; you play *it*."

Loletta fiddled with her wedding ring. As she gazed at it, she realized it was no longer a game. She didn't even think Vernice really got it. This was her life, and she wasn't about to lose it.

"Ms. Jackson? I'm Dr. Lore," said a tall man with an African accent and wearing wide-rimmed bifocals. "I've recommended a few things for your mother."

Ms. Landelton turned her back and gathered her things from the chair beside Loletta, who stood up to greet the doctor.

"We took some blood tests. We think your mother may be at risk for heart disease. Her valves appear weak, and we want to closely monitor her with some routine exams and follow-ups. If you had waited any longer, she could have had a stroke," he said, his hands folded neatly at his waist.

"Thank you, Dr. Lore," Loletta said, shaking his hand. "When is her next appointment?"

"We have her booked to come in every other week so we can keep an eye on her condition and monitor her reaction to the medication. It will be that way for a month or so," he said, turning his attention to the nurse and handing her a folder.

"Are you okay?" Loletta asked Ms. Landelton, who looked tired but still impeccable in her tailored Yves Saint Laurent pantsuit.

"I'm fine," she said, tight-lipped, and walked out the door. Loletta stayed on her heels.

Vernice put her hand on Loletta's shoulder. "I know you have a lot to worry about now. I'm here for you and your mother if you need me. But I say divorce that nigga and take his ass through the dirt if it's true. Expose some shit. Go to the *Enquirer,*" Vernice said, a thread of amusement in her voice.

"Yeah, okay," Loletta said, rolling her eyes as she and Vernice kissed good-bye. As she watched Vernice hop in her Navigator, she knew right there that their lives were going in very different directions.

Kavon was due back in town on Wednesday for a few days. Loletta wanted to do a thing or two before he returned. One of them was meeting with Darva, and she accepted her invitation for lunch at the Four Seasons. Darva was the last person she thought she'd be breaking bread with.

"How did it go with Lady Anise? Is she great or what?" Darva said, as she scooped up a spoonful of ceviche.

Loletta nodded. "She was good. She told me that my mom needed to see another doctor right away. The next day the doctor told me my mom could have gotten really sick if she hadn't come in." Loletta took a small bite of her Balik salmon. She didn't know how much she should reveal to Darva, but if there was anyone who had experience with dealing with other women, it was Darva.

"Is that why you went to her?" Darva asked, her voice echoing with sarcasm. She flipped her blond hair away from her shoulders.

"I had some questions about my marriage. She helped . . . some."

"Lady Anise will get rid of anybody, anywhere. Not in a bad way, but in a very nice, clean way. Sort of like the person forgetting your number or having the instinctual feeling of suddenly moving to another city." Darva winked at Loletta.

And Loletta liked the sound of that and opened up. "Has she done that for you?"

"Of course, except for your little friend. I haven't gotten around to it," Darva said, swishing the champagne around her mouth.

"Vernice is not into Calvin. It may be just a misunderstanding," Loletta said, trying to cover for Vernice.

"Yeah, yeah. Whatever," Darva said, clearly not interested in Vernice. "Be straight up with me. Did she say anything about Kavon cheating? That's why all we wives go see her," she shrugged, more interested in Loletta's business.

"I mean . . . she hinted at that. But I feel so foolish confronting Kavon. I feel stupid that I even went to her—"

"Are you insane?" Darva said, slamming down her hand. "Lady Anise is always on point. She is doing you a favor. You can deal with whatever. That's why we're NBA wives. It's practically in the damn contract. . . ."

Loletta had a bad taste in her mouth. "What if I don't want to deal with it?"

Darva slurped some more of her champagne. She wielded her hand in the air. "We've all been there. We all said we wouldn't deal with it. And here we are, years later. As much as Calvin has his dog ways, I am not leaving. I don't know any other life."

Loletta felt sickened. "I need to talk to my husband."

"Definitely do that. Kavon seems like a good kid. But I wouldn't be too hasty. Continue seeing Lady Anise. See what else she has to say. Don't make any drastic moves without talking to her. Promise?" Darva asked.

Loletta didn't answer back, but lightly shook her head. "I really want this marriage to work."

"Do you love him?"

"Yes, I do. I just don't know if he loves me."

"Well, none of us marry for love these days. It's about convenience and necessity. We all want kids and stuff, and these players don't know what to do with their money so they marry us."

"I don't think Kavon married me for that. He's been in love

with me for some time. At least I think he has," Loletta said, scratching the back of her neck. It was just getting too confusing, she thought. "Would you mind if I ended our lunch a little early?"

"Why?"

"I'm gonna meet Kavon at the airport. I can't wait till he gets home. I gotta see him," Loletta said, leaving her half of the check.

Darva put her hand on Loletta's. "I got this. And believe me. If you ever need someone to talk to, call me. I know it can be a little isolating for a new wife, but we can help each other. No one knows about marriage who isn't married," Darva said.

"I will," Loletta said, as she headed for the door. Somehow, what Darva said sounded sincere and was just exactly the type of support she needed. Neither her mom nor Vernice had husbands, and she wasn't about to let them tell her what to do with hers.

Loletta took swigs of her strawberry banana smoothie as she waited for Kavon outside the American Airlines terminal at JFK. She picked up a turkey club sandwich for him in case he was hungry. She hoped they could have a calm ride home so they could talk. She had this incredible need to see him. Perhaps it was her way of making sure he was coming home to her. She wanted to feel his arms around her, see the warm look in his eyes when he found her waiting. She'd been to the airport before to meet players, usually those she bedded after they called their girlfriends to lie about a flight delay.

Flight attendants and airport personnel gathered at the gate. It was time for Kavon's flight to come in. Loletta's thoughts were drowned out by crying babies and the constant muffled rambling of the PA system. Her knees couldn't stop shaking. What if Kavon wasn't pleasantly surprised, she asked herself. She slipped on her Chanel shades and stood up.

There he was. All six-foot-five of him, taking long confident strides out of the terminal. She saw the gleamy whiteness of his teeth, and his magnetic smile and chocolate-candy skin. She took a deep breath, as if she could smell him from twenty feet away. And when she opened her eyes, she almost choked. Alongside several of the players who were joking and laughing with Kavon was Kia. She held a small, Gucci-logo duffel bag and met Loletta's eyes. She whispered something to Kavon, who looked at Loletta.

Loletta vigorously waved her hand at him, and he did the same. He walked up to her, leaving the players and Kia behind.

"What's up, baby? Everything all right at home?" he asked, kissing Loletta quickly on the cheek.

Loletta touched the place he kissed. "What was that?" She half smiled. "Everything is fine. I just needed to see you."

Kavon hesitantly turned around. "I got some things to do with the team."

Loletta looked over at Kia, who was approaching Kavon. "Kavon, why is that bitch walking over here?"

They both turned around to face Kia, who was dressed in simple fitted jeans and a black tank top. Her long hair had that tussled effect, gathered at the crown with a few gold pins. She looked tanned and refreshed like anyone coming from Miami Beach would. "Hi, Loletta. I finally get to meet you the right way instead of at that crazy game," Kia said, smiling brightly and extending her hand.

Loletta shook her hand gracefully. "Nice to meet you again." Loletta looked at Kavon the whole time. She was waiting for him to dismiss Kia.

"Are you ready?" Loletta asked him as she turned to start walking.

"I said I have some things to do. Go on home without me," he said, his team duffel bag strapped over one arm.

"What kind of things?" Loletta raised her voice slightly. Her blood rushed through her veins. She could feel Kia examining her, but she didn't want to acknowledge her with any eye contact.

"Go home, Loletta," Kavon said firmly. "I'll see you later." Kavon walked in the opposite direction as Kia strolled behind him.

"Kavon!" Loletta demanded as she stood there holding her shake and his sandwich.

"Go home!" he shouted, and he didn't even look back.

Loletta's feet were frozen in place. She didn't walk toward him or away. She only looked on as he walked through the glass doors with Kia, who gave Loletta one final, forged smile before she disappeared with her husband.

Fourteen

In the morning over breakfast, Loletta stole glances at Kavon as he slowly ate his toast and eggs. She could feel the guilt all over him. *He could at least act really nice like most men would after deserting their wife at the airport,* she thought. But he had seemed tense since he crawled in the bed beside her last night. Ms. Landelton was the only one driving the conversation this morning.

"So, honey, are we going to Nordstrom today?" Ms. Landelton asked, politely pouring everyone some more orange juice. "I want to pick up a new set of Waterford drinking glasses."

Loletta chewed her turkey bacon, keeping an eye on Kavon. She wanted him to say something. They needed to talk about a lot of things. She didn't even hear what her mother was saying.

"What time do you want to leave?" Ms. Landelton said, putting her knife and fork down.

"Huh, what?" Loletta said, shaking her head and burying her elbows into the table. She was through eating.

"Are you coming with me to Nordstrom?"

"I don't think I can. Kavon and I have to talk. Isn't that

right? I ain't gonna sleep another night next to you if you keep ignoring me."

Kavon sighed and leaned away from Loletta. Ms. Landelton shot Loletta a surprised look. "Sounds like somebody needs to drink more coffee. A little grumpy?" Ms. Landelton chided.

"Why are we going to Nordstrom?" Loletta put out both her hands for a response.

"Didn't Kavon tell you?" Ms. Landelton said, pushing her shoulders together like an excited bride.

"I'm the last to know about everything around here, I guess." She twisted her body to face Kavon. "Well?"

"Maybe your mother should tell you. I thought she did," he said, with a goofy grin.

"He bought me a house!" Ms. Landelton jumped out of her chair and put her arms around Kavon. She kissed his bald head.

"A house?" Loletta said. She grabbed a cup and guzzled down all the water. "Why?"

"Your mom needs her own space. I thought it would be nice for her to have a nice house, with her own privacy. And it's right down the block. A luxury ranch-style house. Devon Harris used to own it," he said, his shoulders more relaxed.

Loletta pushed her chair back and folded her arms across her chest. "You didn't tell me you wanted to move."

"Oh, honey, stop making a big fuss. I did and I didn't. Kavon surprised me. And I have my own Jacuzzi and a glass ceiling in the den. It's so lovely. All we have to do is go to Nordstrom and start furnishing it," she said, clapping her hands.

Loletta stared at the half-eaten slice of bacon on her plate. Kavon was up to something. This definitely was clouding up the real issues she had with him. She hated to know that he was buying her mother, too. Now she had to watch every complaint she made to her mother about Kavon. Could she trust her? Of course she could, she thought. "Mommy, I'll be ready in a few. I just want to change out of my sweats."

Two hours later, her mother and Kavon racked up tens of thousands of dollars of wares for Ms. Landelton's new home.

Days passed. Kavon didn't give Loletta a reason not to love him or trust him. He helped Ms. Landelton become adjusted to her new home and even paid for all of her medical needs and got her a personal chef to prepare foods to help nurse her back to health. Loletta thought maybe she had overreacted at the airport. She couldn't tell Vernice what happened or that she let it slide because she thought Vernice would be on the phone with a divorce lawyer—on her behalf. She knew what she was buying when she agreed to marry Kavon, and he knew what he was getting. She'd gained so much in being his wife, but she had given up her sense of peace.

This nagging feeling led her back to Lady Anise's office. She had to be sure about Kavon and this other woman. Was it that serious? And what could she do?

"So how is your mother?" Lady Anise asked, with a look of sincerity.

"She's fine. We went to a new doctor, and she's under his care now. And she has her own house now. My husband bought her one. He's been taking care of everything. My mother seems happy."

Lady Anise dimmed the lights and spread the gooferdust on her hands and Loletta's. "Are you happy?"

"Yes."

"It is what you asked for."

"I know," Loletta said, holding her head down.

Lady Anise patted both of her hands together and held them.

"I just want to know if you can get rid of this woman at his office. I think they have something going."

"I told you that."

"And I saw something for myself. Is there any way she can be transferred?"

Lady Anise's eyes stayed half open. "I can do that, but it won't help."

"Why?"

"If you keep fearing her or another woman, there will be another one. And another one."

"So am I causing this?"

"It's a situation you created, sweetie. It first started in your mind; you wanted Kavon and you got him. Now you have to keep him."

Loletta cast her eyes down on her lap; then she looked up. "He's my husband. He should want to stay."

Lady Anise laughed. "Listen to me. She will be at his home in Miami next week. Soon you will get pregnant. Life is going to get very complicated unless you take control."

Loletta had an idea. "I'm going to use some birth control as of this week. And if I do find that woman in my husband's Miami home—"

"Then you will still do nothing." Lady Anise smiled. "You are in my prayers. Because you're going to need them."

The following week Vernice and Loletta were at Ms. Landelton's home, seated in her country kitchen eating a chef-prepared lunch of lobster and avocado salad with tomatoes and citrus vinaigrette. Emmanuel, the chef, a short round man with black and gray hair, came by three days a week. On days he wasn't there, he prepared the meal the night before for Ms. Landelton's pleasure. Loletta and Kavon had the same kind of service, but it was for five days a week. Besides, Loletta thought, her mother spent plenty of time over at their house, so a chef more than three times a week would be a waste. Just because Ms. Landelton had her own home didn't stop her from camping out at Loletta's anytime she felt like it.

"Girl, if I could eat like this at home, I would never have to go out to another restaurant," Vernice said, holding a piece of avocado. "This salad is the truth!"

"Emmanuel is such a doll. He's so quiet too. If it wasn't for the wonderful smell of his food, I wouldn't even know he was here half the time." Ms. Landelton refreshed her glass with more limeade.

Loletta was glad to see her mother taken care of. "Are you keeping up with your medication?" Loletta asked.

"Of course," Ms. Landelton said, sighing.

"Which reminds me—" Loletta went into her pocket and popped a pill.

"What is that?" Vernice asked, with one eyebrow arched in suspicion. "Don't tell me that negro got you on antidepressants already."

"No, silly." Loletta fastened the pill case. "These are for something more important."

"Oh, the hell you didn't!" Ms. Landelton said, inflamed. She snatched the case from Loletta. "You are wicked."

"Why? Because I'm not ready to be a mother."

Ms. Landelton and Vernice looked at Loletta, astonished. Each was speaking a thousand words with her irritated glare. Vernice sucked her teeth as if to say that talking to Loletta was a waste of time.

"The way things are going with you two, you need to have a baby. That's so when you divorce his ass you can also get child support," Vernice said matter-of-factly. "That's what everybody does."

"Honey," Ms. Landelton said, taking a more gentle approach and placing her hand on Loletta's shoulder. "I thought I taught you better than this. You must have a baby. That is the only way to really secure a future outside of Kavon. Do you know how many women out there would vie to be in your shoes?"

Loletta rubbed her stomach. She hated taking any kind of pill that would mess with her natural female functions. She thought maybe a baby would wake Kavon up to the importance of his marriage and family. Maybe he would settle down. But then she said, "A baby won't stop Kavon from cheating."

"Oh, so that is what this is all about," Ms. Landelton said, frowning. "You can forget that. As long as he's Kavon 'Big' Jackson, he's gonna be milking all the cows out there."

"And fucking them too," Vernice said, munching on her salad. She took the salad bowl and shoveled some more onto her plate.

Loletta rolled her eyes at Vernice. She was starting to sound so jaded.

"I don't know why you think you so different now that you guys are married," Vernice went on.

Loletta looked at Ms. Landelton for backup, knowing good and well that Vernice just took a vicious stab at her. But Ms. Landelton cast her eyes to the other side of the room.

"Ain't nobody said anything about me being different. I want to stay married to Kavon. And until I am sure we are stable, I am not having any babies. Point blank," Loletta said, and then a fleeting image of her as a mother passed before her. "But I do want to be a mother someday. And all his friends have kids."

Vernice scratched the edge of her straight khaki weave. With her new hazel contacts and her light skin, Vernice was getting whiter each day, Loletta thought.

"Come on, sweetie. I would love to be a grandmother. No matter what, I will help you with that baby. You will never be alone." Ms. Landelton hugged Loletta tightly and kissed her forehead. "And besides, Kavon needs an heir." She laughed.

Loletta looked at her case of birth control pills. If Kavon were to leave her, she didn't want to be left out in the cold. A baby would give her not only unconditional love, but also undisputed security, at least for the next eighteen years. But Lady Anise's words echoed in her mind.

"Fuck this." Loletta marched to the trash with the case, and as Vernice and Ms. Landelton applauded, she threw in the pills.

Fifteen

Two weeks later, tanning poolside at her oceanfront Miami home, Loletta basked in the delight of the sun as it kissed every nook and cranny of her body. Things were better between Kavon and her. They had a silent agreement of "Don't ask, don't tell." There were still some unresolved issues, but Kavon still made love to her like he did the first time, and showered her with gifts and thoughtful notes every now and again. It was his idea that she join him at the final game of the season in Miami. The Knicks, despite Kavon's stellar season, were not going to make it to the championship. She knew he was down, because it had become quite a burden for him to carry the team alone. One night he scored over forty points. Some papers blasted him for his greed, but others commended him for his leadership. Either way, Kavon felt like he couldn't win. And it was at times like this that Loletta felt the sorriest for him. She didn't want to add any more drama and wanted the season to end.

She slathered an extra coat of suntan oil on her arms and thighs. Her dark skin was accentuated by the red thong bikini that Kavon had requested she wear all day. He wanted to come home and take it off her, he told her. She checked the clock and thought he would be coming in from practice any minute.

Rubbing the lotion on her thighs, she marveled at the blue sea all around her. The mangroves, the blue and green parrots that situated themselves on the nearby tree branches, and the tall magnificent palm trees that towered ever so high. She swore she spotted a dolphin earlier or a manatee, common neighbors to those who live on the water. She closed her eyes and felt blessed. This was the life she was meant to live, she thought. It made her feel alive and rejuvenated. It gave her meaning.

Loletta sat on the pool edge and dipped her manicured feet into the cool water. She moved them around, creating little circles as she caught her reflection. But then she felt a presence behind her.

"Hi, Ms. Jackson," said a woman, in a sultry, raspy voice.

Loletta turned around, and her first reaction was to jump in the pool. "What the hell are you doing here?" she blasted.

"I'm so sorry, I . . . I—"

"How the hell did you get in my house?" Each step Kia took back, Loletta took forward.

"I'm sorry for interrupting you, but Kavon said you were in town, and I just really wanted to meet you and talk to you," Kia said, her eyes pleading for Loletta to curb her aggression. "Security let me through."

Loletta grabbed the towel from her lounge chair and wiped the sweat off her chest. "Look, whatever you need to say to me you can put in a note. I am really here to relax and kick back with my husband."

"Ms. Jackson, I don't know what you think of me, but I really admire you. I mean, you have a great husband, a wonderful home, and you're beautiful. All I want to know is how you did it. Just sister to sister," Kia said, looking comfortable in white cotton knit shorts and a matching white tube top.

Loletta gave Kia the once-over. Her style of dress was simple. She couldn't see how this average-looking woman could even get as far as she had. There was nothing different about her, but her body. It was absolutely flawless, except for the dark-colored scratches on the inside of her arm. She had as many curves as a highway map, but the plain look of your next-door neighbor. Loletta always had a little issue with her obliques and some back fat that she camouflaged nicely with fitted clothes. But everything else on her—from her silky skin, breasts, and ass to her legs—was tight. But as Loletta surveyed her, she thought she could be Kavon's type.

Loletta slowly let her guard down. "I have to tell security to watch who they let in. But since you're here, what do you want?"

Kia walked closer to her. "Can I sit down?" she asked, pointing to the lounge chair next to Loletta.

Loletta shrugged, slipped on her shades, and lay back on her chair.

"First, I just want to say that there is nothing with Kavon and me. I have been a big basketball fan since grade school. But I never had the guts to follow anybody or approach any of the players like girls like you do."

Loletta flipped her shades over her head. "Excuse me?"

"I don't mean it like that. I'm saying that I like the game of basketball. That is why I worked my way up in the association to where I am now. It's all I ever wanted to be."

"Good for you," Loletta said, faking a yawn.

"I'm telling you this because I don't want to lose my job. Kavon mentioned something that you weren't happy and—"

"He did?"

"Yes, and somehow my boss warned me to stay away from the players. My next warning and I'm fired. I'm on probation now."

A smile tugged at the corners of Loletta's mouth. She didn't want to look evil by smiling, but Lady Anise was definitely working out some of her mojo, she thought.

"Well, that is not my problem," Loletta said, turning over on her stomach.

She didn't hear Kia say another word, so she turned to her side. "Anything else?" But Kia just stared at her like a dog checking out a bone.

"What is your problem?" Loletta asked, seemingly irritated by Kia's quietness. She could be wrong, but she got a feeling that Kia was really checking out her goods.

"I'm sorry again, Ms. Jackson. I was just admiring how beautiful you are. I think I've taken up enough of your time. I just don't have many friends. And I really want to ask you one thing."

"What?"

"How did you get this? I would love to have a life like this."

"I know," Loletta said, smirking. "But I didn't get anything; I'm earning this everyday." Loletta stood up to grab her robe and walk Kia to the door. She wanted the woman out of her sight and wasn't going to buy anybody's sob story. One thing she knew about women was that they were manipulative. When Loletta reached for her robe, her foot hit the leg of a small table, where her piña colada sat.

"Damn!" Loletta yelled, as she limped back to her lounge chair. "Adrienna!" She called for the maid.

"Oh, my God, Ms. Jackson," Kia said, helping Loletta to her chair. "Let me get her for you."

Loletta shrugged Kia's hands off her and massaged her ankle, which had a small bruise on the side.

Kia came back with a rag and some first-aid applications. "I think the maid may have gone grocery shopping. I saw a note. But I found these things."

Loletta kept her foot out as she watched in amazement as Kia gently wiped her scar with antiseptic, massaged a light ointment around it, and then sealed it with a Band-Aid.

"Can you walk now?" Kia asked.

Loletta wiggled her ankle. "Yeah, I can walk. Good. I thought I sprained it."

"Looks like it was just a cut." Kia smiled. "I feel like it's my fault."

Loletta looked at Kia good. She couldn't be any older than twenty-five, a few years younger than she. But Kia reminded her of a child striving to please her overbearing mother. She looked sad. "Thank you," Loletta said, straight-faced. "Can I offer you something to drink?"

"I don't want to trouble you. It's just so beautiful out here," she said, clasping her hands together and looking around the landscape. "If you don't mind, I'd love to just lounge around with you."

"Kia, we won't be friends. I still feel you have something for my husband and—"

"Please, Ms. Jackson. I'm like a tomboy. I have a boyfriend. He lives in Brooklyn and he loves me. I don't think I can be no NBA player's wife. I like my men simple, like me."

Loletta raised her chin. "You have a boyfriend?"

"Yeah." Kia blushed. "High-school sweetheart."

At that moment, Adrienna came out to the pool. "Ms. Jackson, I'm back. Is everything okay?"

Loletta smiled to herself. "Everything is fine. Can you just bring us out that pitcher of mojitos, a bucket of ice, and two glasses?"

"Right away," Adrienna said, as she disappeared through the glass doors.

A few moments later, she arrived with her request. Loletta and Kia drank for several hours as they talked about sports, clothes, and the latest industry gossip. Loletta learned that Kia was a fairly intelligent young woman; she'd graduated from Brown and was one of the youngest publicity managers in the Association's history. But with all that she'd accomplished, Kia was stuck on knowing more about Loletta—her likes, dislikes, where she hung out, and her own inside scoop on the industry. Loletta and Kia had finished two pitchers of mojitos before Loletta realized that three hours had passed.

The sun was setting. Kia was sprawled out on the chair beside her, talking some gibberish and slurring her words. Loletta had a blazing headache, but was feeling relaxed and at ease. It had been a while since she'd thrown back alcohol like that.

"Kia, it was really nice talking, but—"

"Hello, ladies," Kavon said, leisurely walking toward Loletta. He smelled their breath from across the room. "Damn," he said, waving the air.

"Sorry, baby," Loletta said, managing to stand up. "We kind of lost track of time."

"And alcohol, I see." Loletta stood up to hug him as they embraced. "What's up, Kia? I hear the office was looking for you," he said.

Kia shakily stood up, gripping the handle of the chair. "I told them I was leaving early. I just had to come talk to Ms. Jackson. I'm a leave y'all two alone," she said, stumbling to the door.

Loletta and Kavon paid Kia no mind as their tongues got lost in each other's mouths. Kavon squeezed the flesh of Loletta's ass in his hands, and rubbed her pussy as they kissed. Then they heard a bang.

"Oops." Kia laughed. She had tripped over herself and was barely at the door.

"Did you drive?" Loletta asked, her hands resting on Kavon's shoulders.

He planted soft, gentle kisses on her sunburned chest. "Let me get you out of this like I promised," he whispered.

"Yeah, I drove, but I will be all right." Kia bent over as she gripped her stomach.

"Girl, you cannot drive," Loletta said, urging Kavon to do something.

"I'll call you a cab," Kavon said, reaching for his cell phone.

"Actually," Kia said, "if you don't mind, I can crash on your couch. My home is almost two hours from here."

Loletta and Kavon looked at each other, then at Kia. Kia rubbed the temples of her forehead. Loletta felt they had a big enough home to have Kia sleep as far away from them as possible. "You can have the guest room in the basement," Loletta said, as she took Kavon's hand. Before they went upstairs, she let Adrienna know to prepare a place for Kia.

In their own bedroom, Kavon was all over Loletta as they cuddled in the bed. He seemed to enjoy having his wife tipsy. He even poured himself a glass of Henny from the minibar he kept in the corner of the bedroom. Kavon gently bit the sides of Loletta's bikini bottom, pulling it down to her thighs.

"Kavon." Loletta giggled as they rolled around the bed. Her breasts were hanging out of her bikini top. He undid the string and slid her bikini top down like the peel of a banana.

"I love these big-ass nipples." Kavan lost his face in her breasts, as he balanced the glass of Henny in his hands. She took it from him and swallowed some.

Buck naked, Kavon staggered to the bar and got a full bottle of Henny and some glasses. He poured the gold, glistening drink into a glass for Loletta and poured another one for himself.

"Oh, shit," Loletta said, spilling some on Kavon's knees. She was kneeling before him on the edge of the bed.

"You sure you don't need something to mix that drink with?" he asked, leaning back in the bed.

Loletta took his thick ebony dick and dipped it in her glass. She playfully stirred it around.

Kavon's jutted out his hips for more. Then Loletta slipped Kavon's Henny-coated dick in her mouth and sucked every ounce of flavor from it. She popped it out of her mouth and said, "It doesn't taste so bad. Like cognac with a twang."

They both laughed. Loletta let her tongue roll all over his tree trunk, sucking it into the wells of selfish satisfaction.

Kavon helped her climb back onto the bed, where he sucked on her thick wet lips. He probed the folds of her pussy with his fingers, securing kisses down the middle.

There was only one lamp on, leaving most of the room in partial darkness. Loletta was in a drunken daze as she breathlessly let Kavon take her to the heights of perfect passion. Afterward, she climbed on top of him, loving him back like he did her, marveling at his perfect rhythm. Then she felt a hand. Then a warm, soft tongue on her nipples. Loletta's eyes rolled back. It was Kia, who had crept in the room a few minutes before. Loletta knelt on the bed beside Kia and sucked her pointy nipples, kneading them between her full, painted lips. Overcome with lust, Loletta didn't want the pleasure feeling to stop. At this point, she couldn't turn back. It was on.

Kavon slid Loletta off him, cradling her onto the bed, her hair flared out around her like a fan. Her heart rushed with excitement about what was happening. Kia bent over in a doggy-style position with her fleshy hips in the air, while Kavon buried his dick inside her. She adoringly licked Loletta to such a sweet, shattering orgasm that she passed out. The scent of alcohol, sweat, and sex clung to the sheets and walls, as three naked bodies lay scattered over the king-size bed, exhausted.

At dawn, when Loletta cracked an eye open, she noticed Kia was gone as quietly as she had come. Loletta convinced herself it had all been a melodramatic dream, as she and Kavon went about their business, albeit hung over, like nothing ever happened.

Sixteen

A month passed. The NBA season was officially over. Kavon had purchased tickets for Loletta and him to travel to Milan to visit her father. They thought it would be a good way for Kavon to unwind after his hectic season. He also got a ticket for Ms. Landelton, who practically demanded to go. Loletta had wanted the trip to be for just the two of them, but her mother complained that she didn't want to be left alone in her condition. Loletta wasn't buying it, and she just took it as another ploy her mother was using to stay in her business and control her life.

There was something that no one knew. Loletta was pregnant with twins. It was something she had planned, and she couldn't think of better timing. Kavon was in his off-season, and they could really be a family now. And she wasn't so concerned about Kia anymore, who she thankfully hadn't heard from.

At home, Loletta and Kavon soaked in the Jacuzzi as they sipped mimosas and read the morning papers. Their bathroom was luxuriously decorated with twenty-four-karat gold-plated sinks and showers, designer handles for the toilet, a one-ton bathtub carved from a solid marble rock, a home monitoring system, and a digital music library that stored their favorite R & B classics. Ms. Landelton called the bathroom a "spa" because it had most of the amenities of a real one.

"Have you heard from Kia?" Loletta asked, even though she had made a promise to herself that she wouldn't mention her.

"She got fired right after the season ended," Kavon said, shrugging. "Haven't heard from her since."

Loletta wanted to jump in their car and drive over to Lady Anise to thank her. Kia seemed innocent, but her adoration for Loletta made her uncomfortable.

There was a long pause; then Kavon said, "I was asking around about your pops. He was the man back in his day." Kavon laid his paper down on the ground.

"He was, but by the time I was born he had been injured, so I don't know much about that other part of his life," Loletta said, flipping through the newspaper.

"I bet your mom does."

Loletta put down her paper too. "And that's supposed to mean?"

"Come on, I can tell by your moms that she wasn't dating nobody broke. Kind of like you." Kavon rested his arms around the edge of the Jacuzzi, as he stared at Loletta coldly.

"Please, don't try to act like you didn't know what you were getting when you married me. I like successful men, and if that means marrying rich, so be it."

"Hey, baby," Kavon said, sliding up to her and massing the soapy water between her breasts. "I ain't got no problem with that. I have always wanted to take care of my woman in every way. You didn't know how much it bothered me to see you go to that dealership job. I didn't like that."

"I know." Loletta smiled, as she caressed his face. She wanted to tell him the good news. That she was pregnant. But something told her to hold on. "I was thinking that after we have a family, maybe I could open a business or something. A lot of players' wives do that."

Kavon pushed the button in the Jacuzzi to get the bubbles started again. "What's the point of being with a man like me if you still gotta work?"

"I don't have to; I want to. I've always wanted a career. Like Derrick Lawless's wife—she opened up a restaurant."

"Your career is being my wife," Kavon said, looking deeply into her eyes like he wanted to read her mind.

Loletta watched the warm bubbles erupt around her, soothing the sore muscles in her back. "I can do that too," Loletta hissed. "But I would want to do something together, like start a business. Isn't there anything you want to start?"

Kavon wrapped his arms around Loletta's waist as he scooted in between her thighs. "I want to retire in a few years and invest. I don't want no business. I got enough endorsements to set me up for life."

Loletta's face turned long. "You mean *us*."

"Right." He smiled.

Loletta, Kavon, and Ms. Landelton arrived in Milan the following week. No one knew her secret. She thought the best time to reveal it would be in front of everyone, as a family. In fact, it made her shiver with excitement when she thought about having twins. Hightower and his family lived near La Scala in the historic Brera district. His home had all the fine trimmings of superluxury. Loletta loved the exotic woods and matte Zimbabwe marbles in black and bronze with oak and bronze detailing the floor-to-ceiling windows.

"This place looks like a freakin' museum," Ms. Landelton whispered to Loletta as they walked along with Kavon.

They were all staying at Hightower's home, which had several guest rooms. It was where Loletta and her mother had always stayed when they visited. Though Loletta agreed that it did look like a museum, Mirella warmed it up with her colorful abstract artwork. Mirella was a dark-skinned, modest, but rich Italian woman. She had a head full of thick, black, shiny hair, which she swept up into a neat ponytail that ended just above the small of her back. It was her signature hairstyle. She and Ms. Landelton always got along fine, mostly because Mirella let her dominate the conversation. Mirella was poised and gracious, and Loletta admired that. She could see Mirella made her father happy.

Mirella had prepared a dinner of all her best dishes. Though they could afford it, she refused to have someone else prepare their meals. The dining room was spread with all kind of delicacies: grilled baby octopus in salsa verde with summer beans and potatoes, homemade ravioli stuffed with lobster, and shrimp sautéed with fresh asparagus and tomato, grilled rosemary shrimp, lamb shanks, crusted chicken breasts, and a huge platter of polenta and gorgonzola salad with tomato, porcini mushrooms, and truffle sauce.

"So I finally meet the famous Mr. Big Jackson," Loletta's father said, as he stood almost shoulder to shoulder with Kavon. They were both around six foot eight inches tall. Hightower gave Kavon a warm but strong handshake, as everybody took their seats around the table.

"Nice to meet you too, Mr. Hightower," Kavon said, putting his arm around Loletta. "We brought you and Mirella a gift," he said, pulling out a red envelope. Loletta wasn't sure what it was because they hadn't discussed anything of the sort.

Kavon handed the envelope to Hightower, who slit it open.

"Hot damn," he said, handing it to Mirella.

"What is it?" Ms. Landelton asked, looking over Mirella's shoulder.

"It's a four-night stay at the penthouse suite at the Sanctuary in Miami Beach. It's been a few years since we been to Miami," her father said, nodding his head approvingly. His thick beard and short fro made him look like a college professor. "Thank you."

"This is lovely, Kavon. It's just in time for our anniversary too," Mirella said.

Ms. Landelton forced a smiled. "Very nice, Kavon. And Loletta."

"And when you guys come to Miami, we'd love you to stay with us too. And if you don't mind, Mr. Hightower, I'd like to take you on, one-on-one at my full-size court," Kavon grinned, still keeping his arm around Loletta.

Hightower laughed, flattered that a young pro would think someone as old as he was still had game.

He was being quite the charmer tonight, Loletta thought. Just like he didn't tell her about buying her mom a house, he didn't even tell her about the gift he had for her father. *He's not the only one good at keeping secrets.*

Loletta smiled on as everyone ate and chatted. She was waiting for the appropriate time. Kavon was dressed in D & G jeans and a sharp white Gucci button-down shirt. He kept smiling at her in between bites and rubbing her thighs under the table. She appreciated how well Kavon treated her family, and she hoped he would be just as happy about a couple of new additions.

Loletta clinked her glass with a fork. "Excuse me, everyone," she said, breaking up the chatter. "I have something I want to share." She put her hand over her stomach, turned to Kavon, and said, "We're having twins."

The table fell silent as all eyes set on Kavon, whose mouth stopped chewing. "Two?" he said, putting his hand over hers. "That's beautiful, baby." Kavon kissed her lightly on the lips.

"Babies! Babies!" Ms. Landelton shouted, as she ran around the table and kissed Loletta on her cheek. Loletta and Kavon were still in an embrace when her father and Mirella also walked over to congratulate them.

"We have to make a toast," Mr. Hightower said, motioning for the champagne sitting in a nearby ice bucket. He popped the cork and poured the bubbly drink into everyone's glass except Loletta's. There was juice for the mother-to-be.

"To Kavon and Loletta. We wish you many more," Mr. Hightower said, as laughter infiltrated the room.

"Many, many more," Ms. Landelton added, as she raised her glass and shot Loletta a wink.

Later on, Ms. Landelton called Loletta downstairs to the wine cellar, as the rest stayed upstairs watching old footage of Hightower's days as a pro.

"Why didn't you tell me?" Ms. Landelton asked, as she looked at Loletta's stomach, which was hidden underneath a fitted, green and yellow Versace summer dress. "You know what this means."

Loletta and her mother talked quietly as they walked around the large cellar that housed rows of vintage wines. Loletta folded her arms across her chest and said, "I know what it means. That is why I waited to say it in front of everyone. Kavon and I never talked about kids."

"Well, I'm glad you waited till now. I honestly think he was shocked. But who cares?" Ms. Landelton said, keyed up with excitement. "Those babies will seal your future. The more babies, the more money he will have to pay if you ever divorce. It's like having insurance on your marriage."

"I hope Kavon doesn't think so."

"Who cares? I can't wait to be a grandmommy. This is fantastic," Ms. Landelton said, as she buried Loletta's face in her.

Loletta hugged her mother back. She was relieved more than anything. Relieved that Kavon looked as happy as everyone else.

"Loletta?" Mr. Hightower said, as she entered the room. "Can we have a moment alone?"

Ms. Landelton adjusted a few strands of her hair away from her face. "Of course, I was just leaving," she said, as she walked past her former husband.

"How are you?" he asked, grimacing. "I'm a little concerned." He walked closer to her.

"Why?" Loletta asked. "With Kavon?"

"Yeah. He seems like a nice person. I know of him, and he's an ace on the court. However, something about you two—"

"What about us?"

"Does he know that your only goal was to marry an athlete?"

"He knows I dated athletes. But Kavon and I go way back to college, Daddy." Loletta walked around him and sat down on a wooden stepping stool.

"Okay, okay," her father said tenderly, leaning against the wall across from her. "I'm just telling you these guys can be unpredictable, and I just don't want you getting pregnant for security."

"I'm not," Loletta said, as she looked up at her father.

"I don't want to see you hurt, Loletta. Just make sure you two talk about this when you get home. He looked like the kiss of death when you told him."

"I didn't see that. He was shocked. I was too when I found out."

"Just talk," her father urged. "He just strikes me as someone who does what he wants, and he will, with or without you being pregnant."

The rest of their stay in Milan went without a hitch, with days spent swimming in the Mediterranean and nights together as a big family. Kavon rubbed her belly until he fell asleep each night, and they made love like he was trying to put in a third.

Loletta was driving with Vernice in her red Maybach over the George Washington Bridge back to Jersey. It had been only a week since she'd returned from Milan nicely tanned and refreshed. They were coming from the spa where they'd each had almond-milk pedicures and manicures, sugar skin scrubs, and an hour of stone massages. Kavon was playing golf with some friends, and Ms. Landelton was in her weekly yoga class.

"I'm gonna be an auntie, I'm gonna be an auntie," Vernice teased, as she reclined back in the passenger seat and admired the cool grayish water down below. "So what you gonna name them?"

"I'm barely three months," Loletta said, as the car crept across the bridge in midday traffic. "Kavon and I didn't talk about names yet. But I know he wants boys."

"How has he been acting?"

"Great. He kisses my belly every night before we go to sleep. He even massages my feet. And he had my favorite Swedish chocolates shipped and stocked in the refrigerator for the next nine months." It dawned on her how lucky she felt, but there was more.

"He sounds like he been taking lessons in kissing his wife's ass from Cliff Huxtable," Vernice said, looking at Loletta through her shades.

"Well, he ain't no Cliff Huxtable. I just think he's been feeling guilty lately. I thought he was fucking around on me."

"So what happened?"

"That girl Kia and I and Kavon ended up getting drunk one night at the house and—"

"No!" Vernice put her hand over her lips. "And y'all didn't invite me to the party?"

Loletta laughed. It was a party in Vernice's book. "It kind of just happened, and she doesn't seem that bad after all. She's like one of those fan types. She ain't like us."

Vernice sat up in her seat and shot Loletta a glare that could stop the traffic behind them. "Are you crazy?"

"What!" Loletta said, turning to her and then back to the road. They were only ten minutes from her house.

"Okay, I see being the missus has really dried up your brain cells. You telling me that you don't think that girl had a motive when she came by your house? Why did she come by?"

Loletta whipped the car around a narrow bend and parked. "Vernice, I don't need your negativity messing up what I already figured out. Can't we just focus on what's good? I'm pregnant. If Kavon is fucking around, he's gonna be the loser, not me."

"How did Kia get in?"

Loletta turned the engine off and rolled down the windows. She could tell where this was going. "Security let her in."

"Doesn't that seem funny to you? How does she know security? They just don't let in any heffa who walks up to the ten-million-dollar home of an NBA star."

Loletta thought deeply about it. She thought maybe security had a list of employees who would be associated with the team and that was it. But then again . . . "You saying that she been there before?"

"Yes. That girl has been all through that house. While you are in New Jersey, she is in Miami. There's no telling what other of his homes she's been in. She could have been in the one we going to now. Your main home."

"Well?" Loletta said, rubbing the back of her neck as she listened to Vernice's reasoning.

"Divorce him."

"It's not that kind of situation."

"Take his money; write a book about it. You can live, girl. You don't need him,"

"Vernice, that may be your answer to everything, but I actually like being married. And Kia was talking about how she admires me and whatnot. She even ate my pussy that night. It was some crazy shit. I ain't never have no man, except Kavon, give my pussy that kind of love. She just wanted to be in the midst of greatness." Loletta smiled.

"Bitch!" Vernice laughed. "That is some crazy shit for real. Kia is crazy. She fucked your man. She fucked your man. Your husband fucked her in front of you. If he could do that with you, God knows what he doing without you."

Loletta put the car in gear at once. She hit the gas and sped down the street to her home. She didn't know what she was going to do with Vernice, especially if Kavon was there, because she was about to come down on his ass like a storm on a parade.

"Kavon! Kavon!" Loletta yelled. She called his name out several times as she paced around the house. Vernice was waiting in the car.

"He not here now, Ms. Jackson. Are you okay?" Adrienna asked, wiping her hands on a towel.

"I'm fine," Loletta said, rubbing her stomach. She felt sick, as if she wanted to throw up. A part of her was glad he wasn't there because she was about to lose it. Everything crashed down on her. Kia was not some adoring fan, but a manipulator. And though she was fired, she couldn't be gone far, she thought. She tricked me into fucking my own husband. Loletta shook the thoughts out of her head. She felt like she was losing it. She wanted to call Vernice in. Her hands were wet, and her heart was thumping against her chest with anxiety. She sat down on the leather couch and counted to three.

Then the front door opened. Kavon walked in with his golf clubs and set them down. He slipped off some white gloves and just stared at Loletta. He was dressed in cream-colored slacks and a green polo shirt. He looked like he hadn't even broken a sweat.

"What's wrong?" he said calmly, watching Loletta from across the door. He didn't even take a step closer.

"You. You. You," Loletta said, clenching her fists. "You fucked Kia."

"Yeah, or did you forget?" he chuckled, putting his hands in his pockets.

"Not then, but before."

"Yeah, I fucked her a few times." His demeanor was composed, as if he had rehearsed this ten times. He walked to Loletta and touched her hair.

"Get the fuck off me," she said, smacking his hand away. "How you gonna just stand there and tell me you fucked her a few times when you told me nothing ever happened?"

"You didn't outright ask me before if I had sex. You asked about some other bullshit," he said, finally raising his voice. He didn't move from beside her, but stood there.

"The point is, you let that bitch in here for a reason. You set my ass up. What happened was probably some fucked-up fantasy of yours. How could you, Kavon?" Loletta stood up slowly to see his face. "How?"

"Sit down."

"I ain't sitting!"

"Sit down!" he said, and pushed her on the couch.

She shot back up. "You are fucking with me, Kavon. You think I'm a damn fool. You had that woman in my house!"

"That was a mistake. Just like you being pregnant is."

Loletta was fixed on his cold smile. "So now the real you comes out. Now you gonna blame me for getting pregnant?"

Kavon paced the floor, growing increasingly agitated. "You knew what you was in for when you married me. And I ain't never tell you," he pointed at her, "that I wanted kids. I was acting like the perfect husband because we was around your family. I gotta take care of you, your mom, and two fucking kids. Hell, no."

"I'm having these babies, Kavon. You can leave me or do whatever you want," she cried, grabbing her pocketbook as she dashed to the front door.

He blocked her way and snatched her up by her neck. The power of his grip nearly took the breath out of her. "You getting rid of those babies. Or I will," he whispered in her ear.

"No, please, Kavon," Loletta pleaded through a gulpful of air. He dragged her across the room before letting her go. She struggled to stand.

"How you gonna call it your house? This place is mine. Just like everything you have. Don't ever think about checking me on my shit. Is that clear?" he asked, his face tightening.

"Fuck you!" She spat at him and tried to brush past him when he grabbed her again.

"I love you, Loletta. I do," he said, twisting her arm so hard she felt it crack.

"Well, I hate you." The tone of her voice scared her, because she didn't mean it.

The next thing Loletta felt was her body tumbling down the endless steps to the basement and her face so swollen she couldn't see out of one eye. She had landed right on her face on the cold cement floor. She couldn't move; her legs felt like two bricks. She couldn't even scream.

Moments later, she heard footsteps. "Loletta!" Vernice said, as she ran down to the basement, skipping several steps. "Oh, my God, I saw that motherfucka run out of here so quick, I knew something happened."

She held Loletta's head in her hands until Loletta opened her eyes to thin slits. "He said he would get rid of my babies, and he did."

"What?" Vernice asked, confused. But then she saw the blood emanating from between Loletta's legs.

The ambulance rushed Loletta to the hospital. That July Fourth weekend she lost the babies. A boy and a girl.

Seventeen

"Why did you have to get yourself so upset?" Ms. Landelton asked over an afternoon cup of tea at her home. Loletta hadn't been out of the house since she returned from the hospital.

"I just found out my husband cheated on me and then had sex with that bitch and me together. I don't know about you, but that made me sick." Loletta blew down on her hot cup of coffee. She was wearing a black Juicy Couture sweatsuit. Her hair was undone, and her nails badly needed attention.

"I don't want to see you lose yourself like this. Look at you," Ms. Landelton said. "No wonder why—"

"Why what? My husband cheats?"

Ms. Landelton squeezed a bit of lemon into her tea. "Honey, you have to keep yourself up with these men."

"Mommy, this is the first time my nails have looked like this in five years. I maintain myself at all times, but I just lost my babies. You and Kavon can get over it, but I can't."

"So what do you plan to do?"

Loletta wasn't sure. Kavon had spent every one of the four

nights she was in the hospital by her bedside. She had a celebrity suite, so there was an adjacent bedroom where Kavon slept. He pleaded with Loletta over and over to forgive him. He was just as upset as she was when the doctors revealed that she miscarried. He even promised to seek counseling.

"I plan to see what happens," Loletta said to her mother. "Just don't plan on me getting pregnant anytime soon. Not until Kavon and I get some serious counseling."

"Baby, the doctor said you can be ready again in a few months. There's no point of being married to a rich man if you're not going to have kids." Ms. Landelton's lips wrinkled as she brought them to the rim of her cup.

"Can you think about what I want for a second? Can this not be about you?"

"It's not about me. It's about the family. You went ahead and got yourself all bothered, and look at what happened."

"I can't believe you're blaming this on me," Loletta said, although she blamed herself even more. "Kavon hit me. He threw me down those stairs intentionally. If I ever went to the police—"

"They'd think you were delirious. I'm sure he didn't mean to. You act like he wanted to kill you."

"It damn well looked like it." Loletta inhaled the mint scent from the tea. She could feel a migraine descending on her. "But now he swears he's changed. And unfortunately, I think I have, too."

When Loletta returned home, Kavon had prepared a dinner for both of them under candlelight. She found a small black box on their bed with a red bow. It was an eight-carat purple diamond ring. She slipped it on without a blink.

The following day Loletta met with Lady Anise in her Upper East Side home. When Loletta entered the small, quiet room, Lady Anise was sitting in a rocking chair. "You didn't listen," she said, her eyes sad.

Loletta sat down. "I got pregnant and wanted to keep the babies, but—"

"It's okay, my dear." She patted Loletta's slouched shoulders. "You have been through a lot. It just wasn't the time for you to have children.

"Your husband needs deep therapy to change the way his mind works. He's very territorial. Very independent, self-sufficient. Children are seen as a burden to him. Another chore. He should be here with you now."

"Can you make him come?"

"I can't make anyone do anything."

"What about that woman we talked about the last time? My husband told me she no longer works for the Association," Loletta said, smiling. "I know they had an affair for sure because he told me. I'm just glad she's gone."

Lady Anise took Loletta's hands and wrapped her thin hands over them. "She's not gone."

Loletta pulled her hand back. "I thought you sent her away."

"I tried to," Lady Anise said. "She is no longer at the job, but she still lives in the Bronx. But she will soon be gone completely. It's a process; I guarantee you."

Loletta didn't like the sound of that. "Is she still with my husband?"

"No," Lady Anise said, gathering her long glittery skirt between her legs. "That is over."

"Are you sure?"

"Absolutely. One thing has changed, and he is sincerely committed to you now, but children are still an issue. But you can work through that."

Loletta let out a loud sigh of relief. "Now I can sleep a little better," she said.

"Well." Lady Anise clasped her hands together, and Loletta did the same. "Pray. Just pray."

"What do you mean, just pray? Is there something else?"

"I'm sorry, Loletta, but I can't do this anymore."

"Do what?"

"This. I feel it's time for you to work on your own problems. I'm not helping you get any stronger. You will need lots of strength to be the woman you are to become. If you rely on me, you won't be able to trust yourself."

Loletta left Lady Anise that day more confused than when she entered. But she realized one thing: she was right. Seeing a stranger wasn't going to solve her problems because the problem wasn't other people; it was inside her.

When she got home an hour later, Loletta saw two packages on the table. One was small and white, and the other was large and brown. She looked out the window. There wasn't a cloud in the sky, the sun shone down on their house, and the green lawn was dotted with white and purple lilies. If she were a painter, she thought, this could be her inspiration. Kavon was shooting hoops in the back alone. She thought both packages were for him, but one of them had both of their names. She took the large brown box into the kitchen to find a knife and tear it open. It was fairly heavy. It had a PO box for a return address. Then it occurred to her that maybe it was something her mom ordered. Her mother loved ordering from catalogs.

Loletta poured herself some orange juice and opened the window to let in the cool summer breeze scented with the sweet fragrance of flowers. Finally, she tore the box open, careful not to damage the contents. When she looked inside, she fell back and gripped the edge of the kitchen island. "Kavon!" she yelled out the window. Her hands shook as she held the knife.

Kavon ran in the kitchen and moved her away from the box. It was two baby dolls, butchered with blood on their clothes and grinning faces.

Loletta cried. *This can't be,* she thought. "Who would be so evil?" Loletta asked Kavon, who held one of the dolls in his hands. A tear ran down his cheek.

"It was probably the wrong address," he said, his back turned. He couldn't look at the pain in Loletta's face. He threw the doll back in the box.

"I'm calling the police," Loletta said, as she picked up the phone.

"Don't." Kavon took it out of her hands. "We can handle this on our own. I don't want to give the media anything else to write about if it ain't about my game. We can do this. *Together*. But I'm really sure it's just a mistake."

Mistake. She had heard that before. But this wasn't a mistake. She sobbed in Kavon's arms. She was still hurting inside, and the pain wasn't just in her womb.

Eighteen

Around four a.m. Sunday morning, Loletta lay awake in the king-size bed with silky smooth, four hundred-thread-count Egyptian cotton sheets. Kavon's heavy hand rested on her abdomen. She imagined that she was mid-term, about to give birth in the coming months. Just in time for the holidays. Images of one baby wrapped in her arm and the other in Kavon's as they sat around the table for Christmas dinner bombarded her. She wanted to be a mother more now that she had lost her twins. She would go about raising kids differently than her mother had. Instead of egging her daughter on to meet stars and "marry rich," she'd teach her to be her own star and "marry smart."

As a child, Ms. Landelton had breathed and studied the success of others but never applied it to herself. She made others do all the work while she benefited. When she was younger, Loletta thought how cool and enterprising her mother was, teaching her self-sufficiency by using other people's money. But inside, Loletta knew that she was different. Things like her husband cheating, and the measure of his love and respect for her, mattered more than never having to worry about money again. Loletta didn't want to place blame elsewhere. She had taught people how to treat her. She silently wished there was someone else to blame, because blaming herself was far harder than blaming others.

The vibrating motion of her cell phone jolted her from her thoughts. She crept across the room to pick it up, but it had stopped. It was an unidentified missed call. But they left a message.

Loletta took the phone down the hall to another room to listen to the message. She couldn't believe her ears. She thought he was a thing of the past. It was Carter. He asked her to call him right away.

"This is Loletta," she said, sitting on the windowsill. She wore a thin burgundy nightgown and flinched when her butt touched the cold panel.

"I know it's late, but how you been?" he asked, sounding like he didn't expect her call at all.

"You call me at four a.m. to ask me how I'm doing?" she asked, speaking low.

"I actually don't want to talk. I want to see you. You took my money, and I didn't hear from you again, baby."

Loletta smirked. She knew what Carter had on his mind the more she listened to his syrupy, baritone voice. "So you want your money back?"

"Nah, not at all. Really, I just want to see that sweet behind again." Carter was one of Kavon's archrivals. They were both at the same level, but Kavon was more commercial, and advertisers loved him for his extravagant style of play. If Kavon was a Shaquille, Carter was an Iverson.

"I'm married; don't act like you don't know," Loletta said.

"Well, at least one of us is."

Loletta's eyebrows creased. "She finally left you. I guess some women have good sense these days."

"I left *her*," he said. "And by the way, being married ain't never stop anyone from getting together for drinks. I'm staying at the Carlyle."

Loletta did want to see him. She didn't know why. But she was still reeling about Kavon and Kia. All she had with Carter was fun, and she needed some of it now. "I'll call you later," she said, and hung up.

"Who was that?" Kavon said. He was standing in the doorway when she looked up.

"Vernice."

At around three p.m., Loletta waited at the Carlyle bar. She wore a Donna Karan white linen knee-length dress and gigantic black shades, her hair softly tousled on her exposed shoulders. The Carlyle was a familiar place for her. She and her mother used to have drinks at Bemelmans before they could afford dinner at the restaurant. They'd often scout out the athletes and business executives in town for the weekend, as well as the regulars. Loletta never had any luck there because she wasn't into white men like her mother was.

The waiter poured her another glass of Chambord and Dom Perignon. "Thank you," she said, staring at the pretty purplish mixture.

"I'll have one too," Carter said, creeping up from behind.

Her eyes stayed on him as she admired his dark blue blazer, white shirt, and dark jeans draping his six-four body. She was still deeply attracted to him, and that only meant trouble.

He slid onto the stool beside her and inhaled. "You smell like a married woman."

She looked at him sideways. "Kavon's cologne is everywhere in that house, even on my clothes."

"That's only a man marking his territory. I can't blame the brother," he said, as the champagne flute touched his moving lips. He picked up her left hand and examined her wedding ring. "Damn, Big must've spent half his contract on that piece. You got the snapper in that pussy, baby."

"Look, let's just get to the point here. I got a check for you," Loletta said, unzipping her Louis Vuitton shoulder bag.

"I don't want your money. And I promise I won't give you any. You look like you doing good for the both of us."

"I'm married to Kavon Jackson. I'm not anybody's 'pay girlfriend'."

"Yeah, but you a paid wife. Not much of a difference," he said, sounding cold.

Loletta ripped the check out of her book and tossed it to him. He tore it in half.

She didn't know what else to do because even his attitude was turning her on some. But her plan was to fall back and let him do the talking.

With each sip of champagne their faces softened as they glanced at each other. The conversation became lighter, brighter.

"It feels good to be single again," Carter said, as he eyed Loletta's décolletage.

"You've always acted single. Married or not," Loletta reminded him. She liked him looking at her. There was just something about Carter that Kavon didn't have, or she thought, it was just something she couldn't have.

"A bit of advice for you. Don't ever let your husband walk all over you, at least not all the time," he laughed.

"Do tell," she said, wiping her mouth. The waiter brought

them another round. "No matter what I do, Kavon never seems satisfied. The only thing that brought us closer was death."

"If I had known you were marrying him, I would've warned you. One thing I've never done is hit a woman, but Kavon would slap the taste out of a seventy-year-old granny if she stepped over the line." He laughed again.

Loletta knew that firsthand. But what scared her most was that if someone had warned her, she probably wouldn't have listened. "Kavon got issues like we all do," she said, coming to his defense.

Carter's massive shoulders touched hers as he moved closer. "I know you got some. Why don't you let me serve you for the night? Make you forget about all those little things at home for a few hours."

Loletta's lips moved but nothing came out. She was close enough to Carter that their lips could touch with neither of them moving. And they did, as Carter's lips lingered gently on hers. The light at the bar was low, making them feel covered and underexposed. She squeezed in the tension she felt growing between her thighs as he licked her flavor from his lips.

"Meet me in room 1276 in ten minutes." He slipped her an extra key.

She felt like she was left holding the bag. It would have been easier, she thought, if they had just walked up together, but it wouldn't have been smart. Carter's drink was untouched. She drank hers down, then his, and then she left.

"Excuse me, miss!" the bartender said.

Loletta stopped dead in her tracks and turned around.

"You forgot your room key," he said, with a friendly smile.

Loletta thanked him and took the keys.

Within minutes, she was in Carter's lavish room nourishing their bodies on a bounty of desire and sheer indulgence.

At around ten p.m. Loletta finally got a chance to leave. After she had combed her hair, showered, and dressed, she was gone. She was relieved when Carter said he was going to Houston in the morning. She didn't need him around whatsoever. She slid her shades on and walked briskly through the hotel lobby. She wondered if she could make it back home in less than an hour. Her car was waiting out front.

Her dark shades made it difficult for her to see as she walked to the exit and out into the dark streets. As she went through the door, she bumped smack into someone walking right in.

"Oh, sorry," Loletta said, trying to get away. She didn't even bother stopping until she heard a voice say, "Can't say hi to an old friend?"

Loletta knew that raspy voice anywhere. "Kia?" she asked, as she stood in place.

Kia walked over to her slowly, with a weird look and wearing the exact same white and beige Versace dress that Loletta owned. "How are you?"

Loletta looked at Kia, horror-struck. "That's my dress," Loletta said, snatching off her shades.

Kia twirled around, holding the hem. "I knew you'd like it."

"That's my fuckin' dress," Loletta said. She had the dress altered to include extra pockets on the side, something that was not in its original design. "You stole my dress." Loletta didn't know whether to run or to tear it off her right there. Something was not right about Kia, and this finally proved it.

"Well," she said, laughing uncontrollably. "What was I supposed to wear home after that night when we all fucked? I can eat your pussy, but I can't wear your clothes?"

Loletta charged at Kia so quick that Kia nearly tripped as she backed away. "Kavon told me everything about you two, and he is finished with you. Don't even think of ever contacting us or trying to come at me like we cool," Loletta said, maintaining her composure as a few curious eyes hung on to their conversation. "So before I kick your ass and end up on the eleven o'clock news, let me get home to my husband, would you?"

Kia sucked her teeth and laughed again. "Um, Loletta?"

Loletta kept on walking like she didn't hear.

"I'll tell Carter you said good night!" she said, from halfway across the lobby.

Loletta had to stop. *That bitch.* She heard Kia's footsteps get louder as she approached.

"What now?" Loletta asked, flinging around. She checked her watch. Kavon would flip if she got home after midnight.

"Nothing." Kia sported an impish smile. "Well, at least not until your husband finds out."

She couldn't downright deny Carter. It was obvious, and denying her feelings would only give them life, she thought. Carter was a player, and she knew he wasn't going to cover for her either. Loletta wanted to acknowledge Kia's comment by getting defensive. Instead she said, "As you know, my husband and I have somewhat of an open relationship," she lied. Then she turned on her heels and walked away.

Kia looked disappointed, but before Loletta could get far, Kia shouted, "Once a ho, always a ho!"

Loletta's life began to change that night as those words rang in her ears all the way home.

Nineteen

Thursday night, Loletta and Kavon headed out to the 40/40 nightclub in Atlantic City. It was Calvin's birthday, and the misty, humid July evening provided the perfect setting for a hot night of gambling and other fetishes. After Kavon won over ten thousand dollars at blackjack at Caesars, Calvin's party was the next stop. Vernice was supposed to meet her at 40/40 since Calvin was playing the family man.

When all three of them pulled up to the club, security immediately ushered them to the ESPN Hall of Fame Lounge. This type of treatment gave Loletta a natural high as she whisked by the long line of average folks vying to be next. Several decorated beds adorned the lounge. Their table had several chilled bottles of Cristal and jumbo prawns. As Loletta and Kavon got cozy on the bed, Vernice stayed far away from both of them. She sat on the black Italian wraparound couch and engaged a few other girls in conversation. Loletta thought that maybe seeing Calvin with his wife tonight was too much. But then again, that had never fazed Vernice before.

"You having a good time, baby?" Kavon asked, feeding Loletta a crispy prawn. He bit into the other half.

"Good." Loletta nodded as she heard one of her favorite rap songs booming throughout the room. "I just hope Vernice is."

Kavon glanced at Vernice, who was chatting it up. "Why you worried about her? She's just playing her position."

"But it must be hard for her. The last time she was with Calvin and his wife, she ended up fucking Calvin and getting caught in our house. I don't want to see her get herself into any issues with him tonight. He act so damn bold sometimes."

Kavon shrugged. "He just being a man. She might as well get on him before Darva gets here," he laughed.

Loletta threw Vernice a look suggesting that she better watch her back tonight. Darva wasn't the fool she played. Vernice smiled awkwardly at her and went back to her conversation.

"My people!" Calvin said, as he gave Kavon a pound.

"This place is beautiful, man. You just gave me an idea of where to have my birthday party. Right, Loletta?" Kavon said, as both men carried on.

Loletta moved up and down in agreement as she dipped a prawn in some sauce. "Or Mykonos," she said, thinking about how great it was to have a birthday party anywhere in the world and not even consider the cost. She kept a close eye on Kavon as he talked animatedly to Calvin. As much as she tried to ignore it, Kavon still made her heart pitter-patter. He looked ruggedly handsome in his white linen Versace suit, which hung loosely in all the right places, complimenting the physique that was as solid as oak. His sharp, prominent facial features and midnight black skin looked even more glorious when he smiled. As she admired him, she remembered what her mother once told her: a handsome man is nothing but ugliness subdued.

Calvin bent down and gave Loletta a firm hug. "Your girl here?"

Loletta pointed in Vernice's direction.

"I'll be back." Calvin grinned as he rolled up on Vernice from behind. She had deliberately worn a very short skirt this evening.

Loletta was amazed at how open he was in his affection for Vernice, at least until Darva arrived. Loletta and Kavon lounged together on the bed, exchanging a few words with folks walking by who knew him. She was feeling relaxed with Kavon, as he gave her his undivided attention in a roomful of attractive young women of all colors, hanging around like monkeys on tree branches. Then Kavon took her hand as they danced their way to the dance floor with the other guests. Kavon opened his arms as Loletta spun around in between them, dropping her hips to the ground while holding a flute of champagne in one hand. Kavon egged her on as they both danced to hip-hop classics in sync and in sweat with the other partygoers.

They danced nonstop for about an hour. This reminded Loletta of her free-feeling partying nights with Vernice. She loved that she could feel that way with her husband. She had thought the feeling of being free was long gone. Then Loletta took Kavon's hand as a slower R. Kelly song belted through the club. She put her head on his substantial chest, and he held her tight like she was going to run. She listened to his heartbeat. She thought of Kavon's heart as secret sanctuary that only she had the key to, but she accepted that it had small rooms that were seldom vacant and that she might never know how to open. Out of the corner of her eye, she spotted Darva and Calvin dancing too. Darva had her back turned to him, and his hand played all over her body and his tongue poked around her ear. Loletta wanted to show Kavon how they were nearly undressing each other, but his body was stuck to hers like peanut butter on the roof of her mouth.

After that song, she decided to look for Vernice. She was nowhere around. It bothered Loletta to think her friend was off somewhere either plotting or stressing. "Baby, I'm gonna check for Vernice," Loletta said, as they went back to their lounge bed. Kavon lit a Cuban cigar, took a long drag, and shook his head. "You gonna run off on me and check for your friend? I thought this was our night."

"It is. I just want to see what she's up to. That's all," she said, liking his little jealous attitude. "I'll be back." She walked out of the room, giving all the female wandering eyes a look they could cash in for a beat-down. Loletta looked over the balcony, which gave a wall-to-wall view of the entire main floor. She couldn't see Vernice, so next she went outside. There was Vernice sitting on a bench.

"Girl, why are you out here when the party is in there?" Loletta scooted Vernice over to sit beside her.

"That's what I should be asking you," Vernice said, smiling. "And I should be asking where you got that bomb-ass Dolce and Gabbana dress. I love the black sequin on that mini!"

"Thank you," Loletta giggled, criss-crossing her legs. "I got it on a shopping spree. Sometimes I have to think of what to buy. I practically have more clothes than I have space for. We may need to move." Loletta laughed, but she noticed how quiet Vernice had become. Sitting on the porch overlooking the bustling Atlantic City boardwalk, Loletta asked, "Is it Darva?"

"Not really," Vernice said, her chin resting on her hand. She flipped her long bangs off her face. Her skin was the color of the inside of an almond, but the summer sun had painted it almost as brown as Loletta's. "I've just been feeling not myself since I seen you at the bottom of those steps that day. *Bleeding*. I just feel bad if I instigated anything with you and Kavon."

"Kavon and I had problems before that day, and we still do. It was an accident," Loletta said, with an uncomfortable laugh. She had tried for weeks to block it out of her mind—and now this.

Vernice shook her head and sighed. "I'm moving."

Loletta's eyes turned as big as quarters. "Why?"

"I don't know," Vernice said, looking out into the distance. "Calvin is never gonna leave his wife. And I need to start thinking about what I need. Seeing you lose your babies because of Kavon scared the shit out of me. Something just clicked for me that I have to start fresh, on a new path."

"What happened to me is nobody's fault," Loletta said firmly, though she knew the truth. "I need you here, Vernice. Where are you going?"

"Back home to Orlando."

"Orlando? There ain't nothing down there but Mickey and Minnie. This is where the money is and the men who are making it. You my road dog." Loletta put her arm around her.

"You married." Vernice snapped, as if she was agitated by Loletta's jovial mood. "How can you stay with that motherfucka after what he did?"

Loletta was done with being nice, but she said politely, "Don't tell me what to do with my—"

"*Husband*. Yeah, yeah, I know the drill. And I know you are really kidding yourself if you think that nigga love you."

"He loves me, and we are both doing the best we can. God knows, I'm far from wife material, and he married me anyway."

"Don't you see something wrong with that?"

"Why is this about me all of a sudden?"

"Because it is always about you. Since you been married, things ain't been the same. I really don't have any other friends. Then you tell me you had lunch with Darva. I didn't say anything then, but that fucked with me. Bottom line, I can't be living this fake life no more."

Loletta took her arm from around Vernice, whose shoulders had tightened up. "I'm sorry if I wasn't the best kind of friend. I've been having problems too."

Vernice looked at her with understanding. "We all do. And trust me, this is no way me attacking you. I'm just angry about a lot of things. Mainly at what I let myself do. I had two abortions for Calvin. My body is just tired of this."

Loletta's stomach clenched. For every "pay girlfriend" that kept the baby, there was one who didn't. She wished she had known, but then she remembered that after the first one Vernice said she was getting her tubes tied. Obviously she didn't. "Wherever you decide to go, I got you. We'll be friends. How much money do you need?"

"Calvin gave me some money. And I didn't even tell him about the abortions because I'd be wasting my breath like I did with those other clowns."

"I mean . . . I may be wrong for asking this. But you know the cardinal rule is to always keep the baby of a rich man. That is your stock."

Vernice smiled knowingly. "True, and I never did. Maybe because deep down I wanted to be a wife before a mother, wanted to have a real family. No amount of money ever changed that. And believe me, I tried!"

A part of Loletta was excited for Vernice. She probably had a better chance at happiness now than she did, she thought. But she wanted her friend, as little as she saw of her these days. "I guess it's gonna be just me and my mom from my now on."

"Come on, now. Ms. Landelton is cool. I know you got your differences, but you know she got you. You and your moms are living your lives; I need to live mine too," she said, standing.

"Why don't you just come back inside? You don't even have to see Darva; we can chill in another room."

"Nah, that's cool. I don't wanna be hiding anymore. I'm just gonna take my ass back home next week."

"Next week?"

"I'll call you, girl," Vernice said, as they hugged in the midst of the crowd waiting to get in the club.

Loletta walked back in and up the long steps to the lounge and caught Kavon dancing—with her mother. Loletta tapped Ms. Landelton's shoulder. "When did you get here?"

"Honey, I just got here. I told you I'd try and make it!" Ms. Landelton danced wildly as she blew into Calvin's gold-plated horn, a birthday favor.

Loletta looked on as her mother did some old school dance with Kavon, who mimicked her updated version of the twist.

"Are you gonna just stand there and let another woman dance with your man? You better get in here," Ms. Landelton said, moving to the side and barely letting Loletta in between Kavon and her. Loletta slowly began to move her hips and feet, but it felt more like she was stepping on her mother's toes.

As Loletta fixed herself a salad on Sunday morning, the blade of the knife kept scuffing her fingers. She couldn't slice the tomatoes with a steady hand because the phone had been ringing nonstop all morning. Each time she picked it up, the person would hang up, or she'd hear what sounded like a woman whispering. The last time she picked up, the woman angrily called her a bitch. Loletta had been used to that happening when she dated other women's men, but she never called any wife's home. It occurred to her that the caller could be Kia, and that aggravated her even more. It was like Kia was building up to something and just wouldn't let go, she thought. But she wasn't going to give her the satisfaction of stooping to her level.

She had hoped one of those calls would have been Vernice. She had called her several times, but was automatically transferred to voicemail. But she understood. She thought perhaps Vernice just wanted to leave before she could be talked out of it, which was exactly what Loletta had planned to do.

Loletta dropped the knife and sauntered out to the living room to answer her ringing doorbell. It was Darva holding a basket of cookies.

"Hi there. I just wanted to bring you some gourmet cookies I had shipped directly from this precious little bakery in Paris. Right on the Champs-Elysées. "Can I come in?" she grinned, wearing a matching blue and white knit sweater and white capris with four-inch stilettos.

Loletta wrinkled her nose. She wasn't really feeling how Darva just popped up, but the cookies did smell wonderful. "I guess," Loletta said, opening her door wide.

Darva pranced in and handed Loletta the basket. "Where's Kavon?"

"He's at his agent's office," Loletta said, inhaling the chocolate aroma emanating from the basket.

"Great. So we're alone." Darva parked herself on the green leather love seat.

Loletta laid the cookies on the coffee table. "Do we need to be alone?"

Darva opened the basket and took out a cookie. She bit into one, letting the crumbs fall on her.

"Can I get you something to drink?" Loletta asked.

Darva ignored her. "I saw you at the party, and you looked fierce in that dress, but stressed."

"I'm good." Loletta took a seat on the white leather couch opposite Darva. "What's up?"

"You tell me. I didn't get to talk to you the other night, but how is everything with Lady Anise, Kavon, and that whole fiasco?"

"Darva, let's stop pretending we're friends. I asked you for some advice that day, and you gave it to me. I think we are pretty even," Loletta said plainly.

Darva ran her tongue across her teeth, dislodging any stuck pieces of cookie. "I honestly don't have lots of friends. And you live so close to me that I just thought it would be nice to at least build some rapport. Sometimes I too need someone to vent to."

Loletta felt uncomfortable. But they were both in the same boat, she thought. Two husbands, up to God knows what. Darva didn't know about her miscarriage, and she wanted to keep it that way. And yet Vernice was gone, and Loletta sure didn't mind the chance to bond with someone, especially a woman who has been there, done that. "Lady Anise told me I couldn't see her anymore," Loletta blurted out.

"Oh, please," Darva said, openly chewing her cookie. "She gets in her mood sometimes. Give her a few months. She told me that twice. And I found that the time on my own really helped me sort things out. I don't need her as much as I thought. I don't feel as desperate."

Loletta moved her head up and down. "Anyway, I think I heard what I needed to know."

"Which is?"

"That woman my husband was seeing is history. She doesn't even work for the Association anymore. I just hope it stays that way."

"Did she move?"

"Well, I bumped into her last week, meaning she's still around. But I'm not worried. Lady Anise said her moving would take some time."

"It sure does," Darva said, grabbing another cookie.

Then it clicked. "You made Vernice move," Loletta said, piercing Darva with a nasty look.

"*I* didn't do anything," Darva said, holding her hands to her chest. "I simply told Lady Anise that I wanted her to disappear. And I guess Lady Anise took it literally. She even said it would be good for Vernice too. I probably did her a favor."

Loletta wanted to get angry, but she was amused. *This shit really works,* she thought. She remembered that Vernice's sudden decision to go back to Orlando seemed to have come out of thin air.

"I'm not a bad person, Loletta, but I love Calvin and I will do anything to keep him. Don't you feel that way about Kavon? It's not like the world is crawling with tall, handsome black men signing twenty-million-dollar contracts for their next job."

"Things are better. Since I saw Lady Anise, he's been more attentive and loving. This is the way it should have been from the gate."

"So who was this girl he was seeing?"

"A girl named Kia who worked for the Association. She tried to come in here like she was my friend, but I peeped her card, a little too late."

"Kia Jameson! She's a fucking predator," Darva huffed.

"You know her?"

"Know her? Do you remember that little 'accident' Calvin had a few years ago when he was cut in the knee and couldn't play?"

"Yeah."

"I stabbed his ass when I found him in bed with her at the Carlyle. I ended up in jail. It was in the papers and everything."

Loletta remembered the story; she just never knew it was Darva and Calvin who were involved. "Oh, shit, so what happened?"

"So I eventually got a restraining order on her. When Kavon came to New York, I guess she found new prey."

"She is also calling my house nonstop today for some reason. And I got the most grotesque package in the mail a few weeks ago with bloody dolls. If I can get proof it's her, I'll have her ass locked up—after I beat it down. Did she ever do those things to you?"

"No. She must really like Kavon."

"She must be *really* crazy. I ain't letting that bitch scare me."

"I'm telling you, Loletta, she sounds like she's gotten crazier. She's not a pretty girl, and those are the smartest. They know men far more than the beautiful ones do." Darva picked up her purse and another cookie on her way out.

"I have to trust Kavon. He's been good to my family. He *is* my family now. And if something does go down, I know we'll get through it."

"You are really trying hard, aren't you!" Darva laughed. "It's okay. You'll be like me soon, and you won't give a fuck anymore."

That was not a pretty picture, Loletta thought, because then she'd just be a shell. Everything would mean nothing.

Twenty

Kia met Kavon downtown at Cipriani's for lunch. Kavon wore big black sunglasses to keep out the August sun and prying eyes but Kia had on a fire-engine red cotton dress. She wanted everyone to see her with Big Jackson. She even dropped a call to her contact at Page Six, who was writing up a mention for tomorrow's paper. She had wanted Kavon from the day she'd set eyes on him when he landed in New York, and bagging him was part of her New Year's resolution.

"Why did you tell her you were going to see your agent?" Kia asked, cutting up a slice of prosciutto.

"Because she'd want to come. She knows she doesn't come with me when I meet my agent." Kavon picked some food from his teeth with a toothpick. He lounged back in his chair like he hadn't a care in the world. "And don't forget today is your shopaversary."

"Of course," Kia said, always up for a shopping spree with Kavon. He'd take her shopping whenever she wanted, and sometimes he'd buy her things Loletta would wear. It had been like this since they started sleeping together before his marriage.

"I called her today and hung up."

"Why?" Kavon said, smiling.

"Because I wanted to make sure you were coming alone. I need to have you all to myself, Kavon. That night we had sex at your house, I loved it. I thought we was gonna be like one big family."

Kavon laughed. "You serious?"

"I am," Kia said, tears welling up in her eyes. "I wanted to be her friend!"

Some people nearby looked over their shoulders. "Calm down," Kavon said, surprised by her outburst. "That was my fault. I shouldn't have let it happen."

"What you mean? If I could have been her friend, I could have moved in and moved that bitch out."

"Perhaps," he said, grinning and swirling his Bellini in the glass. "But I had to stop seeing you for a while after that because she caught on. I didn't think she would have been down for that threesome shit. If my wife could do that, I figured why I need you for."

"You need me because I love you more than she ever will. I have proof," Kia said.

"Look, Kia," Kavon said, sparking a smile that shined like diamond ice. "I know you sent that bloody package to my house. I told you that's the type of shit that gets people put in jail. She was gonna call the damn cops."

"I love you, Kavon." Kia wiped her eyes. "Your wife is playing you. I wouldn't do that to you; I swear I wouldn't."

"Do what?" Kavon asked, roughly chewing his toothpick.

"I saw that bitch with Carter at the Carlyle. She was coming out of his room, half dressed, half drunk."

"Loletta?" Kavon leaned forward.

"And Carter."

"Man, I don't give a shit about Carter. I'll never hate a playa on his game, but Loletta. Damn," he said, biting down tightly on his jaw. "This lunch is over."

"Kavon, wait. We can do this, baby. Just get that bitch out of our house," she said, holding on to his shirtsleeve.

Kavon jumped into his white Range Rover and hit the gas.

Loletta prepared a Cobb salad and brought it over to her mother's house. Ms. Landelton was in a downward-facing dog pose when Loletta walked in.

"Hey, Mommy, I brought you some salad. I know your cook is off today," she said, placing the bowl on the dining room table.

Ms. Landelton slowly came out of her position, dabbed her face with a towel, and walked over to the table where Loletta sat. Ms. Landelton was breathing very hard and couldn't catch her breath.

"Mommy," Loletta said, holding her mother by the chin. There were large red marks on the brown skin of her face.

Ms. Landelton fanned herself. "Water, honey. Water," she muttered, sweat drizzling down her face.

Loletta passed her the bottled water on the table. She didn't remember yoga being a cardiovascular workout. Her mother never looked like this after doing yoga. "Mommy, are you sick? What's wrong?"

Ms. Landelton rubbed her arms. "I just feel achy all over, and I have this shooting pain in my arm. As soon as I stood up, I felt awful."

Loletta touched her mother's forehead. "I'm taking you to

the hospital. You can fry an egg on that forehead." Loletta rushed around for the phone and dialed an ambulance. She immediately gave them the address.

Ms. Landelton struggled to stand, and then fell right on her face.

"Mommy!" Loletta screamed. She got on her knees and put her mother's face on her lap. There was a pulse, and her mother was breathing, but her eyes were dilating. "Please, Mommy, just wait. The ambulance is coming. Drink this," she said, giving her more water, but it just trickled down the side of her mouth. Ms. Landelton was grower weaker by the minute.

Loletta heard the sirens from afar and helped her mother stand up. As soon as the paramedics came in the front door, they took over. They lay Ms. Landelton on a stretcher, secured an oxygen mask over her face, and placed her in the back of the ambulance. Loletta rode beside her mother, praying to God that he have mercy on the both of them.

About ten minutes later they pulled up to the hospital, where the paramedics rushed Ms. Landelton into the emergency room. Loletta ran up to the window. "I'm Loletta Jackson, my mother passed out on me, and—"

"Oh, ma'am, don't you worry; we got it taken care of. Your mother will be just fine."

"You know who she is?"

"Yes, she's Kavon Jackson's mother-in-law. We got the call from the paramedics. You can go right in with her."

"Thank you," Loletta said. There was no paperwork or anything. There was no waiting, no long line to stand in. Kavon was one of the major contributors to the hospital's children's unit. As Loletta looked over and saw elderly men and women waiting and sick babies crying, she realized that being the wife of not only a rich man, but a famous one as well, had its privileges.

After Loletta left a message for Kavon on his cell about what was happening, she waited patiently in her posh hospital suite for word on her mother's condition. Then she saw a young, handsome white doctor approach her.

"Ms. Jackson?"

"Yes?"

"Your mother had a heart attack, and we need to operate."

Loletta put her hand on her own heart, feeling it give out too. She didn't want anyone cutting her mother open. "Is there anything else you can do?"

"It's not a difficult procedure. It's basic. We need to get in there and unclog her arteries. It should take less than an hour. You are welcome to sit in."

Loletta shook her head to consent. She followed the doctor to the operating room. The procedure was done flawlessly and in the time promised. She couldn't get her eyes off her mother on that bed, looking every bit her age. She was frail and gaunt. What was I thinking, letting her live alone, she thought, even if it was what her mother wanted. She needed Kavon with her. She needed someone to hold her hand because right now she felt the loneliest she ever had.

Loletta returned home just before midnight. The doctor had said that Ms. Landelton would be kept for a couple of nights until her condition stabilized. Loletta wanted nothing more than to fall asleep in Kavon's arms. *He must be worried too,* she thought.

When Loletta walked in, the house was pitch dark. She thought perhaps Kavon was upstairs, already asleep. She was disappointed that he hadn't come to the hospital. But then she thought, maybe the meeting with his agent didn't go so well.

She flicked on the lights in the bedroom and found him sitting on the blue Victorian chair near the door, fully dressed, smoking a cigar. "How's your mom?"

"Thank God the operation went smoothly. She'll be in the hospital for several days." Loletta breathed a sigh of relief and kicked off her black Manolo pumps. "Why didn't you come? Everything okay with the agent?"

Kavon puffed out circular clouds of smoke that covered his face. Loletta didn't get what was up with him, but she thought he was acting awfully odd. Whatever it was, she hoped it could wait until the morning. She began to undress and threw on a short silk nightie.

"Everything isn't all right. Found out some things that I ain't too happy about."

"I'm sure he'll work it out for you, babe." Loletta yawned. "Come to bed, and you can work it out on me for now."

"Man, man, man," he said puffing out the smoke. "Is that how you call all them other niggas to bed, or does Carter like doing it on the floor?"

Loletta glared at him. He looked smug and satisfied in his navy blue Sean John suit and white sneakers. "Carter is in my past."

"Why didn't you tell me you met that nigga at the Carlyle the other week? That day you said you had some shit to do with Vernice," Kavon shouted, flicking his lit cigar left and right as he spoke.

"Who the hell you been talking to? Because they got the shit all wrong." Loletta pulled the covers over her, and Kavon snatched them off and flung them to the ground.

"Get up!"

Loletta was terrified; his eyes were red, and he had a cold, distant look in them. "Kavon, I swear I didn't mean for anything to happen. He called me—"

"Get out the bed!"

Loletta slid out of the bed and stood before him. "I'm sorry; let me explain what happened."

"I know everything that happened," he said, with his nose flaring. "Kia said she saw you with that nigga, coming out his room half dressed, all drunk and shit. Man, Loletta how you gonna play me like that!"

Loletta felt like she was gonna go off too. "Play *you*? The hell you doing with Kia, huh? You told me you and that bitch was over. You got back with her!"

"I had lunch. We had a civilized lunch of two people. She wanted to help me, and she did. Since you let that coke-snorting Carter all up in you, we even. Now you can get the fuck out!"

"I ain't leaving, and if anybody should get out it's you! You have the nerve to come up in my face telling me about cheating, when you meet your bitch and have lunch like best friends. And I know you still fucking her. How can you? She's the one who sent that package; she's the one we were arguing over when I fell!"

"Fuck that," he said, and slid a belt off the back of the door. "You let some other man in my pussy, sucking on another man, bitch, you know I will *kill* you." Kavon headed toward her, lifted the belt in the air, and came down on her. But he missed by an inch. Loletta ran out of the room. Her mind raced; she couldn't believe what was happening as he chased her down the long spiral steps. She ran into the kitchen and grabbed the largest knife she could find.

"Now what?" she said, her hands trembling as she held the knife. Tears flowed down her cheek. "I swear, Kavon, you better not put another hand on me."

"So what you gonna do? Get a divorce because you a failure as a wife?" he said with a cynical smile, moving closer. "Your mama is in the hospital, and I'm paying all those damn bills. Medical bills you would never be able to afford. I put food in your mouth, clothe your back, and stroke that pussy so good your ass be asleep till noon the next day. What you gonna do, take your sick mama and go back to your little studio in Harlem?"

"If you take another step closer, I will stab your ass and leave your dick on the kitchen floor."

"Bitch, please," Kavon said to her face. "Give me that damn knife!"

Loletta wrestled with him and kicked him firmly between his legs. He dragged her down with him to the ground. He slapped her so hard across the face that the knife fell out of her hand. She crawled to get it, and he snapped her neck back. But she turned her entire body around and stabbed the knife into the back of his right knee.

Kavon yelled at the top of his lungs, holding the back of his knee as blood spilled out between his fingers.

"Oh, my God! Oh, my God!" Loletta cried, as she too was covered in blood that didn't seem to stop flowing. She darted around the kitchen, finding anything to stop the blood. Kavon lay on his back with his knee slightly bent. She couldn't believe what he had made her do. She couldn't get her thoughts together. She called an ambulance.

In the meantime, she found a rag and tied it around his knee. "Kavon, you made me do this shit."

Kavon's face was covered in sweat as his chest heaved up and down from his pain. Loletta kept muttering prayerful words to herself as she tried to hold her sanity together. All she could think about was his leg.

"I can't play," Kavon mumbled to himself. "Oh shit, my leg, my leg," he kept saying, as he lay looking up at the ceiling.

The ambulance arrived with the police. Three men had to lift Kavon up and put him in a wheelchair; he couldn't walk.

"Ma'am, we need to ask you some questions. This is a domestic violence situation."

"I was defending myself." Loletta looked to Kavon to explain to the cops, but the paramedics wheeled him out.

"Ma'am, we have a right to take you into custody under New Jersey law. You're under arrest. You have the right to remain silent—"

"No, wait!" Loletta begged, her nightgown still covered in blood.

The officers put a blanket around her, secured the cold metal handcuffs around her wrists, and led her out the door. She was held in jail without bond on charges of battery with a deadly weapon.

Twenty-one

It took almost a week to get Loletta out of jail. Kavon had arranged for a lawyer to handle all the details. A bond was posted, and Loletta was released pending further investigation, but with Kavon's lawyer's connections everything was dropped. Loletta walked out of jail feeling exonerated but lifeless. She thought the best thing that had come out of her days in jail was that she and Kavon had time apart. She learned that he had received over fifty stitches, and his knee was severely injured; she had stabbed it to the bone, damaging major tendons, ligaments, and an artery. Kavon would be on the sidelines for the first half of the upcoming season. Kavon didn't visit her or call her, but relayed messages through his lawyer. He was sorry, and he wanted her home.

Ms. Landelton was released from the hospital while Loletta was still locked up. When Kavon returned from his hospital stay, he told Ms. Landelton that Loletta had "accidentally" stabbed him in the leg and was "mistakenly" put in jail.

Ms. Landelton was home on bed rest when Loletta finally visited her.

"How are you feeling?" Loletta asked her mother, who already was looking back to normal with her long fake eyelashes and her makeup in all the right places.

"I was okay until I got home and saw Kavon's leg." Ms. Landelton sat on the couch with her knees pulled into her chest. She wore a comfortable, black cashmere robe and slippers.

"I know; I don't even want to talk about it. I'm sure he told you his side." Loletta hadn't seen Kavon yet. She was dreading it because they had not spoken in nearly a week. Even the pink Juicy Couture sweatsuit she wore out of jail and the car she took to her mother's had been sent over by the lawyer.

"Frankly, I'm disappointed in both of you, carrying on like two ghetto ingrates. You nearly destroyed his career, Loletta. What were you trying to do?"

"I was trying to stop him from beating my ass. You don't know Kavon like I do. He has a wild, crazy streak with a temper that explodes. I hate him when he's like that."

"But what provoked all this madness?"

Loletta explained to her mother about Kia, and what Kavon had found out about Carter. The story didn't make either of them look good.

"I think you should go home to your husband and figure out a way to make this work. You have to."

"But I was hoping I could stay here for a few nights with you until I—"

"No, no, no," Ms. Landelton said, moving her hands around. "You will not put me in the middle of this. Kavon has been nothing but a good son-in-law to me."

"I'm your daughter, and I'm not ready to go back and play wifey right now." Loletta was shocked that her mother was shutting her out like this.

"Loletta, it wouldn't be right for me to harbor you like a

refugee. Be a woman, and stand with your husband in this. He obviously wants to work this out. You should have seen how pitiful he looked explaining the situation to me."

"I can only imagine."

When Loletta got home, she found Kavon sitting in his armchair in their home theater absorbed by *The Matrix,* which played on the large plasma screen. His crutches were against the wall. She opened the door enough to see him with his legs wrapped in bandages, and then closed it back.

She walked up to their bedroom; the bed was neatly made, with an open, airy scent of pine. Adrienna was around, and that made her feel safe. Dropping herself on the bed, Loletta turned over on her stomach and began to bawl. She thought she didn't have any tears left with all the crying she had done in jail. But she had some more she needed to get out. As soon as her tears subsided, she dozed off; she needed to catch up on the sleep she'd missed over the last few days. Despite what had happened, she was happy to be in her own bed.

About an hour later, Kavon walked in the room.

"Loletta," he said softly, as if he didn't want to wake her.

She opened her eyes and saw a blurry vision of him sitting beside their bay window.

"We need to talk, not yell this time." He picked up his crutch and sat at the foot of the bed and stroked her ankle up to her calves.

It hurt Loletta's eyes to connect with his. She looked at the wall.

"The doctors said I'm out for half of the next season. My whole leg is fucked up, and I have to have therapy for months."

"That's not my fault," Loletta said. "I wasn't the one who started this."

"Listen, I'm just telling you because I need you more than I ever have. It's painful for me to walk around here and do things for myself. I need you to support me, even if I never play again."

She looked him in his eyes. "Never?"

"It's possible. It's not just my knee; my entire leg is affected," he said, his eyes red and swollen.

Loletta had never meant to destroy his career. All she was trying to do was stop him that night. He just wouldn't listen to her, but she refused to apologize for anything. "I'll do what I can," she said dryly. She wanted to suggest a nurse, but the last thing she needed was another woman around doing something better than she could. Maybe, she thought, it was her turn to have the upper hand for a change. She also made a promise to never ask him about Kia again. There was a silent agreement in NBA wifehood. "Don't ask; don't tell."

"I just want to say how sorry I am. I was never gonna hurt you that night or lay a hand on you—"

"Kavon, you wrestled me for that knife like you was about to terrorize my ass with it."

His rubbed his chin, which was now covered in a goatee. It made him look even more handsome with his bald head. He didn't answer directly, but said. "We had a fight like most people, and sometimes things get out of hand. Sometimes I do too."

"My point exactly," Loletta said, feeling his hand creep further up her thigh. "But there is one thing I *can* do."

Loletta smacked his hand off and pulled the covers over her. "And that's not something I *want* to do."

Twenty minutes later, she felt a tap on her shoulder. Kavon

was lying beside her. "The doctor said I need to change my wrap three times a day," he whispered in her ear.

Loletta rubbed her sleepy eyes and dragged her feet out of bed. "I don't really know how to do it."

He sat up on the bed and said, "I'll show you," as he unwrapped the bandage.

What was revealed under there nearly made her throw up. Kavon's black skin was purple, with black blotches all over his knee and leg. A large shiny portion stuck out at the back of his knee, which indicated where he got stitches. Kavon explained how the leg became infected and why it was important to change the bandage often. Loletta rubbed his leg with salve and massaged the muscles. While she wrapped his leg with a fresh bandage, Kavon dozed off to sleep.

Later that evening, Ms. Landelton came by for dinner. They all ate in the small intimate dining room, the same one in which Kavon and Loletta had their first date. Kavon had Kenneth Miles, the executive chef from Ida Mae's, one of his favorite Manhattan restaurants, come by to prepare his favorite dish of sweet potato ravioli and spinach salad. Loletta was annoyed that he had planned such an elaborate dinner with her mother on her first night back. She wasn't in any mood to be playing nice. Then, she thought, maybe the dinner was all part of Kavon's plan to get off easy.

After Kenneth explained the dishes, its flavors, and the food and wine pairings, he left. Loletta had hoped he'd stay around to serve. But one way or another, that fell on Loletta's shoulders. She didn't really mind—in fact, she took pleasure in serving her mother and Kavon. But when Kavon had her running around the table for every little bit of salt, pepper, or hot sauce he needed, she drew the line.

"How about you keep everything you need on your side of the table?" Loletta snapped, as she pushed her fork into a tender ravioli. Her mother's face boiled up, but Loletta didn't flinch.

"Sorry, I just wanted some more salt," he said. "I would get it myself, but it was all the way in the kitchen. I hate to be a burden."

Loletta picked up sarcasm in his tone. "Fine," Loletta said, rolling her eyes.

"Mmmm, this ravioli is lovely. Ms. Landelton said. How's yours Kavon?"

"Excellent. I wanted this night to be special. You know, with everything we all went through this week. You look really good for someone who just had major surgery." He took Ms. Landelton's hand and kissed it.

Loletta shook her head.

"Is something wrong?" Kavon asked Loletta.

"Oh, no," Loletta said, forging a smile. "I was just wondering how to make this. The sweet potato filling is so sweet and delicate."

Everyone nodded. Then Kavon began to sigh. "Baby, I need to use the bathroom. I've been holding it in," he laughed, giving Ms. Landelton a sympathetic sigh.

"Ooh," Ms. Landelton cooed, as she gently patted Kavon's hand. "Loletta?"

Loletta took a deep breath, gave Kavon his crutches, and helped him out of his chair. "Thank you, baby," he said, fixing his thick, soft lips on her cheek. Loletta helped him to the bathroom and returned to the table.

"He can really do that on his own, you know," Loletta said, pulling her chair back out. By then her ravioli was cold.

"Dear, he is just being a man. Men need proper feeding and caring. Didn't you read that book?"

Loletta pushed the ravioli around on her plate. "I may have left that one off my list," Loletta said, cutting her eyes away from her mother.

"Honey, just be patient. A wife is a mother, a nurse—"

"Mom, would you cut out the bullshit! If you are so versed in the proper caring and feeding of men, and patience, and wifehood, why weren't you there for Daddy when he became disabled?"

Ms. Landelton turned her attention back to her plate, gingerly picking at her onion salad. "If I had a mother like myself to show me the ropes, maybe we would still be together. I'm trying to help you."

Loletta calmed herself down; she didn't want to get her mother upset, considering what she had just been through. She thought her mother wasn't helping her, but was just helping herself to all of her fixings. "I don't want help; I want your love. And you know this marriage is a sham, and sometimes I feel I'm still in it because of you!"

Ms. Landelton sliced into Loletta's words with a frosty glare. "It's because of me that you're living better than ninety percent of black women in this country. And I have every right to preserve that. I took care of you most of your life, and now you have to take care of *me*."

"And you never let me forget it," Loletta was saying, when Kavon reappeared. She got up and helped him back to the table.

"Did I miss anything?" he asked.

Neither Loletta nor her mother answered.

"Excuse me . . . um . . . could you pour me some more

wine?" he asked, handing Loletta his glass. The wine was right in front of him.

"Is your arm broken too?" Loletta poured him a glass—and two for herself.

Twenty-two

It was Labor Day weekend. Loletta and Kavon traveled to Martha's Vineyard alone. He had told her to invite her mother, but Loletta didn't ask her. She knew her mother would have cheerfully accompanied them.

Three weeks had passed since that first dinner at home, and Loletta was no longer as resistant to playing nurse. She actually liked it because it made her feel secure. Kavon hadn't gone anywhere and was home day in and day out. Due to the spaciousness of their house, they weren't on top of each other either. Their sex life had also returned to fairly normal. She also noticed that Kavon took great pleasure in being served. He seemed to appreciate the things she did, even when he was acting like an outright baby. One night, he woke her up at three a.m. because he had a stomachache and wanted her to rub his belly until he fell asleep. Ironically, they had never been closer.

On Martha's Vineyard they sat in the Jacuzzi in their rented home's steam room as Kavon playfully massaged her feet with the soapy water. Then he reached behind him and handed her a blue box.

Loletta opened it and found a nineteen-inch platinum chain with a diamond-encrusted scorpion pendant that matched his.

"It's twenty-four-carat diamonds. I had it specially made by Jade the Jeweler," he said, with a gleaming smile. "Read the back."

Loletta read both of their names and the date they married. She quickly slipped the chain around her neck. "This is gorgeous. Platinum goes with everything I own," she said, bringing the iced-out pendant to her lips.

As they cuddled in the Jacuzzi, Loletta realized that Kavon hardly ever talked about his being out of commission next season. He seemed to flourish during this rehabilitation time. "Are you still upset about not being able to play?"

Kavon kneaded Loletta's toes between his fingers. "I don't think it'll hit me until the season starts. When everybody goes to training camp, and here I am," he said.

Loletta's eyes examined Kavon's chest, with his platinum chain situated between the scattered tight, wet coils of hair down the center. She slid down to him, wrapping her legs around his waist. "Whatever you gotta do, you have to play this season," Loletta said, massaging his broad chest.

"I'm just following doctor's orders. Trust me, the last thing I want to do is not play. I miss the fans, the rush, the wins, the losses. That's my life."

Loletta traced his eyes with the tip of her forefinger, smearing the moisture from his lids. He closed them and she set her lips on his mouth, tasting the mist of the steam that permeated the room. She pressed and worked her hips against his and squeezed the water from between them. She humped him, not needing him inside her, but getting pleasure from his stiffness on her budding softness.

"I love you." He spoke into her ear as he massaged her ass. He sucked her earlobes between his lips and licked her nipples.

The water began to move as Loletta moved, feeding him one breast, then the next. She grinded her hips into him more, feeling an insatiable pressure build inside her. Kavon found her opening and slid inside her, causing the water to splash around as they pumped their weight into each other. Loletta pinned Kavon's arms against the Jacuzzi, her breasts bouncing uncontrollably as she struggled to orgasm. She felt a warmth discharge in her, and Kavon exhaled loudly.

When night fell, Loletta lay next to Kavon in bed watching the evening news. They had made love repeatedly all day. She didn't want to leave. If Martha's Vineyard could breathe life back into their relationship, she wanted to stay—or at least come back soon. She thought about asking Kavon to buy a house here. That idea excited her. She wasn't even worried about the cost like she usually would be. If she wanted it, she could have it.

"Baby," she said, as she rested her head on his shoulder. "Can we get a summer home here? I mean, right here where we're staying. I love this place. It's right by the Inkwell, restaurants, art shops."

Kavon shook his head at the tragedy being reported on the news. "I'll give you Tommy Mangini's number when we get back. Have him start looking for us." He didn't even bat an eye.

Loletta grinned to herself. Tommy Mangini was Kavon's realtor. She had never met him, but she knew that he only dealt with the rich and richer. While Kavon watched the news, Loletta walked outside to the porch. There she stood just listening to the quiet and watching a few passersby holding hands. She rubbed her stomach, smiled, and looked up at the stars. They glimmered like crystals, one shining a bit brighter than the other. The balmy night was complimented by a sea breeze that whistled through the trees. The houses surrounding theirs were beautiful works of art humming with hundreds of years of history.

She also thought the vineyard was a perfect place to raise children. She wanted to have children again. She fantasized about coming here during the summer with Kavon and their children.

A light, screeching sound distracted her. She looked to her right and left but saw nothing. It sounded like the rocking of an old chair. Then a light went on in the house across from her. Loletta squinted to get a better look. She saw a woman rocking back and forth on a chair. The woman waved.

It was Kia. Dressed in a lacy black nightgown, she sat knitting on the porch.

"Oh, shit." The words escaped Loletta's lips faster than she could think them. "That crazy bitch."

Loletta ran back inside. "Kia's here," she said, her hands stuck on her hips.

Kavon shrugged, while he ate from a bag of Doritos. "I can't tell people where they can travel to."

"Motherfucka, why she wanna come here out of all places? Did you tell her?" Loletta pulled the shades down.

"What are you doing?" Kavon said, giving her a crazy look. "I could care less what she do with her time. I ain't tell her *nothing*."

"We are leaving here right now!" Loletta said, putting on her shoes and looking for her jeans.

Kavon continued eating and ignored her.

"Why are you sitting there?"

"I can't move unless you help me get up," he said, his eyes following her around the room.

Then someone knocked at the door.

Loletta didn't even wait for a second knock. She grabbed a hairbrush, and then flung the door open. Kia was standing there with a basket and wearing a thigh-high sheer black nightie that squeezed her breasts out like melons.

"Are you insane?" Loletta said, hiding her hairbrush behind her back. If Kia took another step, she was going to give her a good whack across the face with the prickly bristles.

"Is Kavon here?"

"Bitch, he *is*. He is my *husband*, or did you forget we were married?"

Kia giggled like a five-year-old. "I just thought maybe it was Carter or somebody else."

Loletta turned around at Kavon, who turned away. "What do you want from us?" Loletta asked, glancing at the decorative basket.

"I just came up for the weekend since this is a popular weekend for us black folk. And when I heard Kavon was here. I wanted to drop off this care package for his leg."

Loletta rolled her eyes. "*I'm* his care package." Loletta slammed the door.

"Don't look at me like that," Kavon hissed as he went back to his bag of Doritos.

Then Kia knocked again. But Loletta ignored it.

"Kavon!" Kia called from outside. "Kavon!"

"I'm about to beat that bitch ass." Loletta took off her diamond earrings and chain. Kavon grabbed his crutch by the bed, hopped to the door, and opened it. "Get the fuck away from the door," he said to Loletta. Then he spoke softly to Kia. Loletta thought that perhaps her half-naked stance had an effect on him.

Loletta slowly put her earrings in their case. She wanted Kavon to scream at Kia, but he took the basket and closed the door gently. "Done," he said.

"It ain't done yet, Kavon," Loletta said.

Then she took the basket that held ointments, herbal teas, and a worn black lace thong and dumped them in the garbage.

At four a.m. Loletta was awakened by a ringing phone. The only person who had their number was her mother. She picked it up on the first ring.

"Yes?" she said quietly, not wanting to disturb Kavon, who was asleep.

"Honey, I hate to bother you—"

Loletta blew down on the phone. She knew it was bad news. "We're sleeping, Mommy. Can this wait?"

"No, I . . . I'm . . . well—oh, goodness."

Her mother rarely minced her words. Loletta was concerned. "What's wrong?"

"I feel sick and weak. I called the doctor earlier, and he said to take the medication, and I have. But I still feel the same way," she said, her voice wary like she was on the verge of tears.

"As soon as we get back Tuesday night, I'll stop by—"

"But that is two nights away. Honey, I'm all alone, and it's making me feel worse," she coughed. "I really feel that the doctor overprescribed."

"Just get a good night's sleep, and I'll call you in the morning."

"Loletta, you know if this wasn't important I wouldn't call.

The last thing I want to do is ruin your R & R with your husband."

Loletta wasn't convinced. She peered over her shoulder at Kavon's naked body and white leg cast. He was sound asleep. She hated to tell him they'd have to leave early.

Ms. Landelton belted out another rough, dry cough. "I don't think I can sleep a wink like this. I have a fever, and it feels like hell."

Loletta didn't want to take a chance, because her mother had just been in the hospital. She thought maybe she should have brought her with them. "Okay, I will be there by tomorrow night. Call me if you need me before then."

"I knew you wouldn't let me down. I just have to get through this right now."

Loletta closed her eyes, wanting to get through her own night. It was already wrought with drama.

Three hours later Loletta and Kavon were eating a breakfast of vegetable frittata, bacon, and toast, prepared by the house's personal chef. It was early enough to still hear the birds singing.

"I'm sorry about last night," Kavon said. "I don't know about you, but I'm not letting it mess up our vacation."

"It almost did." Loletta's eyes were directed out the window at the house where Kia stayed. "Who owns that house?"

Lines formed across Kavon's forehead. "How am I supposed to know?"

He's being defensive, Loletta said to herself. A definite clue but not a giveaway. "I just don't know how she could choose *that* one, right next door to ours. How did she even know where we are?"

Kavon sprinkled some hot sauce on his frittata. "What did

you used to do to find out where one of your favorite athletes was going on vacation?"

Loletta gave him an icy grill. "They *told* me."

Kavon hissed. "Please, those females got their own way. Besides, Kia used to work at the Knicks' office. She got her connects to find out what she needs to know."

"Then you just should have said that instead of asking me." She didn't want to take the conversation any further because she had no proof. "We need to leave today," she said.

Kavon threw his napkin on the table. "Because of Kia?"

"No," Loletta said, sipping an orange mimosa. "Mommy called, and she's sick. She wants me to come down."

Kavon broke a piece off the edge of his frittata with his fork. "I'll arrange for the helicopter to pick you up."

"Just me?"

"Hey, I'm not cutting my vacation short to rush back to therapy. This is my time to kick back before things get hectic again."

"We had planned to stay only two more nights. I don't want to go, but you should have heard how she sounded. I really think we should both go back, especially with that crazy bitch across the street."

"I ain't leaving."

"How are you gonna get around? You can barely walk in that cast."

"I don't need to walk. I'm gonna be chillin'. When I leave, I'll be in a car. I'm good."

Loletta saw he was annoyed that she was leaving. She just wanted to hear him say it, and she would stay. But she thought it was unfair to demand that he go back with her. After they finished their breakfast, Kavon made a couple of business calls, while Loletta ventured out.

She knocked on Kia's door, but there was no answer. Loletta

walked around the back, through rows of begonias, and found a long, deluxe-style swimming pool and a barbecue pit, but no sign of life. She tiptoed up to a window and looked through the slits in the blinds, but the house was dark. "Hello?" Loletta called out, as she walked back to the front. This time she banged on the door.

A petite, white-haired, dark-skinned woman in a purple cotton sundress was on her porch in the house next door. "Who are you looking for, dear?" She tended to a tray of purple petunias.

"A girl who was here." Loletta knew that wasn't much, but she didn't want to get into too much detail with a stranger.

"A black girl with short hair and sleepy-looking eyes, kinda cute?"

"Um, yeah."

"She left a little while ago with a bag. Got in a cab."

Loletta stuck out her chest, thinking that she put the scare in Kia last night, Kia probably couldn't stand it anymore.

"Thank you." Loletta nodded politely at the elderly lady. "Gorgeous flowers." Then she glided back to her side of the street to pack.

Twenty-three

Kia Latavia Jameson was a born manipulator. She never did care for other women's feelings or what they said about her. The difference between women like Loletta and women like Kia was that Kia had no limits. She would do whatever, whenever, to whoever. This time it just happened to be Big Jackson and his twenty-million-dollar contract. It amazed her how easily controllable he was. As a husband, he may have been running things at home, but he was not running her. She didn't care about being labeled a bitch, a whore, or a home wrecker. She'd rather be classified than put away unlabeled and forgotten. She wasn't in it for the money, but she was in it to win. She collected players like players collected trophies. When they got dusty and outdated, she'd clear the shelf for a new one. She wasn't capable of loving anybody but herself. And loving herself wasn't something she was good at either.

Kia sat in the blood-filled tub, a small razor in her hand. She pricked helplessly on her wrists and forearms. It didn't hurt. She had been doing it for years. She was an expert at it, too. She didn't cut through any veins; she cut vertically, not horizontally, and kept the cuts in the same square-inch area. In case anyone asked, the cuts would look like a simple burn.

The sight of blood brought on a feeling of excitement. It was almost like being in a trance. She liked her own blood. When it flowed out of her skin, it made her feel pure and clean.

She had seen Loletta looking for her earlier. She heard her footsteps as she walked around the house. She even heard her talking to old Ms. Semple. Kia had watched from the top floor. When a black SUV picked up Loletta, Kia walked out and thanked Ms. Semple for looking out for her. She had known that Loletta would be bold enough to come over. With that in mind, she paid Ms. Semple a couple of twenties to cover for her. That way she could stay in peace and be as close to Kavon as his next breath. It was in fact his house that she was staying in anyway.

But he hadn't called her yet. It was ten p.m. From the bathroom window, she could see the TV on in his house. This was how it was done. She called him mostly; he rarely phoned her. His role was to be responsive; that was how she controlled the situation. Men did it with women all the time.

Kavon reminded her of most of the players she knew. Wives were like a new pair of shoes. They would eventually wear and tear through the stress of being married to a high-profile man who women clawed each other over. Kavon was always open to a better offer—teamwise and familywise. She had some feelings for him, but her trysts were never about the men. They were about the women. And for the life of her, she couldn't see how Loletta got as far as she did. After all, Kia was the one who had the Ivy background, the bomb-ass sex, the killer head game, and the right words.

She hated Loletta more than she loved Kavon. She hated that a woman like Loletta could grow and change, that she could be given so much for doing so little. Kia hadn't changed. Her mother disowned her when she got pregnant by her father at sixteen. She later put the severely disfigured baby up for adoption. She had no friends because she had taken on the effortless task of bedding their men. She was arrested for assault and battery on an NFL player and his wife. She was hospitalized after another player's wife broke a champagne bottle on her face, requiring major eye surgery and many stitches. She almost went blind. But instead of deterring her, she wanted more.

Abortions were routine for Kia. When she saw a baby leave from a "cut" in her body, as she described it, she turned to cutting herself. She wanted other things to leave too. Like thoughts, memories. It was her brains that got her scholarship after scholarship. No one expected her to be like she was, and that gave her access.

Kia wrapped herself in a yellow towel as she focused on her reddish, sore arms. She dabbed a cotton ball with peroxide and tended to the cuts like a mother would. Once she cleaned them, she massaged on an antibiotic ointment that made them heal fast. Tonight she planned to see Kavon, and she had the perfect thing to cover her wounds. She looked through her bag and found her satin arm mittens. They were like long black gloves minus the hand. They went up to her elbows, hiding all her imperfections, and were smooth enough not to irritate. She had sex with Kavon several times while wearing them, and he just though she was being freaky.

She tied her red, silk robe around her and slipped on a set of high-heel, furry leopard-print slippers. The block was quiet; the only sounds were a few owls and a passing car every now and then. She snuck across the street in a catlike movement, careful not to dig her heels too deep into the dirt. She climbed the steep steps to Kavon's door and knocked.

After a minute or so, he opened the door to let her in.

Kia disrobed at the door. "I was hoping we could get started out here."

Kavon looked behind him like he was asking for permission and then joined her on the darkened porch. A screen protected it from bugs. However, anyone passing by could see in if they looked hard enough.

"What took you so long?" he asked.

Kia lowered her ass on his lap. He had on a pair of blue and white stretch boxers that hugged his muscular thighs just right. "I was taking a long hot bath, getting myself all ready. Who knew we would have it this easy?"

"I couldn't have planned it better myself," he said, stroking the back of her neck and shoulders. He planted a kiss on both of her nipples. "I wish she hadn't seen you though."

"I don't want to talk about her right now. I wanna make love," Kia said, putting her legs over his lap, facing him. "Do you love me?"

Kavon chuckled. "I do," he said, losing his face between her breasts.

Kia kept her eyes on him. His lips were getting acquainted with her shoulders, neck, breasts, and earlobes. "I think it's time we do this. Time that we be together."

"I'm doing what I can, but Loletta is all on top of me," he said.

"Why don't you just tell her your knee ain't that bad?"

"If I told her that, she would have gotten in my ass about you after I told her I knew about Carter. It was my way of getting a little sympathy for fucking up."

"Look, Kavon. You either end shit with her, or I'll end it for you. I'm your damn wife right now. She ain't here."

Kavon held her chin and kissed her deeply. She inhaled his

breath as he breathed through his nose. She didn't just want all of him; she wanted to be a part of him.

"I don't know how much longer I can wait," she said in between breaths. "I want us to get our own house."

Kavon held her shoulders and looked at her. "If we were getting married, then maybe. Or if you got pregnant, I would definitely look out for you."

"You know I can be a good woman to you. We can open a business, like a restaurant."

"Yeah, I could see that," he said, knowing he had told Loletta that was out of the question. He was a different man for every woman.

Kia bubbled up inside and uttered, "I'm pregnant."

"You are?" Kavon asked, a small hint of happiness in his voice.

"No, but I want to be." She laughed, getting on her knees and cradling his dick in her hands. "Until then, I'll just keep swallowing."

Kia and Kavon romped for at least two hours, up, down, and all around the porch. She fucked him with fervor, like she was trying to make a baby. But he wore a condom, which he insisted on. After he came, he dozed off to sleep on the mat, the last place they did it. While he slept, Kia slid the semen-filled condom off him and went into the bathroom. Using a suction tube she urgently sucked the semen out of the condom, hiked one leg up on the sink, and inserted the white fluid inside her.

When Loletta finally got to her mother's house a little before midnight, she found Ms. Landelton with her feet perched up on the couch, watching *Dr. Phil* and eating Cheetos.

"Sweetie, great you made it," Ms. Landelton said, pointing

to the plasma TV screen. "I had no idea he comes on so late over here. Do you know that he is doing a show where his ex-girlfriend comes on?"

"Aren't you supposed to be sick?" Loletta asked. She put her hand over her mother's forehead. "With a fever 'as high as hell'?" Ms. Landelton's forehead felt normal.

"I'm feeling better. I did what you said, and I tried to sleep."

"You could've called and told me," Loletta said, tucking her dampened hair tresses behind her ears. She was sweating even though she was wearing a short, summer dress. "I could've saved the trip down here. I'm calling Kavon." Loletta unzipped the small pocket in her Louis Vuitton weekender bag and pulled out the phone.

"Honey, you're here now. Actually, I was just kind of lonely," Ms. Landelton said, sucking cheese powder from her thumb.

Loletta was about to tell Kavon that either she was coming back or, at the very least, she arrived safely. But after the phone rang for the tenth time, she hung up. She tried his cell next. When that call went to his voicemail, things became all too clear. The question became, Was she going to do anything about it?

Loletta spent the night at her mother's house. When she woke up in the morning, her eyes were red and puffy. She hadn't slept a wink. It was eight a.m. and her mother was buried under her covers in the room next door. Loletta washed her face and did her morning ritual just like she was home. After freshening up, she heated some water on the stove for tea. She stared at her cell phone, waiting.

Then it rang.

"Loletta, it's Darva!"

Not now, she thought. She wanted it to be Kavon. "Hi," Loletta said curtly.

"Listen, if it's not too much, I want us to get together for breakfast at the Four Seasons. There's someone I want you to meet."

"Darva, I am in no mood to meet and greet anyone. I am tired and have a lot going on right now."

"That is why you need to meet this person. Please be at the Four Seasons at ten a.m.—"

"But—"

Then the phone clicked off. Loletta held it in her hands wondering what could be so urgent and who they knew in common. Vernice came to mind. That didn't make sense, but it would be good to have her friend to vent to, she thought. She hadn't heard from Vernice since she moved, and she prayed that everything was okay. She gathered that she'd hear from her once she settled down back home.

"Why the long face?" Ms. Landelton asked, as she shuffled into the kitchen wearing white and green bunny slippers.

"Just thinking. I wish I hadn't left Kavon like that. I should've made him come," Loletta said, blowing on her hot mint tea.

"I know *I* would have," Ms. Landelton said, sticking a croissant in the microwave.

"Thanks for letting me know that," Loletta said, squeezing a lemon into her tea.

The tea burned Loletta's mouth. She couldn't believe how ungrateful her mother was at times. *Everything is always about her,* she thought.

Ms. Landelton spread strawberry preserves on her croissant and poured some of the hot water into a mug. "I mean, come on. Not many women would leave a man like that for their mother. I have a wonderful daughter."

"You just want me to know that you wouldn't do that. Somehow that doesn't make me feel better." Loletta spilled some of the tea on her lap. All she wore was a long Knicks tee-shirt, and her thighs were bare. "Damn," she said, drying herself up. She didn't know why, but she felt way off-kilter this morning.

"Honey, you are just way too intense. Can't take a joke." Ms. Landelton hopped up on the kitchen counter. For her age, her yoga had given her the bone density of a twenty-year-old.

"Whatever," Loletta droned.

"I think you could have avoided all this if you had just called me. Maybe if you had checked in with me before you left, then I could have told you to hold off," she said, rocking her feet back and forth.

"I came here because you sounded like you were gonna pass out if I didn't come. Let's just drop this."

"Have you heard from Kavon?"

"No, I haven't. He's probably upset because I dumped everything to come here only to be made a fool of."

"You did it to yourself. I swear, if I was working with everything you had, I would be so happy. I would feel like the luckiest girl. But you're so grumpy."

"And you're so fucking selfish!"

"Excuse me?" Ms. Landelton said, sliding off the counter. "How dare you!"

"You know what, Mommy? I think you purposely say and do stuff just to fuck with me."

"Loletta, you have never spoken to me like that before," Ms. Landelton said, holding her chest.

"And you've always spoken to me like I'm below you or like I just can't do anything right. For you to tell me that you wouldn't have come is a real blow. Especially at this time, when Kavon and I are having issues. Which, according to you, is my fault too."

"I want an apology," Ms. Landelton demanded.

"For what? For speaking my mind like you would do? I never stand up to you. It's always you getting me to do something that you can benefit from. You really could care less how unhappy I am with Kavon, but I'm with him because I made a commitment to him, something you have no clue of."

Ms. Landelton leaned against the counter, her croissant half eaten and her tea getting cold. "Let me tell you something. I've worked hard for everything. I paid my dues. Nothing in this life is free. If you want certain things you have to give up other things. You have to decide what you want to give up. I am under no circumstances going to support you leaving Kavon. I too have things vested in this relationship. My health and my lifestyle are not things I'm going to compromise because you can't control your husband."

"I've given up everything to be what you want me to be, and to be Kavon's wife. So I have a Maybach, unlimited credit cards, VIP access to anyplace. But I can't sleep at night. I don't have peace of mind. I want peace in my marriage, and that I am not willing to compromise on."

"You act like all those things you have are burdens. I taught you how to get those things. You were the best dressed girl in high school and the most envied. You had the most sought-after R & B stars picking you up from school and giving you money just to keep them company."

"Oh yeah, Mommy, that is something I am ever grateful for," Loletta said, rolling her eyes at the ceiling. "Maybe if you didn't blow your divorce settlement money and every penny Daddy sent us, I wouldn't have had to do all that."

"Admit it, honey; it's addictive. You chose this to be your life. You are well over eighteen, my dear," Ms. Landelton said, as Loletta rose from her seat.

Loletta dumped her tea into the sink. "If it's addictive, maybe it's time for rehab."

Twenty-four

Loletta waited for Darva at a table reserved especially for them. The moment she thought about calling Kavon one last time, she saw Darva and a white-skinned woman approach her table. Loletta put away her cell phone.

"Good morning, Loletta!" Darva said, throwing her arms around her. Loletta shifted her feet to keep from falling. "You look so good in that white Chanel suit. You go!"

"Thanks, Darva," Loletta said, eyeing her friend.

"This is the woman I wanted you to meet. This is Clara Barnes, Kavon's ex-wife."

Loletta's mouth flew open, but no words came out.

Clara took Loletta's hand and gave it a firm, friendly shake. "I'm Clara. Nice to meet you."

Loletta feebly responded. "Same here," she said, but she felt like a fish out of water. She wanted to choke Darva to death. She was in no mood for an inquisition about Kavon. Immediately, she put up her guard.

The waiter filled everyone's glass with sparkling water. While Darva ordered lunch for the table, Loletta inspected every inch of Clara. She was petite, very attractive, with lush brown hair. She reminded Loletta of Ashley Judd.

"I'm Hispanic," Clara said, chuckling. "Everyone thinks I'm white. So rest assured, Kavon likes women of color. Unlike most of the NBA."

"No, sweetie. It's those NFL players who like white women. I happen to be married to Calvin because basically I trapped his ass." Darva laughed. "And I have a little flavor to savor." Darva snapped her fingers like a black girl.

Loletta couldn't help but laugh. For some reason she was relieved that Clara wasn't white. She liked that she knew some things about her husband's history, and she remembered Kavon liking his girls dark and sweet.

"I hate those NFL bitches. They think they are so much better than everybody," Darva said, as she buttered a warm roll.

"Everyone knows the MLB wives are the most paid," Clara added. "Baseball players are the highest paid athletes in the business."

"For a game that takes nine hours, they should be," Loletta chimed in. "But I could never get into baseball. I like to see my men sweat a little."

"Me too," Clara said.

Then Loletta looked at her. It was so awkward to be with her husband's first wife. What are they supposed to do? Trade notes? "Um, can I ask why we are all here?"

The waiter returned with fresh rolls and an assortment of frittatas, bacon, French toast, fresh fruit, and steamed asparagus. "This was my idea, Loletta," Darva said, touching Loletta's hand. "Clara wanted to meet you to talk about Kavon."

"I'm not here to be nosy, but I thought maybe I could be of

some help," Clara interjected. "Darva told me there're some issues."

Loletta looked at Darva, who was smiling sheepishly, but she wasn't upset, only embarrassed for herself. "There are some things we're working out," Loletta said, taking some asparagus and a few slices of French toast.

"Did Kavon ever tell you why we divorced?"

"He said that you couldn't handle the life or something. I really don't remember." Something in Loletta didn't want to let Clara in, but another part of her told her to listen and learn. "What kind of husband was he?"

"Okay, well . . . ," Clara said, folding her napkin over her lap. She obviously didn't want to go in that direction. "He was almost the perfect husband. We would garden together in the spring. He'd plant his favorite flowers—yellow chrysanthemums, if I remember correctly."

"Chrysanthemums?" Loletta asked. She didn't even think Kavon knew how to say the word.

Clara went on, as Darva stuffed her face with bacon and listened in. "He loves to paint. I think it's dry acrylic paint. That was what he did on his downtime after the season. He also used to write me these poems. I mean, they were a bit corny, but they were cute. We ended up writing them together for each other. He'd write one line; I'd write the other—"

"Oh, hell no," Loletta said, clasping her hands together tightly. "That is *not* Kavon."

"My point exactly."

"Kavon is a good cook, but he can't do any of those things you mentioned," Loletta said.

"Kavon couldn't cook boiled water if he had to."

Darva chuckled as she smeared butter on her asparagus. "Sounds like two different men. Clara, isn't there more?"

"More?" Loletta asked, astonished.

"There was Kia. She has always been around. At first, she would come by and she was quite friendly. Really kept me company sometimes. But eventually I knew something was up when I found her panties in my laundry."

"Ewww," Darva said, cringing in her chair.

"She's been around that long?" Loletta said.

"She had this little vicious dog she used to travel with. One day she and I got into an argument. She was coming over way too much. We ended up fighting in front of my house, and her dog attacked me. Mauled me all over my chest," she said, pulling down her blue V-neck blouse. Loletta noticed the dark stitch marks. "And with one word from Kia, the dog stopped. She just sat there until she was satisfied with what that mutt had done to me."

"What did Kavon do?"

Clara guzzled her entire glass of water in one gulp. "He basically told me I shouldn't have been outside. He blamed *me*. I don't know what those two got for each other. I filed for divorce the next week. It took me four years. I'm out, but Kia is still in."

Loletta hissed and said, "The girl is completely dick-dumb over Kavon." Darva jumped in. "If I may add something. I took a little psychology course in college, and it sounds like it's more than that. They both have severe personality disorders. Kavon may be suffering from deep inadequacy issues, and all that drama Kia creates feeds his troubled self-esteem. Kia gets the same thing from him because he keeps accepting her behavior."

They both looked at Darva, amazed. Loletta thought she made sense, but it was too easy to excuse Kavon's behavior on psychological grounds. "I can deal with a couple of women after my husband, but when it's one woman, that means it's deep," Loletta said. "And what Darva said makes sense."

"What do you mean?" asked Clara.

"Darva made me understand what needs to be done. Kia needs to be shown that her behavior is unacceptable."

"I tried," Clara said.

"I did, too," Loletta said, "but I don't think I've been hard enough. I can't just lie down and let her control my marriage. If it wasn't for Kia, Kavon and I would be just fine."

"Do you really believe that?" Clara asked.

Loletta looked down on her plate. No, she didn't. From what she learned today, it felt like she barely knew him.

"All I am saying is that if you stay, you need to understand that Kia will always be an invisible third party. Can you deal with that?"

Loletta didn't answer.

"I'm not telling you to do anything, but I've never been happier since I left Kavon. I'm seeing a wonderful man now, and we have plans to get married."

"Who?" Loletta asked.

"He's nobody you know. He's rich, but he's a selfmade man. He's a real estate mogul, and we just bought a home together in the Bahamas. I could never go back to a broke man. I love this lifestyle. But if I'm gonna marry rich, I'm gonna marry smart."

Loletta couldn't eat anymore. "Have you ever met Kavon's family?"

"No," Clara said. "He cut them off over something trivial that had to do with money. He claimed they were using him. He didn't even accept their calls. He was sending them money though."

"Yeah, he still does."

"Just understand that it's not anything you did wrong. It's just something very wrong with Kavon, and I don't think any one of us knows what it is."

"Why doesn't he just marry this girl then?"

"Because then it would kill whatever it is that he's getting from the relationship," Clara said. "She'll just become his wife, and he'll get rid of her too. She probably has more permanence in his life as his girlfriend, or whatever she calls herself."

"I heard she even follows the team bus in her car," Darva added. "She would chew Kavon's food for him."

The three women sat around the table for another hour, and Loletta made a promise to keep her meeting with Clara to herself. Loletta left the restaurant with a new weight sitting on her shoulders. It wasn't she who was destroying the marriage, and that made it even harder to fix.

Loletta couldn't get home soon enough. As she parked the car and removed her travel bag from the trunk, she noticed a man in a baby blue jacket and white slacks at her door. He was a tall white man with a receding hairline, and handsome, chiseled facial features.

"Coach Randall?" Loletta said, as she walked up to him. "How are you?"

"Loletta, good to see you," Coach Randall said, adjusting his dark-rimmed glasses. "I was just about to knock on your door. Kavon home?"

"No," Loletta said, turning the key in the door and letting Coach Randall in. "He's away until tomorrow."

Coach Randall followed Loletta inside the house and sat down on the leather sofa. "Oh, well, how is he feeling?"

"Can I get you something to drink?" Loletta asked, as she put down her bags. "Adrienna!"

Adrienna appeared from upstairs. "Yes, Ms. Jackson?"

"Can you bring us some lemonade with ice?"

Adrienna nodded and walked quickly to the kitchen.

"So how's Kavon doing?"

"Oh, I'm sorry," Loletta said, playfully tapping her head. "I just have a lot on my mind. Kavon is still on crutches, but I think he's getting used to not playing for the first half of the season. He was crushed at first."

"He's still on crutches?" Coach Randall asked as if that was a revelation.

"Yeah," Loletta said, as Adrienna served them lemonade. She passed one to Coach Randall. Adrienna put down the pitcher and walked away. "I was wrapping his legs like every other day."

"Loletta, we have Kavon scheduled for the full season. He's our star. We had the best doctors run tests on him, and they assured us he was ready."

Loletta didn't know what position to take. She didn't want to get Kavon in any trouble. It was clear to her that she was the one who was misinformed. "Coach Randall, I'm sure Kavon is ready. You know, sometimes men like a little extra attention, and maybe he was looking for some."

Coach Randall drank some of the lemonade. "Well, as long as he didn't hurt himself again, he's good to go. I was just stopping by to see if he was ready for training camp. We need him this season more than ever. And he's ready."

"Yes, he is," Loletta said with a grin.

"He's a good kid, a real special kind of guy."

"Oh, *very very* special," Loletta said, raising her glass.

Coach Randall finished his drink. "Thanks so much for the lemonade and the chat. I guess I'll see you at the season opener?"

"Of course." Loletta walked Coach Randall to the door and stood there until he drove away.

Loletta fixed herself a drink at the bar under the staircase. She mixed some vodka with a glass of lemonade on the rocks.

She walked up to the bedroom with a bottle of Grey Goose, closed the door, and sat in the quiet stillness. Her first inclination was to call Kavon and curse him out for lying and using her sympathy to his advantage. She didn't mind taking care of her husband; she minded being taken for a fool. She didn't understand why he would lie to her about his season starting. How was he going to keep playing that off? she thought.

She dialed his number. "Kavon."

"What's up, baby?" he said, sounding like he was asleep. It was two p.m.

"I called you several times since I got back."

"I know; I just been asleep. You know, resting my leg and all that," he said in a drowsy voice.

"Resting your leg, huh?"

"Yup. How's your mom?"

"Good."

"Anything else going on?"

She wanted to tell him about Coach Randall, but passed. "No, I'll see you tomorrow," she said.

Then she hung up and disconnected the phone.

Twenty-five

A week after Kavon returned from Martha's Vineyard, he and Loletta, along with Ms. Landelton, decided to spend a weekend at his Los Angeles home. He carried his crutches like he couldn't live without them, and Loletta let him, knowing that her time would come. It was Loletta's first time visiting the house with Kavon, because it was usually rented by one of his celebrity friends. He admitted that the LA house wasn't his favorite because of all the media and all the activity going on around him. Loletta hadn't confronted Kavon yet about his knee or what she had learned from Clara, because timing was everything. She wanted to be smart and not react as he would expect. If the best way to catch bees is with honey, Loletta was coated with it that weekend.

Loletta, Kavon, and Ms. Landelton had lunch at the Ivy, a celebrity power dining spot on North Robertson Boulevard. It was Loletta's first time dining there, and she didn't see how a restaurant that looked like a worn-down cottage could be the place where the likes of Jennifer Lopez and other Hollywood stars wanted to be seen.

They sat on the coveted patio where the flashing cameras of the paparazzi were nonstop. To her right were the Hilton sisters with friends, as well as a young celebrity couple who had recently graced the cover of *People*. Loletta felt starstruck, but played it like she was around those folks all the time. A few women approached their table for Kavon's autograph, which he politely signed. She signed a few, too.

"You know, I really think we should spend more time in LA. I love this!" Ms. Landelton said, as she enjoyed her crab salad.

"I prefer Miami," Loletta said, smiling brightly at Kavon, who agreed.

"Me too; something about being so close to the Caribbean. It's like the French Riviera but closer." Kavon caught the stack of napkins that almost flew off the table in the fall breeze.

"I can't wait to hit Rodeo Drive." Ms. Landelton looked at Loletta. "Can you?"

"I was up all night wondering whether it should be Rodeo or Sunset," Loletta said in a mocking way. "I already did my shopping this afternoon. I am actually tired of trying on clothes."

"You are the only woman I know who gets tired of shopping. It gives me a rush. After three hours at Bergdorf Goodman, I feel like I can do a triathlon."

Kavon and Loletta laughed. Ms. Landelton was telling no lie. It was her fix, and Loletta wasn't about to get on her about that.

"You know, walking around this morning I saw so many restaurants owned by celebrities. It's like everyone has a spot down here," Loletta said, nursing an Ivy gimlet.

"I think Dennis Mckay's father opened a rib shack somewhere in Hollywood. It supposedly served high-class meat that he imported from Japan," Kavon said, totally disinterested. "Too bad it barely lasted six months."

"I guess these people have money to throw away. Instead of giving it away to charity, they go ahead and blow it," Ms. Landelton said, her lips tightened in distaste.

"I would love to open a restaurant," Loletta said excitedly. "What do you think, Kavon?" Right off the bat, her mother would have something negative to say, she thought.

"You don't know *jack* about restaurants, never mind how to open a business," he said, poking fun at the thought.

"Keyshawn's wife most likely didn't know jack about opening a restaurant, but she did. And it survived . . . I think," Loletta said, looking down at the street below her. "We can do it together. It would be so hot with all your famous NBA friends, and—"

"That's not the point. You heard what you mother said, and I don't want my money blown away on some fancy idea. You can find other things to do." Kavon looked at Ms. Landelton, who was of the same opinion.

"Like what?" Loletta asked. "Join some NBA wife committee where they bitch and moan all day under the guise of charity and doing what's right for the children? I want to be out and about. I am tired of just sitting around. You have your basketball, and I want my restaurant. I can hire a business consultant to help us."

Kavon shook his head and rubbed between his eyes.

"Loletta, come on; can we at least eat in peace? The man doesn't want a damn restaurant. There are some very nice, prestigious charitable organizations we can join together," Ms. Landelton said, moving her chair more to the right so she'd be in a paparazzi photo of the Hiltons.

"Whatever," Loletta said, pouring a ton of ketchup on her fries. "I want something of my own, even if I have to use my own money."

Kavon laughed. "Please, what money?"

Ms. Landelton gritted her teeth at Loletta, signaling her to shut up.

Loletta didn't know what money she was referring to either. She barely had five thousand dollars of her own in savings. And a restaurant would take at least six figures. "Kavon, what are you gonna do when basketball is over? We need to build something together. Every other couple is doing it."

"I got a Nike endorsement, Gatorade, and Coca-Cola. I could live off those alone if I stopped playing tomorrow. I don't want to do nothing else but cheese for the camera and be a beast on the court."

Ms. Landelton beamed with pride.

"Spoken like a true negro," Loletta said, smiling but serious.

"Listen, baby," Kavon said, putting down his turkey club sandwich. "I know things get a little routine when your husband is making millions. But I work hard, and I need you there for me. Not in some restaurant killing yourself just to get bashed by critics. I don't want to see you disappointed."

Loletta rescinded her push for a restaurant. She didn't really want to open one alone, but with Kavon, thinking that it would give them something to work toward together. But he didn't get it; maybe he never would.

While Kavon took Ms. Landelton on a shopping tour of Rodeo Drive, Loletta drove back to the house. Her cell beeped with a text message from Carter.

Loletta smiled at the simple message: "Call me." It gave her an idea.

"Hi, Carter; it's Loletta," she said, speeding down the LA highway in Kavon's shiny silver Bentley.

"Where are you?" he asked. "I hear lots of wind."

She rolled up her windows. "I was driving with the windows down. And before you go any further, we can't have sex anymore. I want to work on my marriage or what's left of it," Loletta said.

"How you know that's what I want?" he said with a cute chuckle.

"When I left you the last time, I bumped into Kia, and she threatened to tell Kavon and she did."

"Kia Jameson? Come now, everyone know she's a looney tune. Nobody fuck with her no more."

Loletta stayed silent.

"Oh, well, Kavon is. That's one—"

"—crazy bitch, I know," Loletta said, sucking her teeth. "But look, I may need you to help me out."

"I don't want to get involved in all that."

"No, silly. Money. I think I want to open a restaurant."

"Yo, that is a hot-ass idea. I was thinking of doing the same thing. Derek Marbury and Lebron Lewis was gonna get down with me on it. If you serious, we can ask them to be investors. I'll talk to them."

"Really?" Loletta said, cutting off the car in front of her as she caught her exit.

"We can blow that shit up. I know mad people in the rap industry. They'd even put it in some of their rhymes. We can have mad heads rolling through there."

Loletta wished Kavon had reacted this way. "Okay, well let me know what they say because I can make some serious bank with that."

"What about Kavon?"

"He's not into it, but every NBA wife needs a business. What's the point of marrying these niggas then?" She laughed, feeling like her old self.

"You wrong, you wrong." He laughed with her. "But so true, baby."

Loletta ended her call with Carter. Her heart fluttered a bit thinking about him. What if she were single? she thought. Would they even have a chance? But then she remembered his notorious womanizing reputation, including the paternity suits. She thanked God for the things she had, and the things she didn't. She didn't know what she would do if Kavon ever had a child with another woman.

In the morning, after her jog along the beach in front of Kavon's house, Loletta stopped at the nearby Jamba Juice for a smoothie. While she waited on line, she saw a petite woman with her hair in a ponytail; she thought about Kia. But the woman was light-skinned. When she turned away from the cash register to leave, Loletta was in disbelief.

"Vernice!" Loletta jumped.

Vernice turned around with a straw stuck to her lips. "Girrrrl!" She put her arms around Loletta as the two giggled like kids. "What you doing here?"

"I should be asking you," Loletta said, as they caught a seat by the window.

Vernice sighed and dipped her straw in and out of her smoothie. "I went to Orlando and stayed only a week. I was bored out of my mind. So I took the last few hundred dollars I had and came out to LA. I got here last week."

"Why didn't you call me? I was thinking about you."

"I didn't want to call until I had something to talk about. I barely even have a place to stay right now."

"Where are you?"

"I am living with like three other girls in this house in Long Beach."

"If you need money, just tell me how much," Loletta said.

"I got a job as a bartender at this hot spot, and I already met me somebody with money."

"Who?" Loletta was more than curious because she thought Vernice was through dating the rich and paid.

"This actor named Matthew Sealy. He was in an HBO movie with Halle Berry recently. He got the prettiest eyes," Vernice said, blinking hers playfully. "We only went out a couple of times, but he's nice."

"You told me you were through with rich men," Loletta said, hitting Vernice's arm.

Vernice covered her laugh. "I meant athletes. Here in LA is where the actors are. So I got me one," she said.

"Wow, well, just be careful. Play the game. Don't let them play you," Loletta advised. "And I can see you keeping yourself up."

Vernice patted her stomach and flipped her brand new ponytail weave, which landed at the middle of her back. "Yeah, I had to lose like twelve pounds. I am working on five more. These bitches out here ain't no joke. I gotta keep up."

"I hear ya," Loletta said, feeling jealous that Vernice had a chance to make her life over. It sounded exciting to her.

"You okay?" she asked. "How's Kavon?"

"Girl, we are like up and down. That girl Kia is around still, and I just don't trust Kavon anymore. Something about that whole thing rubs me the wrong way."

"Divorce him."

"Vernice, I haven't done anything else with my life. Marrying rich was probably the best thing I've ever done. I would feel like a failure if I divorced him. There are wives who have dealt with more and still hold it together. I think in time we can work it out. Our marriage is still pretty new and all."

Vernice said, "Call me if you ever need me. I should have my own place soon."

"Cool," Loletta said, then paused for a moment. "I stabbed him, Vernice."

"*What*? You are officially a desperate NBA wife. And he still stayed with you after that? He must love your ass."

"He better," Loletta said.

Vernice intertwined her fingers with Loletta's. "I do respect you for hanging in there. Don't think I've ever undermined that. I don't know what it means to be married, so I can't speak on it. I know you are doing the best you can. I'm sure Kavon will see that soon enough."

"Oh, he will," Loletta said.

When Loletta got back to the house, her mother was sitting on the beach in an Indian pose, doing a meditation. Loletta waited by the kitchen window until she saw it was clear to sit with her. She wanted to tell her about Vernice.

Loletta pulled a blue pashmina shawl over her against the wind that blew up from the water. She joined her mother on the blue mat that she was sitting on. "Hey, Mommy," she said, hoping she wasn't interrupting her.

Her mother opened her eyes. "Oh, there you are. I thought you would have been back from your jog before now."

Loletta slipped on her shades in the blaring light of the sun. "I bumped into Vernice at the smoothie shop. She's living out here now."

Ms. Landelton dug her feet in the sand. "Why?"

"She didn't want to stay in Orlando. She looks good and happy."

"What is she doing with herself?"

"She's bartending," Loletta said, taking off her sandals. "And she's dating an actor. That guy Matthew Sealy."

Ms. Landelton frowned and said, "What a disappointment. Those actors' careers barely last a year or two. She should know better."

"She's sworn off athletes. And LA is the land for actors and models."

"Well, I'm just glad she is okay. I kind of miss her," Ms. Landelton said, rubbing some suntan lotion on her bare arms and shoulders. Then she squirted some into Loletta's hands.

Loletta spread the lotion on her skin. "I miss her too. I know I'll see her again."

"Did you tell her to save us a ticket to the Golden Globes?" Ms. Landelton laughed, as she kicked her feet around in the sand.

"Where's Kavon?" Loletta asked, looking around. She hadn't seen him when she got in.

"He said he was going to see one of his friends."

"But his car is here."

"Somebody picked him up." Ms. Landelton folded her legs, closed her eyes, and opened up her palms.

Loletta wasn't going to let her mother get away with suddenly acting like she was meditating. "Did you see who it was? Was it a woman?"

"I don't know," Ms. Landelton said, aggravated. "I couldn't tell one way or another." Her mother stood up and pulled off her top and bottom sweats to reveal a simple black tankini. "I am going for a swim."

"I can't believe you won't even tell me. As nosy as you are, I know you were all up in that."

"I'm nosy, but I'm minding my business on this one," Ms. Landelton said, and ran off into the cool ocean water.

At the end of the weekend, the family was back in New Jersey. Kavon had blindfolded Ms. Landelton and Loletta. They both knew they were in for a surprise. Loletta wanted it to be Kia's head on a platter, but Ms. Landelton was expecting much more. As soon as they got out of the car, Loletta and her mother spotted their spanking new rides tied in red ribbon. Ms. Landelton dug her sleek black Porsche. But what Loletta received made the big fuss she made about Kavon seem like child's play. It was a one-of-a-kind, powder blue Lamborghini with "MRSBIG" on the plates.

Twenty-six

"Loletta!"

Loletta turned down the sound on the plasma TV. She was checking out the latest Denzel movie in their home theater. She walked out to the hallway and shouted from the bottom of the steps. "What, Kavon?" She was tired of him and his little act.

"Bring me some of the cheese corn in that blue tin can," he yelled back.

Loletta huffed and muttered several words to herself as she walked angrily to the kitchen. She poured Kavon a bowl of cheese-flavored popcorn, shoveling a few in her mouth. She took long strides up the stairs, skipping a stair or two, and barged right into the bedroom. She held the bowl in her hands at the door.

"Mmm, I can smell that all the way up the steps." Kavon gave a big-toothed grin. "Oh, snap!"

"What now?" she said, as she walked over to the bed where he lay in his boxers.

"Could you bring me some soda?"

That was it. Loletta pulled down his boxers and dumped the load of cheese corn inside. "Maybe you'd like some nuts with that too?" she asked, smiling wickedly.

"Is you on your damn period or something? Now I got cheese powder all over my dick!" he said, standing and shaking out the popcorn that stuck to his hairs.

"Oh, now standing up ain't so fucking hard!" Loletta said, sticking her finger in his face. "Why don't you go get your own damn soda?" Loletta pushed him toward the door, but he held on to the frame.

He spun around, naked, with little yellow specks all over his middle. He grabbed her by the throat. "Are you out of your damn mind?

Loletta bit his wrist hard enough to make him whip his hand away.

"*When* do you plan on playing?"

"Shit," Kavon said, as he sucked on his wrist. "Did Coach Randall call?"

"He came by and said you were perfectly fine and that you were on the schedule for the full season. You lied about being sick, like a little bitch."

Kavon strolled toward her with a swagger and nudged her in the shoulder, pushing her back on the bed. "So what?"

"You had me looking like a fool for two months, running after you, helping you piss, and all that. Don't think I don't know that you did all this to avoid the real issue—and that's that bitch."

Kavon pushed her again, his eyes glazing over like he was in a mood she wasn't.

"Kavon, get the hell off me," she said, finally backed up on the bed.

"I still fucked you every night, didn't I?"

Kavon stood before her with an erection straight enough to sit a glass on. He took her hand and brought it to his dick. Loletta took her hands away, but not her eyes. She wanted anything that would make her feel better. Kavon got on his knees and blessed her cleavage and neck with kisses. "I'm sorry, Loletta. I just wanted some attention. I just wanted to be closer," he mumbled, as he kissed her all around. He pulled down the straps to her thin, white Lycra top. She was wearing no bra.

Loletta turned her head from side to side. She put her hands up against his chest to push him away, but his solid weight didn't move an inch. "I don't want to do this, Kavon; please, not now."

He climbed on top of her in the bed and rubbed his hardness against her pussy. "Just a little bit," he said.

"Get off me!" Loletta said, pushing him off her with her feet. She jumped off the bed, and grabbed her pocketbook and keys.

He sat on the bed, holding his wrist. "And you got the nerve to ask me why I got another woman on the side? Do what you good at. Get me a Band-Aid."

Loletta went into the bathroom, grabbed the Band-Aids, and threw the metal can at him. She didn't know where it landed, but before he could get far, she dashed out of the house and into her car.

By the time the first game of the season rolled around, Loletta and Kavon were sleeping in separate rooms. It was her idea, and each night he would climb into her bed and hold her. She didn't know what to do to satisfy him. He seemed more loving when they were arguing. She didn't want to live a life that was so volatile, but she wasn't ready to walk away either. No woman just walked away, because before the door closed another woman would be taking her place. She didn't know whether she was staying because it was right or because she didn't want to see another woman get it right. It was just how it was. "Mo' money mo' problems" wasn't just a song anymore.

Mid-October saw the first game of the season at the Garden. Loletta and Ms. Landelton sat in the first few rows and watched Kavon and the Pistons. He ran and jumped without a glitch. There weren't any more crutches or bandages. He was like new, and the more she saw him jump for an alley-oop, the more irritated she became.

"Go, Kavon!" barked Ms. Landelton, as he scored another two points, giving his team the first lead for the night.

Loletta clapped. As much as it bothered her, she admitted to herself that her husband did look good out there. She felt proud to be his wife. If he could put that much determination and strength in his marriage, everything would fix itself, she thought. As the game progressed, Loletta realized there was a woman in the back row to her left who was constantly shouting Kavon's name.

"Mommy, that girl is really driving me nuts," Loletta said, covering her ears. She situated the popcorn between her thighs.

"That is just a fan. You should be honored." Ms. Landelton clapped her long, red manicured hands. "Oh, dear, did you just see that awful pick Clay Rogers did on Kavon?"

"Huh?" Loletta said. She wasn't looking at the game, but at the black woman with the blond wig and black sweater hat.

"Loletta, your husband is out there. You shouldn't let some stranger outroot you. Root for your husband!" Ms. Landelton grabbed Loletta's hands and fake-pumped her fists in the air.

Again, the young woman squealed when Kavon made a slam dunk, giving the Knicks a ten-point lead. She called Kavon's name out repeatedly. It was Kia.

There were seven seconds left on the buzzer, and it seemed like the entire stadium was on its feet. She cheered on loudly with her mother and thousands of others. She couldn't hold back the excitement. Then she saw that Kavon was on his back, not moving.

Team doctors and coaches ran to his side. Loletta dropped her popcorn as she and Ms. Landelton headed to the court. Kia was there and did the same. It was mass confusion as Kavon lay on his back, semi-conscious after the elbow of another player hit his head. Loletta pushed her way through, catching sight of him as the doctors hovered over him, taking his pressure, checking his eyes, his heart rate.

Loletta knelt by his side and started shaking his face around. "Kavon, honey, wake up," she said, her body shivering with fear. She rubbed his forehead as his eyes rolled around in his head. TV cameras swarmed around her, and reporters' mikes hung over her like tree branches. Ms. Landelton stood by Kavon, while Loletta conferred with the team doctor.

There was a short, red-haired, male reporter standing a few feet away from her. "Mrs. Jackson, what did you see?" he asked, but it wasn't to her. It was to Kia.

"Well, I was in my chair, and when I saw my husband—"

Loletta didn't know what happened next. She stepped over Kavon and plowed her fist into Kia's face. Security stepped in and broke them apart.

"Who is Mr. Jackson's wife?"

"I am!" Loletta said, waving her ring in the officer's face. "Get this woman out of here now!"

"I'm pregnant!" Kia said, holding her bloody nose as Loletta was beseeched by photographers.

Kia yanked her arm away from the officer and ran to Kavon's side; he was already being lifted onto a mat. She groped his face and kissed his hands, and said, "Kavon, don't worry, boo; you'll be better, and soon we can have our baby."

"I want her out, or I'll take her out!" Loletta said to the officer, as reporters followed her every move. They seemed more interested in her than in Kavon, the star of the night. "Do it now, or I'll start a commotion in here you've never seen the likes of."

The officer immediately grabbed Kia and escorted her out of the building. Kia kicked and spat at the officers as the TV camera flashed in her direction. Loletta ignored her, and followed the mat that carried her husband out of the building. She couldn't believe what she was up against.

Loletta slept at the hospital with Kavon, while Ms. Landelton went home. Kavon had suffered a concussion, and the doctors kept him overnight just to make sure he was okay. Loletta let him sleep while she flicked the channels on the TV.

"Good morning, *Ms. Jackson,*" a nurse said, as she rolled in two trays of breakfast and the morning newspaper. The bowlegged, young black nurse handed her the paper first. "Ms. Jackson, I usually don't work this unit, but I had to come see you. I really like how you regulated on that woman's ass last night. It's time for those groupies to stop messing with those married men. Even if they got money and all."

Loletta looked at the nurse like she was crazy. "What?" she asked, as she poured herself some orange juice.

"Check it out for yourself." The nurse pulled out the *New York Post,* and on the back page was Loletta sticking her ring in an officer's face, as he held on to a deranged-looking Kia. *"Call Me Ms. Jackson If Ya Nasty"—NBA Star's Wife, Loletta Jackson, Causes Stadium Brawl.*

Loletta laughed so loud it woke up Kavon. She shoved the

paper in his face. Kavon turned to the story and read for what seemed like hours. Then he slammed it down. "I'm getting fined 500K for your little act last night."

"My act? How about that dumb-ass ho who was talking to reporters about being your wife? I would have killed that bitch if all those cameras weren't there," Loletta said, fuming.

The nurse smirked and crept slowly out of the room. Kavon scratched the white wrap around his head. "What is this shit?"

"It's karma. You lied about being sick; now your behind really got knocked out on your back. You are so lucky that the Knicks won last night," Loletta said, as she passed his tray to him. It finally occurred to her that they were functionally dysfunctional. *There is no way a normal marriage can work like this,* she thought, as they both ate their breakfast.

"So now you a star. The article had only a few lines about my injury," he said, wiping toast crumbs from his mouth.

"Well, maybe because it wasn't that serious."

"I was unconscious!"

"Semi," Loletta said, as she spread butter on their toast. "What you did do was cause the brawl indirectly. I don't ever want to see that woman at any of your games. I'm putting her on the security list."

"You can't do that," Kavon said authoritatively.

Loletta sucked some jam from her fingers with a teasing giggle. "I bet you didn't think I could do this either," she said, throwing the paper in his face.

He caught it and glared angrily at the back page again.

A week before Halloween, while Kavon was playing in Denver, Loletta found herself attending the grand opening of Darva's new handbag boutique, "D. Bags," on Madison Avenue. Darva had sent her an invite weeks ago, and Loletta thought it would be a good idea to see how a business was run. Darva had owned her own business before and had the experience.

Loletta arrived at the tail end of the grand opening. She had run late at her spa appointment.

"Hey, precious!" Darva said, flinging back her blond hair and wrapping Loletta in a tight, friendly hug. "I see you have been making headlines. You've made us wives so proud."

Loletta noticed that there were a few people still around, including Calvin, enjoying the last of the champagne and conversation. "You know, I didn't expect it to make the news. We have been inundated with calls from the media asking more about my relationship with Kavon. *Extra*! said they want to profile us. But Kavon turned them down. I did an interview with *Sports Illustrated*—well, at least a sidebar next to the bigger story on Kavon."

"That is huge. Have any of the women's magazines called?"

"The Knicks office got a call from an editor of *Glamour*, who said they wanted to use me for a photo shoot about NBA wives called 'Behind the Bench,'" she said, keyed up at the thought of posing for a national magazine.

"That is fantastic! When is it?"

"Tomorrow. That's why I couldn't follow Kavon to Denver."

Darva sat her down on one of the cute pink sofas.

"Okay. I think this is the best thing that happened to you since you married Kavon. Really. Think about it. Now you are known not just as a wife, but as a personality. You can write a book, open up a business, and all that. Work it," Darva said, flashing a smile.

Loletta scratched her ear, unsure of this empire Darva was speaking of. "But," she said, "I've been wanting to open up a restaurant and build something up for myself."

Darva whipped out the article from her back pocket. "Then this is the way to do it."

"You have been carrying the article around?" Loletta asked, flattered.

"I showed it to everyone tonight. I'm even going to paste it up on the wall behind the register. You should have been here earlier. A few folks asked if I knew you." she smiled.

"Who was here?"

"Just a couple of big-name rappers, models, and some media folks, like *People* magazine," Darva said, like nothing impressed her anymore.

But Loletta was impressed. "Nice," she said, looking around the boutique with all its pink and red decor and colorful handmade bags. The cheapest bag started at four hundred dollars.

"Hey, Ms. Superstar," Calvin said, as he grabbed Darva from behind. "You almost had my man taken to the mental hospital instead of the regular one," he said to Loletta, looking casual in baggy dark jeans and a black button-down shirt. "Man, it's about time somebody kicked that bitch's ass again."

Darva turned around and locked her lips on his. Loletta was embarrassed sitting there while they kissed, and he had his hands all over Darva's ass.

"Okay well, um, I'm gonna see if there's any cake left." Loletta walked to the other side of the boutique, where a nice, fat chunk of red velvet cake waited with her name on it. She walked by a mirror and stopped when she saw her reflection. *Damn, I look good,* she said to herself. She had to admit it—the attention she had been getting the last couple of weeks really boosted her self-esteem. She posed to the left and to the right in her fitted designer jeans, white Prada boots, and hunter green vintage Chanel, off-the-shoulder blouse. She had gained some weight around her thighs, and her skin glowed, but she attributed that to the spa she had just come from. Her hair was black, shiny, and longer than it had ever been. Kavon may not be good for her soul, but the marriage had been good to her body. She put the velvet cake on a plate and dug in, savoring the moist cake and licked the white frosting off the fork.

"I was just about to take that home," Calvin said in a joking manner, fiddling with his diamond-embellished, platinum Rolex. "Shoot!"

"Please, Calvin, this cake has been here all night. Consider it eaten," she said, lifting the cake up and taking a big chunk out of the side.

Calvin began to laugh. "So you one of them women that eat and don't gain weight?"

"Sometimes," Loletta said, pouring herself a glass of champagne.

"Can I have a little bite?" he asked, but before she could react, he broke off a piece.

"Damn, I think you could have gotten a fork," Loletta said, in a lighthearted way. "I'm gonna see if Darva needs any help cleaning up." She tried to walk around him, but he stopped her.

"Can I have another little bite?"

"Calvin." Loletta laughed nervously. "Get out of my way before your wife makes the papers this time."

Calvin dropped his hands around Loletta's waist. She was up against his chest and could smell his cologne. She didn't want to overreact to keep things under control. She wasn't the slightest bit attracted to him because he was her friend's husband and not so easy on the eyes.

"I like a woman with a little fire in her. Let me eat your pussy right here, right now, with Darva in the next room," he said, bringing his hands around to the zipper in her jeans.

She splashed what was left of her champagne in his face.

"This pussy has Kavon's name and tongue all over it, you nasty fuck," she said. Then she flew out of the room.

"Loletta?" Darva said, as she followed her out of the door.

Loletta didn't want to say anything, but she was so disgusted with Calvin she didn't care. "Your husband just came on to me very hard, in the back room."

Standing at the door of her boutique, Darva pleaded. "That's just Calvin. He's a big flirt."

"Yeah, okay," Loletta said, throwing a napkin over her slice of cake. "I'm out."

"Loletta, you can't let every little thing bother you."

"I'm not gonna stay around and let your husband feel on me," she said, with one foot out the door. "Why do you stay with him?"

"Why do *you* stay?" she said, with a sinister smile. "When was the last time you heard of an NBA athlete divorcing? This isn't Hollywood."

"No, it's worse. It's pure hell," Loletta said, and hopped in her black waiting sedan.

As she got closer to home, her confidence waned. What Darva said proved that if she divorced Kavon, she would be a complete failure.

Twenty-seven

Kia waited for Kavon at the Denver hotel room. She was surprised to hear that Loletta was staying behind. She actually wanted her to come, so she could stir some more drama. Through her own grapevine, she had heard about Loletta's *Glamour* spread. What she had planned had backfired. She had thought her affair with Kavon would at least cause a rift between Kavon and Loletta, but instead it made Loletta almost famous. Kia cut the article into little pieces with scissors, jabbing her fingers at times. She also cut up an article on Page Six about Darva's boutique opening, where there was another mention of Loletta.

Kia grabbed a bottle of Hennessey and drank as much of it as her body could take at once. When her eyes began to tear up, she put it down. She was pregnant, and she despised the feeling, as well as the thought of being a mother. Children always sickened her with their demands and unreasonable behavior. But this time she had no plans of aborting the baby. Kavon didn't know yet, but once he found out, she'd have to take better care of herself. She was convinced that he wanted his baby, because in her world he had asked for it.

She stared up at the ceiling, her body naked, smelling like Kavon's sweat and cologne mixed together. She was barred from appearing at his games, and it burned her up to know that Loletta was responsible for that. Kavon never would have done that, she thought. He was well aware that it would drive her over the edge. She hadn't ever attempted suicide, but it was a thought.

Kavon turned the doorknob at two o'clock in the morning. Kia was up watching television. He mounted the king-size bed and kissed her forehead. "Hold on," he said. He dug out his cell phone. He walked to the adjoining room, where she heard him tell Loletta he was in and everything was fine. She heard him say, "I love you too." Kia unplugged the phone in the bedroom in case Loletta called to double-check. The phone had been ringing all night, but she hadn't picked it up. She figured that in due time everything Loletta had would be hers anyway. And she had the ace in the hole—Kavon's baby.

He walked back in the room somber, his face down as he undressed. "You know we lost today," he said. "Did you watch the game?"

"Um, no, I fell asleep," Kia said. She didn't want to tell him what she had really been doing.

"What's this?" he said, looking at the half-empty bottle of Henny. "You was drinking?"

"I missed you," she said, her nails sliding up and down his muscular, defined back. He smelled fresh from the shower and looked edible in his gray, Italian suit.

Kavon turned around and caught her tongue with his. She slipped his wife-beater and boxers off him and climbed on top of his naked body. Strands of her hair danced in his face. She pushed it back. She kissed his eyes, his nose, and his ears.

"I have to tell you something," she said, pressing her breasts into him. He slipped his fingers inside her butt cheeks, walking them down to the wetness between her thighs. He slid his finger in her mouth.

"Mmm." She giggled, running her tongue over her lips.

"What you gotta say?"

She jiggled his long platinum chain, wrapping it around her fingers. "I'm pregnant," she said, lying down on his chest. She listened to his heartbeat go from normal to amplified.

"You sure it's mine?"

"Yes," she said bluntly.

Kavon embraced her back. "Are you keeping it?"

"Yes," Kia said, with tears welling up in her eyes. "I want this baby so bad. I am so excited to be a mother. I just need you to be by my side."

"Kia, I still got a wife. I have to tell Loletta," he said, rolling over on top of her. "But right now, it's about just you and me."

As he entered her, Kia realized that nothing after this moment was going to be the same, even if he belonged to someone else. They were both ready to pay the price.

The Tuesday after Halloween was Kavon's thirty-first birthday, and Loletta set up a get-together at the house with some folks. She invited some of his teammates and their women, as well as Darva, Calvin, and Ms. Landelton. She didn't really want to invite Calvin, but not doing so would raise questions from Kavon. Adrienna prepared the hors d'oeuvres and table settings, while Loletta made sure there was enough Grey Goose for everybody.

"Adrienna, when you're done, please give me a final bottle count for tonight. I'm just gonna set up some things in the living room," she said, as she rinsed her hands in the sink. She picked up several batches of fresh white orchids and arranged them in vases all over the first floor. She took the gold and white balloons that she had ordered and let them float up to cover the ceiling. Taking her time, she put small, scented votive candles along the steps, and wherever there was a flat surface. She didn't want to hire anyone to do this. She appreciated decorating her home and adding a little bit of her own style. While she lit the final candles, she imagined the same ones on every table in her own restaurant.

Kavon was still showering when she entered the bedroom to place the leftover orchids in the wooden African vase beside the television. She didn't want anything to mess up this day and was keeping tight reins on Kavon. There was no way she was going to let him out of her sight, and he seemed okay with that. Adrienna had served them an intimate breakfast for two on the outside porch to ring in his birthday, but then had to make extra when Ms. Landelton popped up. It pleased Loletta to see that Kavon was actually happy with something she was doing. He looked relieved and satisfied. She hoped he liked his birthday gift just as much. It was the hardest thing, she thought, to buy something for a man who had everything. But with her mother's help, she decided to get all the photographs of his game-playing and assemble them in one huge six-by-eight-foot frame for his game room, which was like a museum dedicated to himself. Darva had suggested a place where they could get the job done professionally, and it came out superb. Loletta's eyes welled up when she saw how much Kavon had accomplished since college. His body was in superior form, as were his skills. With age, he was just getting better.

"Yeah, I like that," he said, nodding at her flower arrangement. "Those look real good over there."

"I know. Who would have known I was good at stuff like this?" Loletta took the towel from him and patted him dry from his head to his feet.

"I wish it was my birthday everyday," he said, locking his arms around her as he sat on the bed.

"It doesn't have to be your birthday for us to get along. We made it to seven months, and I think we can make it to seven years and more," she said, her hands on his shoulders. She let them travel down to his dick. Getting on her knees, she held his weighty meat in her hands, licked down its length, and sucked it deeper in her mouth.

Kavon breathed in and out deeply like he was having palpitations. Loletta's tongue journeyed down to his balls, daintily licking them. Kavon grabbed the back of her head, guiding his dick back into her mouth. She gripped his thighs for balance and sucked his dick until her jaw ached, slobbering and making sounds, just as he liked it. But he was softening up.

She slipped it out of her mouth. "What's wrong?"

"I got something to tell you," he said, signaling her to sit beside him.

Right then, she felt her stomach fall out of her. She had a hunch that it wasn't about his next big contract.

He rubbed his cropped beard, something he had let grow in the last couple of days. She liked his new look and thought it made him look sexier, more mature. He thought it was a nice change to welcome in another year in his life.

"Well?" she said, wiping her mouth. "You ain't never ever got soft on me before."

"I'll just come out with it," he huffed. "Kia is pregnant."

A woozy feeling overcame her as she tried to stand. She sat back down on the bed. "How could you do this?" she said, in a low voice.

"I'm sorry."

She belted a slap across his face. This time he didn't hit her back.

"How could you do this!" she yelled at the top of her lungs. "Loving you is killing me."

She went for the door, but she couldn't leave; she didn't know where to go. "Is she gonna keep it?"

"Yes, but I didn't ask her to. That was *her* choice," he insisted.

Loletta knew he could have an influence on her to abort it, and she wasn't buying it.

"Okay, so what do you plan to do? Play daddy?" She followed Kavon around the room as her eyes reddened with tears. "I want a paternity test."

"It's mine!" he snapped. His words had enough power in them to make Loletta step back.

Kavon adjusted his black slacks and put his head through his charcoal sweater. "I think we have guests coming."

"Fuck them. I ain't going downstairs. I can't do this with you," she said, crying hysterically into her hands.

Then the bell rang.

"I'm going downstairs," he said, sweeping by her with a cold shoulder. "We'll talk about this later."

She grabbed the back of his shirt to stop him. "Kavon."

But he tugged it away and kept moving.

Loletta watched as he ran down the steps and happily greeted their guests like it was all good.

Throughout the evening, Loletta stayed in the background. She was courteous to all, even Calvin. She didn't want to make her guests feel uncomfortable by holding on to her attitude toward

Kavon. All she wanted to do was crawl under her sheets and drown in a bucket of tears until she fell asleep. She didn't know if he was being genuine or desperate, but Kavon was unusually affectionate all evening—rubbing her shoulders, asking for her input in conversations, kissing her, and giving her the first bite of his birthday cake. She was as used to hiding her feelings as she was used to brushing her teeth every morning. Dating athletes and music stars, she'd learned to put up or shut up. But there was always room for change.

Loletta was able to sneak a piece of Kavon's pineapple cream-cheese cake to the darkened home theater. Kavon was one thing, but she didn't want to see Calvin smiling in her face for much longer. Everyone else was outside or in the living room, and Loletta could hear their animated voices and Kavon's booming laughter. She sunk her fork into the cake and sailed away in her own misery. She thanked God for life's little pleasures.

"Loletta, are you in here?"

Loletta quickly swallowed her last bite of cake. She didn't want to give people the idea that she was binge eating, when she really just wanted some privacy.

"I know you're in here," sang Ms. Landelton.

Loletta switch on the lights in the room. "Oh, I was just looking for something," Loletta said, studying the carpeted floor. "I'll be right out."

Ms. Landelton put one hand on her jutting hip. "In the dark? And I see that you have been having your own little party over here," Ms. Landelton said, eyeing the empty plate with globs of cream-cheese frosting.

Loletta picked it up and dumped it in the garbage. She walked to the door to leave.

"Not so fast, honey. What is up with you tonight?" Ms. Landelton asked, closing the door behind her. They turned the lights down low and took a seat.

Loletta stared at the gigantic plasma movie screen looking down at her. "Kavon did something awful."

"Well, I figured out that much. Tonight you just looked lifeless, like a robot. All talk, no feeling." Ms. Landelton adjusted the twisted strap to Loletta's black halter dress.

"What did he do?"

"Kia is pregnant. He got another woman pregnant," Loletta said, her words unwinding gradually out of her mouth.

Ms. Landelton began to stare at the blackened movie screen. Both women waited for the right words to come.

Loletta rested the back of her head on the chair and slid her body all the way down. "I'm dreading tonight when I have to sleep next to him."

Ms. Landelton gave her a Kleenex from the green leather, Gucci purse that she had borrowed from Loletta. "Sweetie, you *can* get through this. Stuff like this happens."

"How?" Loletta asked abruptly. She blew down hard on the tissue. "I hate him."

"Now listen. This was obviously a mistake. Perhaps he can convince this Kia to abort it. If not, we'll get a paternity test."

"He told me that the baby is his without a doubt. He said it like he was offended that I asked," Loletta said.

"I must say he doesn't look like he has a care in the world tonight. He's looking very handsome and relaxed."

"Are you here to help or make me even more upset?" Loletta pressed her fingers together as she tried to compose her thoughts.

"I'm here to help."

"I have to do something," Loletta pleaded. She looked at her mother, poised in a white Donna Karan pantsuit. She wanted her mother to give her the plan, the breakdown of her next step. She didn't give herself credit for coming up with anything as conniving as her mother could.

"Okay, so she keeps his baby," Ms. Landelton said, sitting up straight and seeming pensive. "Have you suggested that you two fight for custody?"

Loletta's foggy mind hadn't contemplated such a move, but she wished she had. "That may actually work. Kia is totally unfit to be a mother, and I would never trust her with any kid, never mind Kavon's."

"Then good," Ms. Landelton said, patting her lap. "Tell him that is what you want to do. You would be totally supporting him and crossing out the other woman. Not to mention avoiding some hefty child support."

Ms. Landelton put out her hand for Loletta to take, and they rejoined the party hand in hand.

"Thank you for holding yourself together tonight," Kavon said, as they both undressed for bed in different corners of the room. "I had a good time today. This was one of my best birthdays," he said, trying to add a jovial mood to the stress-laden vibes Loletta was giving off.

"Glad someone had a good time," she said, thinking to herself how much better it would have been if they could just be normal. She also realized that Kia hadn't once reared her head today, and that concerned her. Then again, she thought, Kia probably already thought she'd won.

Loletta got into bed dressed from head to toe. She had on an ankle-length white and blue silk nightgown, and socks and panties. She wasn't letting Kavon's smooth talk get to her tonight, and she could tell he was already starting.

He slipped under the covers right next to her and asked, "Can I touch you?"

Loletta pulled the covers up to her chest. "No."

"Are we still married?" he asked, talking lightly into her ear. He lay on his side with his head resting on his right hand.

"Yes, but I'm very upset about everything," she said. "I can't think of you having sex with her so freely. No protection, nothing, like you weren't even thinking of me, of us."

Kavon's eyes took on a deep feeling of yearning, as if her words were turning him on. He touched her, his fingers playing in her wavy hair. "I messed up, but I can't take it back. I swear this will never happen again."

"I am so tired of hearing you say that," she said, pulling her head away.

"Loletta, if I could fix this I would. And I did use protection. I always do."

"Well, then it must have broken. Now she's gonna be in our lives forever. Thanks to you and your brilliant moves."

"I don't have to listen to this," he said, turning on his back. "Either we gonna work this out, or we ain't."

Loletta saw that he was finally showing some signs of stress. "I want us to fight for custody."

Kavon quickly turned back over to her. "Hell, fucking no."

"Why not?" Loletta said, staring at him intensely. "She would be an unfit mother, and I will see to it that we get that baby."

"Listen, Loletta, Kia ain't never kill nobody. If you do that, she's gonna go off. All I gotta do is send her some money every month."

"The hell you are!" she said, rolling up to him. "Don't you see that is a part of her plan? Bitch probably can't take another abortion. She is not well. She can hurt that child."

"I don't want us to have the baby," he said, sitting up on the edge of the bed.

"I don't understand why you care so much. You seem to forget that I lost both of your babies, and you ain't never bring that up again after that week. But now some ho is pregnant, and you ready to lay down your motherfuckin' life and pockets!"

Kavon grabbed the wife-beater that lay on the floor and slipped it on.

"Where are you going?" Loletta asked, tearing her covers off.

"I gotta go someplace to think." Kavon put his dress shirt and jeans back on. "One thing I know is, I don't want to fight for custody. That baby is not *ours*."

Loletta thought she might as well be sitting buck naked on the icy sheets of Antarctica by the way Kavon sounded. She didn't know where his disdain for her came from, and she felt it like a boulder dropping on her from the sky.

"I'm trying to work this out with you. Do you want to be alone with this baby and Kia?" she asked, her voice cracking from the dry, sore throat that was doing its best to hold back a well of tears.

Kavon took a dark blue baseball cap that sat on the chair by the window and put it on. "I just wanna be *happy,*" he said, and jetted out the door.

Twenty-eight

On Thursday, Loletta's father flew into town for twenty-four hours to attend a business meeting regarding opening a branch of a popular coffee shop in Milan. The residual checks from his old basketball days were few and far between.

Loletta met her father inside the Bull and Bear at the Waldorf-Astoria in Midtown. When she got the call that he was in town, she dropped everything and was at the hotel in less than an hour.

"Why didn't you tell me you were coming? Can you stay longer?" she asked, as she scanned the room of white-collar workers and investment-banker types. She and her dad sat at a quaint table in the corner.

"Baby, they just told me two days ago. I closed the deal today. And I have to get back to Milan tomorrow to meet with the lawyer before he goes to Morocco for vacation." Her father poured some honey in her tea. "Is that enough?"

"Yes," she nodded, recollecting the distant memories of him teaching her how to ride a bike when she was six. All the while her mother thought it was foolish. Ms. Landelton complained that bike riding would lead to tomboyish behavior, which would "confuse" all the "cute, athletic" boys at school.

Her father looked deep into Loletta's eyes. "Are you all right? I know I came here for a business deal, but I feel you need me."

"Oh, I'm fine," Loletta said, waving her hand carelessly in the air. "Just going through some changes."

Her father's gray-speckled eyebrows raised up to his forehead. "Bad changes?" He cupped his mug of coffee with both hands.

Loletta thought she might be able to get a man's perspective on it all, something she'd missed living with her mother all these years. "Kavon got another woman pregnant. And he doesn't want us to fight for custody. But I don't feel right with another woman having a piece of my husband somewhere out there."

"Who is this woman?" he asked, with a somber expression. He was much older than Kavon, and Loletta was his only child. But with almost twenty years in the NBA and CBA, he had seen it all.

"A woman who used to work at the Knicks office. And to make a long story short, she's obsessed with Kavon. She would do anything to keep him," Loletta said, touching the rim of her hot cup to her lips.

"And you would too," Hightower said matter-of-factly.

"He's my husband." Loletta responded defensively, but she knew her father was going somewhere, and she forced herself to listen.

"First of all, I think it is mighty noble of you to want to take this baby in and give it a real family." He chuckled to himself. "I don't even think your own mother would go there. Actually, most women would want that woman and child as far away as possible. Why did you *really* suggest that? Is it because you lost the babies?" he asked, lowering his voice around the bustling restaurant crowd.

"A little bit," she admitted, wiping a strand of loose hair away from her face.

"But it wasn't your fault that you fell and lost the twins," he insisted, loosening his black pinstriped tie.

Loletta only smiled, because her father did not know the whole story and it was too much to recount.

"Listen, I gotta be honest. I don't like Kavon. There's just something off about a man who is disconnected from his own mother and family. I can go on with some other reasons, but I think you can do better."

"Kavon is one of the richest players ever. I should feel lucky that he chose me," she said, digging her heels into the ground, frustrated at herself. "Why can't I feel lucky, instead of trapped?"

"Baby, you gotta do for yourself what's right. If you want to stay, just be aware that this baby won't be the last. And that there will be other women."

"If I move on to another man, he may cheat too. Cheating does not discriminate," she said.

"True, but the point is that Kavon basically knows you will stay for that money. He can do whatever he wants. You didn't bring anything into this relationship that he didn't already have. In his mind, he doesn't need you. You need *him*."

Loletta didn't like the sound of this, but it couldn't be any truer. She had allowed herself to be in this situation, to marry a man who she didn't even really get to know beyond his fat multimillion dollar deals.

"Just think of what great things you can accomplish without him. I'm sure you met some well-connected people as his wife. You gotta be working with something, Loletta. *Anything besides a pretty face and a body*. You can't let these men win. Every king has to fall," he said.

"Daddy, you really 'bout it, 'bout it." She laughed. "I was thinking about starting a restaurant, but Kavon wasn't hearing it."

"You can do it without him. Stop being afraid. As carefree as your mother seems, she lives her life based on fear. I know you're not like that. That's why you are so torn about all this."

"But you're telling me to leave my husband and everything Mommy has raised me for. I don't want to let her down, including myself. I can do this. If he doesn't want to fight for custody, I can live with that. I have one more try left in me," she said, drinking her lukewarm tea.

"I don't mean for you to leave. That is on you. But sometimes a man never knows what he really has until he loses it," he said.

"Is that how you feel about Mommy?"

"No." He laughed. "But you were the best thing that came out of it. I'm so glad you're more like me. You really *are*," he said, patting her shoulders.

She smiled. It was exactly what she needed to hear. Now she just had to believe it.

After Loletta left her father at about five o'clock, she decided to visit an old friend. Lady Anise. She had promised herself that she was going to go it alone, but she found herself desperate again for direction.

She walked up the cold concrete steps of Lady Anise's imposing brownstone just a few blocks north of the hotel. It had been months since she stood there. All the curtains were pulled in, but there was a light on in the top floor, where Lady Anise held her appointments. Loletta rang the bell several times until a young Mexican woman let her in.

Loletta was about to explain that she was dropping by unannounced to see Lady Anise, but the young, tan-skinned woman told her to go upstairs, as if they were expecting her. She held on tightly to the banister as she climbed the steep, gold-carpeted steps in her black Manolo heels. By the time she reached the top, she thought she had pulled a muscle in her thigh.

"Hello, Lady Anise?" Loletta said, as she tapped lightly on the wooden door. She inhaled the fresh scent of peppermint coming from the inside.

Lady Anise opened the door and welcomed her with wide open arms. Loletta hugged her awkwardly. She felt like a child returning home.

"Oh, my dear. I knew you would come back." Lady Anise pointed for Loletta to sit in the familiar cedarwood chair and then dimmed the lights.

"Maybe because you can foresee the future," Loletta said, taking Lady Anise's hands.

"No, that's not why," she said, waving her finger. "It's because I had strong dreams about you. I usually dream about my clients before they come." Lady Anise lit a small white candle and laid it on the table between them, where stems of incense emanated smoke.

Loletta looked at Lady Anise's long, olive-toned hands, which looked like rice paper wrapped in green, thin veins. Her hands felt warm and soothing as Loletta squeezed them. Then she said, "I need help. Quick help."

Loletta knew the routine. She sat patiently as she breathed in and out, calming herself. Lady Anise did the same, but as each second passed, Loletta's hands became tighter and her breathing turned deeper.

"What do you want to do?" Lady Anise asked, with her eyes closed.

"I don't know. If I stay, I don't think I can ever trust him now that he has a baby with another woman. If I leave, I'll feel like a failure to everyone and will be wondering, 'What if?'" Her decision rested on Lady Anise's response, she thought. Whatever it was, she was ready to act.

Lady Anise opened her eyes. "Ms. Jackson, you may not like what I am about to say. I see this situation far more clearly than you can because I am not close to it. You are the only person who can help Kavon be a better person. This life is about sacrifice. If you leave now, that young lady will be with him, and they will both go downhill together. You have the power to change things."

Loletta blinked profusely as her mind wrestled to untangle Lady Anise's advice. She had mixed feelings about it. *Why do I have to be the one to help him?* She needed the help, she thought.

"You have the power to change things," Lady Anise repeated, wrapping her gold and salmon-colored scarf around her neck. "Change yourself, and then everything around you will change."

"I see," Loletta said, letting go of Lady Anise. "I guess it's on me. It always is," she said. She started to leave.

"Ms. Jackson," Lady Anise said, as Loletta sauntered to the door. "You have a duty to fulfill, and I know you can do it. I want you to take this." Lady Anise opened up a cherry-stained wooden chest. She took out a folded paper and handed it to Loletta.

Loletta read it. "What is this for?"

"Read it at night. Every night. It will make your path easy."

Lady Anise closed the door, while Loletta stood there and reread the note several times.

That night, while Kavon was out of town for a game, Loletta fixed herself a grilled cheese sandwich to take up to bed with her. She had the entire three-level mansion to herself. It was ten p.m. She and Kavon had spoken several times that evening, and he was now on his way home from his game in Philadelphia.

When she got to her bedroom, she flipped on the television to catch the evening news. She felt like a kid whose parents were away for the weekend. With all the tension mounting up between herself and Kavon, she was relieved to have some hours alone to process her thoughts. Whenever she wanted to cry again or dig through all of Kavon's belongings, she pulled Lady Anise's note out from under her pillow.

My apparent enemy now becomes my friend, a golden link in my chain of good. Loletta recited this over and over, in between bites of her sandwich. Each time she said those words, she felt ridiculous. She could no way think of Kia or even Kavon as a friend, and there was no way any good could come out of this betrayal. She turned off the TV, lay on her back, and pushed herself to recite the words some more. What Lady Anise had said, she thought, was good—up until the point when she handed her the paper. *This is bullshit,* Loletta thought, angry that no one understood. She crumbled up the paper and threw it in the trash. She was finally convinced that she was in this alone.

A few days later Loletta and Ms. Landelton spent the day lunching and getting their nails primped and polished at the swanky Daddy's Diva Salon in Soho. Sipping martinis, they both had their feet up as every nook and cranny of their toes were attended to.

"You know," Ms. Landelton said, popping the olive in her mouth, "I never knew the beneficial qualities of milk until I bathed my feet in it. I mean, we all know the stuff about the calcium and the bones, but who would have thought it could get rid of calluses."

"Yeah, who would have thought?" Loletta said, as she thumbed through an issue of *Glamour*. The one she was to appear in was months away, but she needed something to put her attention on. Otherwise, she'd have to spend the time talking to her mother about Kavon, something that took more energy out of her than a good sex romp.

"Do you think we should pick up those Prada shoes for Kavon we saw earlier? I don't think it's right to go home empty-handed to him," she said, looking over at Loletta.

"He has at least fifty pairs of Prada shoes. I'm sure another won't hurt. I bought him some new ties this morning at Nordstrom. He doesn't like wearing the same one twice," Loletta said. "He's going on four hundred now."

"But there are only three hundred and sixty-five days of the year," Ms. Landelton said, completely perplexed.

"I know. He loses a lot of them," Loletta said curtly.

"Do you think he liked that birthday gift we got him?"

"Yes," Loletta said, closing the magazine. "Remember that big ole wet kiss he gave you on the cheek?"

"Oh," Ms. Landelton said shyly. "And you were so rigid when he kissed you."

"And you know why," Loletta said, watching the young attendant carefully apply her white nail polish.

"How's your father?"

"Good."

"Did you tell him about Kavon."

"Yes, and he was really helpful. He's worried about me, and so am I," Loletta said.

"No, no, honey. You are strong. Listen, I'm gonna leave the two of you alone tonight. You two need *quality* time."

"Thank you, Mommy." Loletta said, pleasantly surprised that her mother believed in her. Her mother sometimes did little things like that. One time, her mother cooked when Loletta was seeing a member of Jodeci and had lied about her cooking skills. Her mother fixed some smothered chicken wings, mac and cheese, and greens in order for Loletta to woo him. It must have worked, because she was his girlfriend for six months and used his money for shopping sprees for herself and her mother.

Loletta turned to her mother and kissed her cheek.

Loletta fussed with her keys to open the front door of the house. She had several keys, and the one to her Lamborghini looked strikingly similar to the front-door key. She shook her head at how many people would love to have that problem.

"Here, let me help you," Ms. Landelton said, taking one of Loletta's shopping bags. Then the door flung open. It was Adrienna, looking troubled.

"Thanks, Adrienna," Loletta said, as she and Ms. Landelton passed by her. Loletta noticed that the living room wasn't the way she had left it. An unrecognizable black trench coat was thrown over a chair. "Everything okay?" she asked Adrienna.

Adrienna just looked down and shook her head. "I have something in the stove."

Loletta watched her scurry off.

"What does it take to get good help these days?" Ms. Landelton said, pouring herself a drink at the bar. "You did ask a question."

"I know," Loletta said, with a bad feeling in the pit of her stomach. She was afraid to talk, move, or even blink. She wanted time to stand still for a moment until she put her finger on it. Then she saw them.

Kavon and Kia walking down the steps hand in hand. A glass smashed to the ground as Ms. Landelton jumped at the sight. That explained the look on Adrienna's face, Loletta thought, as she too cringed inside. There Kia was, in her house, holding her husband's hand as if they were making a grand entrance. She was dressed in a lacy black dress with an empire waist, black satin arm gloves, and sparkly heels. Kavon was in his usual loungewear: a gray sweatsuit and sneakers.

Loletta felt cornered. She looked to her mother whose grim eyes were glued to Kavon and Kia. She wanted her to say something first. *The hell with it*, Loletta thought, as she stepped forward.

"What is this?" she asked Kavon in a composed manner. She didn't even acknowledge Kia, who stood by, holding Kavon's arm.

"It's over; I want you out," he said, offhand like it was no big deal.

"I want to talk to you upstairs now!" Loletta said to him as she walked up the steps, but he didn't budge.

"Kavon, maybe it's best if we call the police," Kia said to him, but loud enough for all to hear.

Loletta marched back down the steps. She wanted to rip into Kia, or the both of them, but it was too much.

"What the hell is going on here! This is my house too. I live here. This woman is crazy. Can't you see?" she pleaded with Kavon.

"Don't make me call the cops if I don't have to," Kavon said, looking at his watch. "Kia and I have plans tonight."

Ms. Landelton crept to a corner of the room and didn't say a word. Loletta wanted her to say something, anything. But she was mute.

Loletta walked over to one of Kavon's mantels and picked up a trophy. "You think all of this makes you a man? When you can't even come to me like a man and tell me you want a divorce? You humiliate me like this. Why?"

"You humiliating yourself. It just so happens that I did some thinking, and you wasn't a part of it," he said, letting go of Kia and moving closer to Loletta.

Loletta threw the trophy across the room and smashed the wall-to-wall mirror behind the couch. Kavon grabbed her and wrestled her down to the couch. "You getting the fuck out."

"I'm calling the police to handle this bitch!" Kia said, dialing her cell phone.

Ms. Landelton shouted, "Kavon, whatever it is, I'm sure Loletta's sorry. This is all a misunderstanding!"

Loletta kicked and spit at Kavon to let her go, but he dragged her along the hardwood floors to the door. "Do I have to kick you out, or do you want to leave with a little pride?" he said, with a twisted smile. He rubbed the sweat from his forehead.

Loletta grabbed the wall to help her stand up. Her right arm was bruised and swollen. "You both should have just shot me dead, because this hurts way more," she said, holding her arm. "I don't care if I have to stay up day and night, but I'm gonna destroy everything you worked for. Everything," she said, through her tightly clenched lips. "And bitch, you're next."

Loletta's hair was disheveled, and her face scratched by Kavon's rings. She looked to her mother. "Mommy?" she said, noticing her mother had not advanced to the door.

Ms. Landelton sat curled up on the couch, her head shaking uncontrollably. "I can't go," she said.

"You are welcome to stay, Ms. Landelton. This has nothing to do with you," Kia said, sitting beside Loletta's mother.

Loletta wanted to drag her mother out of that place, but her mother made her choice. Loletta mustered enough strength to bend down, pick up her handbag, and walk out alone. She heard the door slam behind her with a thud.

Twenty-nine

Loletta had approximately five thousand dollars of her own savings. She checked in at the posh Carlyle. She couldn't bear to downgrade. She was degraded enough and needed to build a wall around herself that could give her what she had lost. Her mother's behavior was what ripped her apart the most. It killed her to know that her mother chose her own security over their bond. Perhaps *she* had too, she thought. But if her mother was a hopeless case, at least Loletta still had a chance to make a life. Where most daughters would run to family in this type of situation, she had no one. She could fly to Milan, but it would just be a place to hide when what she needed to do was get her life in order. Her room at the Carlyle was quickly depleting her bank account. Kavon had frozen her access to his money. But there was one person she knew who would have her back, because she had his during their affair.

She gave him a call hoping he would be in town. "Carter, it's Loletta." He was still out on disability. She didn't care about his past or whether or not he slept with Kia. All she cared about was making a power move.

"What's up, lady?" he said on the other end. "You sound *bad*."

"Thank you," she said, rolling her eyes. She pulled out a piece of tissue from the box on the nightstand. "I need some help. Kavon and I are getting a divorce, and he cut off my access to our accounts. Can you get down here?"

Carter hesitated for a moment. "Are you by yourself?"

"Yes. My mother decided to stay with him and Kia. Just give me a loan, and I swear I will pay you back with interest. I'll even give you my diamond ring as collateral," she sniffled. "Or damn it, keep it."

"Hold on, hold on," Carter said, growing concerned by the second. "You don't have to give me a damn thing. I'll be right over."

"I'm in room 1506." She hung up.

It didn't take long before Carter was knocking on her door. He was wearing a light blue parka, black sweats, and a white team tee-shirt. It looked like he came directly from the gym.

"So what's good?" he said, sitting on the Victorian-style, paisley love seat. Then a grimace came on him when he looked at her face. "That negro beat you?"

Loletta patted her swollen cheek, which had several scratches from her struggle with Kavon. "He held me down on the couch and hit me a few times," she said, holding her head down. She was embarrassed. Carter was used to seeing her look sharp, but now her face looked like she had been in a schoolyard brawl. Even her costly outfit looked cheap and tattered.

"C'mere," he said, rubbing the seat next to him. He placed his soft thick lips on her face, kissing her scars, and caressed her face with his hands.

She pulled away. "Carter, I am in no mood for sex. If that's what I have to do, then forget it," she said, shaking her head.

"I ain't here for no sex. You still my people. I hate to see your pretty face all banged up. You know you can take this to his coach," he suggested, his arms around her. "You need to be held right now. That's all I wanna do."

Loletta let her shoulders relax as she cuddled up into his arms. She didn't care whose arms they were; she did need some love, some affection. Anything that made her feel safe, even for a few minutes. Loletta chewed on her fingernails as she replayed the day's events over and over in her head.

"Loletta? You gotta do something. As a matter of fact," he said, digging in his pants pocket, "here's my divorce lawyer. You ain't going back to that shit, are you?"

"No," she said, taking the card from him. "There's a lot of things that are gonna be different from now on. I gotta start living for myself. Fuck everybody."

"Baby, I'm telling you, if you call my lawyer, he will have you sitting up pretty in just a few months. Believe me, Kavon will want to get this over with as fast as possible, before people catch on."

"But we only been married less than a year. We had no prenup."

"That ain't the point. Call him. He is like the motherfuckin' mafia of divorce lawyers. Call him before Kavon does." Carter handed her his cell phone.

Loletta dialed the number, got a voicemail, and left a brief message. When she hung up, she actually felt better. The biggest move turned out to be the easiest one. She wondered if the real fight was ahead.

"Now," Carter said, unzipping his sports bag. He pulled out his checkbook. "For the real business at hand."

"Carter, I just need a few thousand to hold me until I decide what to do. I may end up going to Milan, to my dad."

"Why? You can do everything you want to do right here. This is the time to get yours, and there is no better place than our beloved United States."

"What you saying?" she asked him, noticing the smile in his dark brown eyes. His thick eyebrows made them look deliciously outstanding.

"You told me you wanted to start a restaurant. I got people wanting to invest in a good business venture. I can hook you up with my business manager, and we can get this poppin'. It'll be yours—your name, your ideas. We'll be the silent partners, of course, for a percentage. Everybody's doing it."

Loletta began to smile too. "My own restaurant? People investing in my dream?"

"Yes, but you gotta act fast. No one likes to deal with people who don't know how to move money. This is what I'm gonna do for you," he said. He scribbled down a steep six-figure.

Loletta's eyes bubbled with water. "Oh, my God," she said, slapping her hand over her mouth. "I can't take this."

"Take it," he said, pushing her hand back toward her. "And I know somebody else who can really hook you up on another idea."

Loletta planted a big, fat wet one on the check and started rambling. "I want it to be a Mediterranean-style restaurant, all French and Italian dishes," she said, her mind imagining a red carpet at her grand opening.

Carter laughed. "Hey, you should throw some soul food up in there."

Loletta looked at him like he was nuts. "We doing this high-style, high-cuisine. Black folk need to experience other things besides mac and cheese." She laughed too, feeling hopeful for a change.

"Have you ever thought about writing a book after all that press you got a few months ago?"

"A book?" Loletta asked, her attention fixated on Carter's next proposition. She had no idea that he was so entrepreneurial or even this motivating.

"I got some people at Creative Artists Agency. They are always looking for some celebrity to write a tell-all. You could write about all your years chasing the light, the dream. I don't know too many females who get promoted from groupie status to wife status."

Loletta closed her eyes a bit as she focused in on what she had to offer. It was a rare thing to get "wifed" by an athlete who knows your "pay girlfriend" past. But whatever she had done, it was enough to elevate her to a position where few women sat, especially not black women. She had earned her gold star. Unfortunately, she had lost so much on her way there. "I can do it, but I want it to be more inspirational than anything. I want people to learn from my mistakes. Sometimes what glitters is shit under the sun, not gold," she said, grabbing his cell phone. "Who do I call?"

"Slow up a bit," he said, taking his phone away. "I can give you the info, under one condition."

Loletta knew what was coming.

"You have to sign an agreement to promise that you won't tell my story. That's all I ask," he said, with an intensity that showed he was in it for more than a book.

"And what else?"

"Let's just say that I think everybody needs to know who the real Kavon is. And now with him and Kia together, that shit is only gonna cause more drama for all of us," he said. "Get to it *first*." Carter pulled out another business card from his wallet.

They looked at each other like it was on. Whatever "it" would be.

"Thank you," Loletta said. She was armed with the ammunition to rebuild her life, and she had no plans on running short.

Loletta made one of her most satisfying trips to the bank since her marriage to Kavon. She had deposited a small chunk of Carter's loan in her checking account, and the rest sat secure in her savings for her restaurant plans. As she was crossing West Fifty-sixth Street at Seventh Avenue, she thought about calling Vernice. She had put off calling her because she would have to relive the whole painful story again. She had thought she should take some time to get herself together first, but Carter helped her see that there was a life waiting for her. She wanted Vernice in on it.

"Hey, girl," Loletta said, struggling to get a little pep in her voice. She stood on the corner and braved the rain. Where was the black sedan with a driver now? she thought.

"Loletta! You know I tried to call you and see how you was, but some woman picked up your phone," Vernice babbled out, as soon as she heard Loletta. "Who *was* that?"

Loletta signaled for a cab, but each one of them was full during the rush hour. The rain matted her hair down on the sides. She used her Prada handbag to protect it. "There's been some changes," Loletta began, as she frantically ran to a cab that had stopped a few feet in front of her. She slipped in and began to recount to Vernice everything that went down.

After she was done, Vernice was dead silent.

"I should have called you the minute I got to the Carlyle," Loletta said, dabbing the corner of her eyes. "But it didn't really hit me until I slept alone that night."

Vernice spoke as if she was on the verge of tears as well. "I'm on the next plane over there. We gonna take that motherfucka out!" Vernice said. "And if Kia wasn't pregnant, she'd be going down too."

Loletta smiled, but even the baddest beat-down wasn't going to solve this. "I am moving on with my life, Vernice. He's gonna see for himself that he didn't get the best of me. I got an appointment with the divorce lawyer tomorrow."

"Is your mom going with you?"

"Please," Loletta hissed. "She stayed with Kavon."

"What? Not Ms. Landelton. I never thought she'd go out like that."

"She did. All because of how wonderful a son-in-law he'd been, buying her out with cars, a house, an expense account," Loletta said, as she pointed to the driver to pull over after the next light.

"Loletta, I'm about to go get my tickets. You can't be going through this alone. Please don't try to shut me down. I'm here for you," Vernice said, sounding sympathetic.

Loletta paid the driver and exited the car. "Girl, I really need someone here who is on my side and not looking for a 'lil extra somethin'.'"

"You mean like Carter?"

Walking through the hotel lobby, Loletta said, "Not him. But he gave me some money and even the lawyer to go to. He says he wants to help me with opening my restaurant."

"Girl! That is hot. A restaurant? Now you know you have to come to LA for that shit. I can be your assistant manager." Vernice giggled.

"Maybe," Loletta said, smiling at the numbers on the elevator as she rode up to her floor.

"Did ya fuck?"

"Hell, no!" Loletta said. "I just left my husband."

"Don't even try that. The best way to get over old dick is to get on top of a new one."

They both laughed out loud. But Loletta was in no mood to start sharing out the goods. "Vernice, I have no patience or fortitude to be laid up with any man right now. I still love Kavon, and it wouldn't feel right laying up with Carter or anybody."

"If you really meant it when you said you would move on, you would get Kavon out of your system the old-fashioned way. No therapy, no spiritual counseling, nada," Vernice said.

"Look, I have to go, but don't worry about your tickets. I'll have the concierge book and send them to you. Don't be surprised if I go with you to LA," Loletta said, her stomach jumping at the thought of starting over.

"Okay, no problem. As long as you promise me that if I hook you up with a fine-ass man, that you will at least go out on a date."

"Promise. But for now," Loletta said, as she finally reached her apartment door, "I'm celibate."

The next day Loletta rushed back for an appointment with Louis Ray Corbett, Esquire, to discuss her divorce settlement. She had arranged a meeting with him during Bemelmans tea hour. When she arrived, he was already seated and being served.

The courteous male waiter pulled out Loletta's chair, as she greeted Corbett, a stout man of average height, wearing thick glasses and a blue pinstriped suit. "So nice of you to meet me on short notice. It's not like I was expecting to get divorced today," she said, with a feeble smile.

Corbett stood up and greeted her, a mole on his chin moving as he spoke. "When I heard Carter referred you, I made it my business to be here," he said, waiting for Loletta to sit.

Loletta wasn't as struck by his looks as she was by his record. She trusted Carter's word because his divorce settlement was an example of Corbett's skills. Carter's ex-wife got alimony that wasn't much higher than a minimum-wage salary. It didn't matter if it was right or wrong, but Carter won. After briefly looking over the menu and placing their orders, Corbett didn't wait another second to get down to business. "How long were you married?" he asked, pulling out a small, black leather notepad.

"Um, almost eight months," she said, her hand slightly shaking.

"No prenup, right?"

"Right. We married so fast, it wasn't something we thought of."

"Honestly, Ms. Jackson—"

"Call me Loletta, please," she said, wincing at the sound of a name that once made her proud.

"Loletta, he may have already had plans to divorce you when he married you. Meaning he didn't plan to stay married long."

The waiter placed down the steeping teapot and beautiful china teacups. They waited until he poured their tea. Then Corbett continued. "If we can prove that he married you under false pretenses or for malicious reasons, we can walk away with something."

Loletta stirred her herbal tea as she listened. It had never dawned on her that Kavon had planned all this. But she wasn't about to put anything past him.

"Did he sign a major contract while you were married?"

"No . . . I mean, yes. Well, we were dating when he signed his twenty-million-dollar deal with the Knicks. Then we got married a few months later," she said, not sure what Corbett was getting at.

"Did he buy any new assets?"

"Besides the regular vacations, some gifts he gave me. My standard of living was never so carefree and top-of-the-line," she said.

Corbett jotted down a few things in his notepad and chewed the end of his pencil. But Loletta wasn't feeling his mood; it made her incredibly nervous.

"Here's what we have, Loletta. Since there is no prenup, you basically go back to the same things you both had when you entered the relationship. That is standard procedure."

Loletta's forehead began to pound. "You mean I get nothing? Nothing for the hell he put me through?"

Corbett sipped his tea. "That is where *I* come in. I've never done anything to standard, but I've exceeded standards and expectations. We may have to get our hands dirty, but we can make this work."

"Work? I need a guarantee that my ass is not gonna be out in the streets when this is through. I need Kavon to pay; even if I strike a million dollars tomorrow, he owes me something," she said, looking for the waiter.

"Right, and this is how I see it—"

"A cranberry and vodka, please," Loletta said, when the waiter appeared. He nodded and was off to fill her request.

Loletta looked at Corbett, who had a little smirk on. "Loletta, I assure you there is no need to be nervous. I do these types of cases all the time. We can get alimony—and *good* alimony. We need to go over everything to prove malicious intent. But—"

"But what?" Loletta said, leaning over the table.

"You may not get a flat-out settlement. But the alimony you receive will uphold the standard of living and taste that you were accustomed to," he said, opening his arms to indicate the Carlyle as an example. "We're gonna hit him where it hurts."

The waiter placed Loletta's drink in front of her. She picked it up, held it in the air against Corbett's teacup. Corbett said, "In Mark Twain's humble words, to get the full value of joy, you must have someone to divide it with."

That was something Loletta could definitely drink to.

Thirty

"Mommy, it's me."

On Loletta's fifth night at the Carlyle, she made up her mind to call her mother. Her feelings of anger and rage at Ms. Landelton were dwindling to sadness and confusion. It didn't matter if they never spoke again, as much as it mattered that her mother was safe and okay.

There was a deafening silence on her end.

"Mommy? Are you okay?" Loletta asked, as she glanced at the clock. It was one a.m.

"Yes, baby." Ms. Landelton slurred in her sleep. "Where are you?"

"Where are *you*?" Loletta retorted.

"I'm at my house, where you should be." Ms. Landelton began to awaken. "You *really* disappointed me."

The last line felt like a punch to the stomach. Loletta wrapped the phone cord around her index finger so tight the tip turned bright red. She closed her eyes, took a deep breath, and counted to three. She didn't want this to be another fight. She had fought too much lately. "Can I ask you something?"

"What."

"Why did you stay? What kind of life can you possibly have with Kavon and that woman?"

"They don't have anything to do with me. Kavon bought me a house and a car that are rightfully mine. He made no suggestion that *I* had to leave." She coughed and continued. "Besides, Kia is really a basket case. I don't see that lasting more than another few months."

Loletta continued winding the cord around her finger. "I don't get how you can even look him in the face after how he treated me. He can't respect you if he doesn't respect me."

"Who said anything about me looking in his face? He still puts money in my account, and I am well. In fact, I'm investing. Just because you ruined your life, why should I lose out? It would be very unfair."

"If you stay there, I will never come see you again," Loletta said, her mouth rigid with anger at the thought of seeing Kavon or even anything that was associated with him. "I just can't. The wounds are too fresh."

"Well, suit yourself." Ms. Landelton yawned.

Loletta didn't know how her mother could be so cold. There had to be some type of resentment, or unresolved feelings, she had for Loletta as a person, Loletta thought. There was just no love, or at least not love as Loletta defined it.

"I'm getting a divorce, and I can get that house you're in and turn it over into our names. He bought it for you, but he's paying for it."

"Damn right he is." Ms. Landelton snarled.

"Don't you see that he can stop anytime? Divorces get ugly,

and you don't know what people will do out of spite," Loletta said, trying to talk some sense into her. It was almost as if she were brainwashed by a fantasy that she lived in by herself.

"Honey, look, it's too late to get into this," Ms. Landelton said. "You are out of your mind if you think I'm paying for this kind of mortgage. I couldn't possibly do it."

"*I* can. I have a plan after this. I'm writing a book and opening a restaurant, and you can come live with me," Loletta said. "Or you can stay where you are, and I'll pay the mortgage." Loletta wanted to take back those words. The mortgage was a hefty five figures. It wasn't the money, however; a part of Loletta didn't want to feed her mother anymore or sustain her over-the-top lifestyle. The thought made her feel awfully guilty.

Ms. Landelton began to roar with laughter, which permeated Loletta's ears. "You write *and* open a restaurant? You like silk and lace, not grime and grease. Plus you don't even have any business sense or savvy. You'll end up on the nine-to-five grind again."

Loletta wanted to pull the cord out of the wall at that point. Her mother spoke her fears, and it hurt. She hated the way she disabled her, and she wasn't going to have it. "And what have you done that's been so business savvy besides piggybacking off everything I get and every relationship I'm in? Your divorce settlement from Daddy slipped like water through your fingers. If anything, you're the one who sounds like she won't have a pot to piss in."

"Loletta, you do what you have to do. I'm only doing what I know. I think you're foolish to get a divorce before you even sit down with Kavon and—"

"You're crazy!" Loletta shouted, crying and laughing at the same time. *"I'll see him in court."*

"You're making a big mistake. A big, big one," Ms. Landelton said, her voice trailing off.

"I've made my biggest mistakes already, and you're about to make yours," Loletta said, slamming the receiver down hard enough that it fell on the carpeted floor.

At that moment, Loletta didn't want to do anything but move, as far as she could, to a place where she could reinvent herself. It was obvious to her what the problem was. She didn't love herself enough to make anyone love her back.

On Wednesday evening, it dawned on Loletta that without Kavon or Ms. Landelton, she had nothing to do with her time. It was eight p.m., and she had just eaten a wonderful room-service dinner of filet mignon and a decadent slice of cheesecake. Usually she'd need to nap her meal off, but tonight she didn't want to sleep away her worries. She wanted so much to call Kavon and ask him when and where did everything go wrong. But every time her heart led her to pick up the phone, her mind told her to put it down. As much as she disliked the thought, divorcing him was the best thing. She regretted not leaving him on her own. She wanted to hold on to her anger, but she couldn't. She was more angry at herself than anyone else. She thought perhaps a stroll downtown was what she needed. She didn't want to shop or get her nails done; she just wanted to be around others and disappear in the midst of their evening goings-on.

The cabbie dropped her off at the corner of Fourteenth Street and Seventh Avenue. Couples walked down the street embracing, a man with a red sweater-hat argued loudly on his cell phone, and a group of rowdy teenagers stepped quickly past Loletta to catch the turning light. She walked south on Seventh Avenue, reveling in the extraordinarily warm November weather. With a gray and white cashmere shawl wrapped over her shoulders, she peeked in the brightly lit bakery and colorfully decorated shop windows along the avenue. Loletta stopped at a pizzeria for a treat she hadn't had in months.

"Let me have a slice, please," she said, to a dark-haired man wearing a white shirt and pants. While Loletta waited, he popped a cheesy serving in the oven.

"Want a bag?" the man asked when her pizza was ready.

"No, thanks." Loletta paid him and walked out of the store munching on the pizza. A black Escalade pulled up beside her at the red light, and the driver's-side window rolled down.

"Can I get a bite?" Carter asked.

Loletta wondered if she was being tested by the Lord. "Are you stalking me?" she joked.

"Get in," he said, unlocking the passenger door. Loletta thought about it for a moment. If she got in, there would be no easy way of getting out, she thought.

Before the light turned green, she climbed in the truck with her pizza half eaten.

"If I had known I was gonna get into trouble, I would have stayed my behind in the room," she said, biting the crispy crust. Carter reached over with a free hand and took the slice from her.

"Damn, this some good pizza," he said. He handed her back the slice.

"You got some nerve," she said, shaking her head as she looked at the C-shaped part cut out by his mouth. "Where are we goin'?"

"Where do you wanna go?"

Loletta wanted to go back to the Carlyle, but she liked being out. The evening weather was beautiful, she thought. "Wherever is fine," she shrugged.

"Cool," Carter said, as he threw a grin at her.

In minutes, they were in his loft apartment in Tribeca. There was very little furniture, but a chocolate leather sofa sat up against an open-faced brick wall, and three butter-leather armchairs were gathered around a fireplace. Carter was in his kitchen shoveling cheese-and-caramel popcorn onto plates. She couldn't get over looking at him and his strong muscular physique slathered in jeans and a white sweater. Not that she was turned on, because she had seen that and more on Carter. He looked just like a regular guy, she thought, not the seductive, big-dick-swinging, pimp-daddy-playing baller that he made himself out to be.

"How's your injury?" Loletta asked from the living room.

"It's good; my hand feels like it's back to normal. Coach says he wants me back when I'm one hundred percent normal. You know, I'm known as the three-point man," he said, flicking his right wrist in the air.

Carter stepped down a few steps into the sunken living room, holding two heaping bowls of popcorn. "My mom buys this for me every year around the holidays, like five gallons," he said, handing her a bowl.

"I know this popcorn; this is Garrett's from that store in Chicago. Mommy ordered it once from Oprah's "favorite things" show. She was always trying to get tickets to be in that audience," Loletta said, feeling a deep pain inside her.

Carter put his arm around her, but Loletta stiffened. She moved away, closer to her side of the couch. "I want to thank you again for that lawyer. I'm sure he told you we met."

"No, he didn't. But I knew you'd do the right thing," he said, digging his hands in his popcorn.

"Wanna watch a flick? I got the new Chris Rock movie

right here." He sauntered up to his DVD player and slipped in a disc.

Carter sat back down and respected Loletta's space. They both stole awkward glances at each other as they laughed at all the right scenes.

Some popcorn fell inside the cleavage of Loletta's purple mohair sweater. She picked them out of her blouse one-by-one. Carter looked on like he wanted to give her a hand. She quickly adjusted her blouse.

"Want some of my popcorn?" he asked.

"I'm fine," she said, glancing at his long, extended legs. The tent between his thighs looked like he was packing a .357. She looked back at the screen, reminding herself of her self-imposed celibacy. But he was on such good behavior, she thought. Kavon was still a part of her, and that made it harder for her to do anything with Carter. *I'll wait till after my divorce*, she reasoned.

"Do you want something to drink?" he asked, getting up to go to the kitchen. He put the movie on pause.

"Sure," she answered, scooping the popcorn into her mouth. *That swagger he has is so sexy,* Loletta thought, as he walked away. When he returned, it felt like every pore of her body opened when he sat back down. She breathed him in and out.

He handed her a bottle of Vitamin Water. "Like the movie?" he asked with a tight-mouthed smile.

What she wanted to watch was him on his knees losing his nose between her thighs. She squeezed her legs together and nodded. "I think I'm moving to LA," Loletta said. She didn't know why, but she was curious about Carter's reaction. They had grown somewhat closer lately.

"What for?" he said, his eyebrows slanted in confusion.

"I need a place to start fresh. Vernice wants to help me set up the restaurant."

Carter's disappointment soon receded. "If that is gonna make you happy, I think it's great. It's good that you have somebody to help you set up the business. It can get hard sometimes."

"I know," Loletta said. The movie was now becoming background noise.

"I got a house outside Beverly Hills if you need a place to stay," he said, now sitting just a few inches from Loletta. She didn't see him move, but he was definitely closer. "It's an eight-bedroom pad with everything you can think of—Jacuzzi, gym—"

"Thanks, but no thanks," Loletta said, knowing that a year ago she would already have asked for the keys. "I'm staying with Vernice."

"Oh," he said, putting his finished bowl on the ground. "I'll make sure to look you up when I'm out there."

"That's cool, but I really just want to focus on what I got to do there. I'm not going there for fun and games."

"I wouldn't be looking you up for fun and games," he said, his hands resting on her thighs. She parted them slightly.

"I can lend you my baby Benz out there until you get your own ride," he said.

"No, I'm okay. Vernice has a car, or I'll rent one till I'm ready to buy." She couldn't believe herself, turning down free gifts. Her mother was probably right that she had lost her mind, she thought. However, she felt strong and empowered. It wasn't like she wanted to stay with Vernice in less than stellar surroundings, but it was about her integrity. She was tired of compromising it for life's little trinkets.

"Hey, with Mr. Corbett, you can probably get the cars Kavon gave you," Carter said, his knees touching hers.

Loletta got up and walked to the kitchen. "Well, the more

the better, because the cars are mine," she said, putting her plate in the sink. Carter rolled up behind and wrapped himself around her.

Loletta inhaled deeply and put her hands on Carter's clasped hands around her waist. He nestled his face in her hair, and said, "I have to ask you something I never have before."

Loletta exhaled hard. She felt Carter press against her, and this time she wasn't moving away. She kept still.

"Can I make love to you right here, right now?" he whispered, swaying their bodies from side to side.

Loletta stared at the wall in front of her. *Yes, yes, yes,* she thought. But her body was so tight, it wasn't budging; she couldn't relax. She held her head down.

Carter twirled her around, lifted her up by her waist, and sat her on the kitchen counter. The cold granite finish made her butt flinch as she spread her legs. She gazed into his eyes. She didn't want to answer in fear of turning him away. He kissed her forehead, her nose, her lips, and found a perfect little space between her legs.

"I just want to make you feel as beautiful as you look," he said, unbuttoning her jeans. He pulled down her zipper.

Loletta pressed her hands into the counter as she leaned her upper body back slightly, her body calling him. The rough bristles of Carter's five-o'clock shadow teased the nooks and crannies of her neck. She gripped his back, totally taken in by his weight and power. Her pussy throbbed so hard it hurt.

Carter slid her jeans off and then her white chiffon thong. He threw them over his shoulder and got down on his knees. He set his lips lovingly on her aching flesh.

He helped himself to the little bit of her that she was willing to offer. But it didn't take long before that little bit turned into the full entrée of liberation that Loletta had been seeking. An hour later, they had blessed every corner of his loft with their grace.

"Are you sure you ready to give this up for my crib?" Vernice asked as she camped on the couch eating a basket of grapes. She had arrived the night before.

Loletta looked around her suite. It was a sight to be envied, but she didn't want to dwell on it. "I will be fine. My focus is not on whether I have Egyptian cotton sheets on my bed or filet mignon for dinner. As long as I can have a good night and peaceful sleep, I'm good. You do have a bed?"

"Yeah," Vernice said, picking one of the purple lilies from a vase by the sofa. She sniffed it. "I have a pullout couch that's all yours."

Loletta folded the last of her clothes into her suitcase and zipped it shut. "Good," she said. She made a note to herself to buy those Egyptian cotton sheets anyway.

Vernice got off the couch and helped Loletta bring her two suitcases to the front door for the bellboy to pick up. "You sure you ready to do this? You handled all your business?"

"Yes," Loletta said, looking in the mirror by the front door and brushing her eyelashes with mascara. "The lawyer told me he is working out some details. When the court date is set, I'll be back in town. It's nothing to fly back and forth for a few months. I just don't want to wait here and be a sitting duck. I want to live my life now."

"And Carter?"

"What about him?"

"Are you still celibate?" Vernice grinned. She had picked up that something was different about Loletta. She just knew her girl like that.

Loletta rolled her eyes at her and then cracked up laughing.

"I don't know where you came from with that crazy celibacy shit," Vernice said, putting on her black leather jacket. "Ain't no one dick worth the sacrifice of all the dicks in the world."

"I don't know, girl. There's just this thing between Carter and me. But I really can't go there. At least not now."

Then the bell rang, and Loletta let in the bellboy, who quickly took her luggage. She and Vernice followed him out.

When Loletta heard the cab door shut, she realized her life was about to take another wild turn. Next week was Thanksgiving and she was going to be thirty. Like the moth longing for the flame, she was on a search for a new life, one much greater than the old. She held no anger at Kavon, because she knew that she had brought her own madness to their marriage; both of their madnesses married, and her heart had bled and she had called that love.

Epilogue

ONE YEAR LATER

To avoid the onslaught of the press into Kavon's private life, and under the advice of her lawyer, Loletta settled out of court. She was awarded 3.5-million dollars and the two cars Kavon had bought her. She thought Kavon had already made her pay for every dollar. Corbett assured her that she received slightly more than she would have if they had gone to court. She didn't know what Corbett kicked to Kavon's lawyer, but it worked out for everyone. Loletta, however, refused to sign a gag order. Her book, *Diary of an NBA Wife*, would be in the stores in a few months.

She and her mother were still amiss. Their relationship had suffered profoundly and would never be the same, but Loletta was okay with that. After Kavon broke up with Kia, Kia took him to court for child support for their four-month-old daughter. During this time, he had to ask Ms. Landelton to leave because Kia wanted the house. It was only right since she had his child. Ms. Landelton packed up her things, and within days she was in LA. Loletta thought her mother's timing was suspicious;

just when she got her cool millions, her mother was at her door. But this time Loletta wasn't falling for the drama. She quickly bought her mother a house, close but not too close. She also gave her a job at her restaurant, Loletta's, as vice president, a loaded title that kept her mother out of her hair, but well taken care of. After all it was her mother, and she wasn't about to see her struggle, no matter what they'd been through.

"Ms. Hightower, this is compliments of the chef," the waitress said, setting down a delightful plate of dessert for Loletta and her guests at Loletta's special table.

"Tell Jeff I said keep the sweet talk coming, but he ain't getting another raise," Loletta joked, but she had something better for Jeff—a promotion to executive chef. She dipped her fork in the luscious creation. Some of the best things about having your own restaurant, Loletta thought, were that you could eat well anytime for free, as well as have a place to hang out and meet new people, a place where they could kick back if they felt like it.

"We have two guests outside who demand to see you right away," Vernice said, as she stopped by Loletta's table. She was now manager of the place, and a good one, too.

"That's one thing I gotta get used to—when you own a restaurant, you are always on call," Loletta said to Darva, who was seated beside her. Darva was now officially separated from Calvin.

"Here, finish this," Loletta said, handing a slice of cake to Vernice, who happily obliged and took Loletta's seat at the table. As Loletta passed by, she greeted many of her guests. Several were A-list singers and Hollywood producers, who Darva had helped lure in with her publicist Rolodex. Loletta felt exquisite in her red chiffon, halter-top Dior dress. She hoped that the mystery guests weren't the LA police, because she was still waiting for her liquor license. Thankfully it wasn't.

"Hey, you," Loletta said, wrapping her arms around Carter and Damon Miles, both partners in the restaurant. Damon was a successful venture capitalist who made his money from other people's businesses.

Carter held her for a second too long. She slowly slipped his hands off her. "Think you can get a table for us, someplace near yours? There's gonna be about five of us."

"Sure," Loletta said, signaling to the hostess. "Maria will take care of you."

"Who's gonna take care of you?" Carter asked with an intensity that made her heart patter. Then he walked away, turning back to look at her. That was something she had built a wall against. She didn't need anybody, because everyone who she thought she needed eventually disappointed her. But Carter was different; he was still playing, but he wasn't all about basketball. He was about using it to get to places he wanted to be. He enhanced her, and he could love her. Her heart was on the mend, and he might just be the person to heal it. *Whenever,* she thought.

Loletta walked back to her table and saw Carter and his friend mingling with the other folks there. She finally realized a truth. Maybe Lady Anise was right. Everything happened for a reason. She was moving closer to what she really wanted in her life, and moving farther away from everything she feared.

Leslie Hassler

Maryann Reid, award-winning author of several novels published by St. Martin's Press, enjoys writing stories that unveil the inner lives of powerful women in distress or good girls gone bad. Her work has been published in *USA Today, Glamour, Newsweek,* and more. She is from Brooklyn, New York. Follow her at maryannreidinc.com.